Root Bound

Written By
Tanya Karen Gough

Copyright

Published by:

Baba Yaga Press
PO Box 21146
Stratford, ON N5A 7V4

http://www.facebook.com/emmaseries
http://emmaseries.blogspot.com

Print Edition ISBN–13:   978-0-9878506-0-7

Ebook Edition ISBN–13: 978-0-9878506-1-4

Printed in Canada and the United States of America

Cover Design by Tanya Karen Gough

Cover Photo: "Rays of Light" by Petr Kratochvil

Public Domain Pictures: http://www.publicdomainpictures.net

"Roots" photo sourced from: http://www.public–domain–image.com/

First Edition: (June 2012)
10 9 8 7 6 5 4 3 2 1

For my mother

Faery Song

Shed no tear! O, shed no tear!
The flower will bloom another year.
Weep no more! O, weep no more!
Young buds sleep in the root's white core.
Dry your eyes! O, dry your eyes!
For I was taught in Paradise
To ease my breast of melodies, —
                            Shed no tear.

Overhead! look overhead!
'Mong the blossoms white and red, —
Look up, look up! I flutter now
On this fresh pomegranate bough.
See me! 't is this silvery bill
Ever cures the good man's ill,
Shed no tear! O, shed no tear!
The flower will bloom another year.
Adieu, adieu — I fly — adieu!
I vanish in the heaven's blue, —
                            Adieu, adieu!

                                        John Keats

Table of Contents:

Chapter One: Creaks & Squeaks

They'd started moving at dawn, Emma curled up half asleep in the front seat, her father at the wheel. They'd been driving for hours and hours in the hot autumn sun along a plain, open highway that never seemed to change. Nothing to see but miles of farmland and small, dilapidated towns, most not much bigger than three or four ramshackle houses with a corner store at an intersection, followed by more seemingly endless flatlands and scraggly trees. The only thing keeping her awake was the ukulele poking her playfully in the ribs.

Town farmland farmland farmland town.
Grass grass tree grass grass cow tree grass town.

The landscape repeated on itself endlessly, droning past while the sun beat through the window. She struggled to stay awake, but the heat and the monotony tried hard to get the best of her.

The car didn't help, either, with its puttering exhaust and that funny clunking sound it made every few seconds like syncopated jazz back beat:

Clunk, chug–a–lug, chug–a–lug. Clunk, chug–a–lug.

Then there was her dad improvising softly hummed tunes while he drove:

Dum–di–dum–di–dum–diddily–dum.

They continued on their way; the farm country outside the window maintained a form of visual harmonics:

House, house, cow–tree, house, tree, cow–cow.

By the time the city appeared in the distance, she was half dazed, and between the warm sun and her drowsiness, she no longer knew what was what. The sudden shift in the otherwise unchanging landscape seemed strange and unnatural, as if they had chanced upon a magical kingdom. Oz maybe, or Xanadu, or Olympus.

"Dad? Where are we?" she mumbled, not quite sure if she was

awake. His voice floated back in the sweltering heat.

"Almost there, sweetheart. We're almost there."

From a distance, the city was all glass and steel and stone fortresses, surrounded by a moat of highways flowing with a steady stream of cars. But the magic peeled back as they approached, revealing a harsher reality. Shiny glass and reflective steel gave way to poor tenement housing and old, rickety train tracks. Rows of laundry on clotheslines flapped crazily in the wind like streamers, crisscrossing the space between the fatigued buildings, seeming to hold them together and keep them upright. But then she blinked, and for a moment she saw them as regal banners welcoming her, and the crooked antennae on the rooftops flanked them like regimental soldiers in glistening armour.

The highway landscape quickly began to repeat on itself too:

Houses, clotheslines, children, cars, cars.

She snuggled into her seat and watched the buildings pass.

Houses, clotheslines, children, cars, cars.

Bored, she picked up a storybook that was wedged between her leg and the car door.

It had been her mother's book, wonderful, big and heavy, with a well–worn cardboard cover and chock–full of folktales and legends from places all over the world. Greek and Norse mythology, folktales from Asia and Africa, even ghost stories and fables. She had read it cover to cover a hundred times, until the spine was all wobbly and the pages faded with use and years of accumulated fingerprints and smudges. Her father smiled.

"Hey, that's a great book! Want me to tell you how it ends, or do you want it to stay a surprise?"

Emma frowned and moaned, "Daaaaad."

They could both recite the stories by heart, and he began to do so, quickly twisting key details and making the whole thing ridiculous. Minutes later, they were both giggling, and another five miles passed before she finally settled back down to read.

She decided to start reading it from the beginning, in honor of this new leg of their journey. She flipped past the preface, which she secretly thought was rather boring, to the first page of the first story and dove headlong into ancient Greece and Rome.

By the time they pulled up to the old, crumbling brownstone apartment building that was going to be their new home, the sun was starting to sink. The light cut across the street like a pointer beam, bouncing off the apartment windows and making the glass blink in the flickering light like lazy eyeballs half asleep in the heat.

Her father got out of the car.

"Well, kiddo, this is it. Stay here a moment while I make sure they left the key for us, k?"

"K," Emma nodded sleepily.

"And lock the doors."

"Uh huh." She nodded again and tried to stretch awkwardly in the cramped seat overflowing with boxes and bags.

The light struck her face, and she blinked, and for a brief moment she was sure the house blinked back. She frowned while she tried to decide if blinking houses were normal. Then she realized it was just a curtain on the third floor, flapping in the wind and making the sunshine on the window flicker and wink. She let out her breath, not realizing she had been holding it in. She flipped through some pages in her book, looking at the pictures, to distract herself.

Just then her father came back outside.

"Emma, come on up and see the new place." His voice was deep and musical and carried easily through the car windows. She shook off the last of her sleepiness and unfolded herself from the car seat.

"On my way, sire," she called back, waving her arm in a fancy bow.

"And grab a box while you're at it, will you, princess?" he called back with a laugh.

Packing and unpacking was something Emma had become very good at. They had moved twelve times in the past five years, each time following a series of musical gigs that kept her father moving across the country and back again and again and again.

Emma opened the car door and stepped out onto the curb. The hot sun felt different on her skin without the windows intensifying it. It was a sharper heat in some ways, but the evening breeze also made it feel less severe, unlike the car heat that spread throughout the interior and made her feel like a Christmas turkey. A shiver ran down her back.

She pulled a couple of her father's bongos from the haphazard pile of instruments in the back seat and crossed the quiet street to the entrance. Her father looked down at her from the top of the stoop.

"So, here we are. What do you think?"

She finally took a good look at the building that was about to become their new home.

It was a five–story apartment block, with a brick facade and plain stone windowsills. The door was old and made of peeling, cracking wood. The ornately carved frame might have been beautiful many years ago, but now it was worn and faded, and the tree motif had nearly disappeared. The overhead doorjamb also sagged a bit, giving the front an organic but somewhat sad feeling, like a droopy upper lip. Many of the upstairs windows were open, with faded curtains flapping in the evening breeze. One or two of them had air conditioners, but they didn't seem to be turned on.

She smiled thinly. "It's great, dad. Home, sweet home."

She climbed the uneven concrete steps, one hand gripping the surprisingly detailed iron banister. Her father reached down and relieved her of one of the bongos, then took her other hand in his as she reached the top. He smiled down at her and pushed on the door. It swung inwardly with a groan.

The foyer was dimly lit. The tile floor was cracked, and exposed wires stuck out of the walls where light sconces once had been. There was an old fashioned elevator cage with an iron mesh door, but it was clear it hadn't been used for years. A sagging staircase wound upward past banks of old, dirty windows.

They trudged up to the top floor and walked down a long hallway to the end, passing several doors. They were all closed. The hall was terribly quiet, except for the rustle of the boxes against their clothes and the occasional clink of objects shifting in their containers as they walked. Moments later, they arrived at the door to their new home, and she waited patiently while her father unlocked the door.

"Ready, kiddo?" He grinned like a clown as he pushed the door open. "Ta–da–a–a–a–a!"

The entrance opened into a dark hallway that ran to the left into a small kitchen and living room area with two large windows, covered in heavy, dusty curtains. Looking down the hall to the right, she saw three doors, which turned out to belong to a small bathroom and two separate bedrooms, respectively.

"Really, Dad?" Emma squealed in delight.

"Yes, honey, really. For as long as we're here, you've got your own room. Pick one."

It had been a long time since she'd had her own room. They had mostly lived in one–room apartments, where Emma slept while her father played music at local hotels and clubs and musical shows and wherever he could find work.

She pushed the door open cautiously, revealing a single bed, a small plain dresser, and a simple white rollup blind in the window. The bed was already made, and she discovered her father had somehow managed to sneak her favorite teddy bear and her storybook out of the car while she was daydreaming. They were sitting on the bed, welcoming her, when she walked in.

Her father placed his hand on her shoulder.

"Can't promise I can make this one stick, princess," he said, "but I'll do what I can. In the meantime, we'll do the best we can with what we have, right?"

Emma placed her hand on his. She smiled. He smiled back. It was a warm, strong smile, but she could still see the traces of sadness behind his eyes. The sadness never really went away.

"That's my girl. Always such a trooper." He stroked her hair for a moment, then pulled her in for a hug. Emma hugged back. She wanted to say something to help, but she had no idea what to say. She never did. So she just hugged back and waited for the moment to pass.

They went back downstairs and began carrying in their few possessions. The apartment turned out to contain a pair of beds, dressers, a kitchen table, a ragged, but otherwise clean tweed sofa and an upright piano. Her father had already brought his saxophone in, not taking any chances with leaving his livelihood in the car on the street. He played every instrument imaginable, but it was usually his sax and piano playing that put food on the table. Emma struggled with the smaller boxes, while her father brought in the suitcases and boxes of sheet music.

They raced down the stairs for another load, and by the time she got back up to the top floor on their third trip, Emma's legs were starting to shake.

She stood on the landing, panting for a moment. The hall was so strangely quiet and dark. She took a step, and then another. As she passed by the first apartment door, she noticed it was open slightly. Just a crack.

"Don't dawdle, Emmakins. It's getting dark," her father called out from deep within their new apartment.

Emma grunted in acknowledgement but found herself oddly drawn to the door. A vertical shaft of bright white light pushed against the doorframe. She figured it must be the sun, shining through the window and right up against the door. But as she stepped away, a strange moaning sound came from inside. Her heart jumped, and she made a beeline for her own apartment door.

The apartment building had been eerily quiet up to that point, and except for the noise beyond the slightly ajar door on the top floor, Emma hadn't seen or heard a single sign that any soul beside herself and her father occupied the building. She felt sweaty and dirty as they climbed up the stairs yet again, and she was starting to find it difficult to breathe in the stagnant air, as though she and her father had already used up what little oxygen there was.

By the fourth trip down the stairs, Emma found herself looking longingly at the broken elevator. She wondered if it might suddenly start working if she wished hard enough.

BANG!

She was on the staircase on her way back up, barely past the first landing above the lobby, when a heavy metal door near the entrance swung open with a creak and slammed shut with an ear–splitting bang.

CRASH!

Startled, Emma stumbled.

The box in her hands flew out, tipped sideways and spilled toothpaste and soap in all directions. A bottle of shampoo rolled back down the stairs to the first landing where it spun like a merry–go–round before finally coming to a stop.

Emma dove after the bottles to re–collect them, so she never really saw anything other than the stairs until the woman stepped foot on the landing. At that very moment, Emma stood up with the bottle of shampoo in her hand and found herself face to face with an old woman. Her breath struck Emma in a hot, stifling blast.

"Cat got yer tongue, child?" croaked the woman with a squint.

Emma almost dropped the bottle again in surprise and fumbled with it she tried to step aside, but her heel caught the banister, and she almost fell down the stairs herself. Her father leaped back down the half flight, still balancing the box he was carrying in the other, and caught her arm at the last instant. Emma caught her breath. She looked timidly at the old woman, and she opened her mouth to apologize. She suddenly felt overwhelmed, tired, confused and off–balance, but at the same time, she was rooted to the spot.

"I …"

"Yep, jest as I suspected. Yer child's a mute or an idiot?" she growled, turning suddenly to Emma's father. He was taken aback almost as much Emma was. She had never seen her father surprised like that before.

"I … er … I mean, she …," he sputtered.

"Oh, I see. Runs in the family, does it?" cackled the woman. "Idiots. One branch of the family goes rotten, and the next thing you know, whole tree runs sickly with them."

She pushed her way past them, and they looked at each other with a look of surprise in a private, voiceless conversation:

What was that?

I have NO idea!

Me either!

Emma and her father collected themselves and their boxes and proceeded silently back up the steps, trailing the old woman by a half a flight. By the third floor landing, Emma had nearly caught up with her. She made a move to pass in the corridor, but the woman stepped onto the next set of stairs and cut her off. Emma looked back at her father. He shrugged. So Emma followed the old woman step by step up to the fifth floor. The fatigue in her legs made her painfully aware of each and every step she took.

The woman turned down the hallway in the same direction as their apartment.

Oh no, Emma thought. *She's heading straight for our place!*

Instead, the woman stopped abruptly, in front of the door to the mysterious apartment with the strange noises Emma had heard earlier.

The old woman threw the door open and a blast of brilliant light filled the hall. She stepped inside and slammed the door behind herself. The hallway became very dark, very quickly.

Emma and her father hurried down to the end of the hall, opened the door to their apartment and scooted inside.

They closed the door and looked at each other. She'd never seen her father look so surprised. The expression on his face made her giggle. Seconds later, his mouth twisted from shocked "O" into a smile and then into a grin, and soon he was laughing too. This only made Emma laugh harder, and she sank to the floor, laughing so hard her stomach hurt, the box of soap and shampoo still in her hands.

They made short work of the rest of the boxes and carried the last of their luggage into the living room just as the last rays of sunshine finally disappeared, and the sky turned black, or at least as black as the sky can get in a city at night. They cleared a small space between the boxes in the living room. They opened the curtains and windows to help clear the air and managed to dig out a pot and a can opener to make a simple supper of soup and bread. By the time the dishes were done, the city had lit up the sky outside the window like an urban nightlight, and skyscrapers dotted the distant horizon like a river made of constellations.

Her father pushed back his bowl and sighed contentedly, the way he always did after a meal. Emma stood up and reached for the bowl to clear the table.

"Hon, go rest. I'll clean up here," he said, placing his hand on hers. She looked at him, ready to protest, but she could tell from his face that he meant it. So while her father tidied up the few dishes and puttered about, humming a complicated tune from one of the many pieces he was always composing, Emma curled up on the sofa with her storybook to read some more Greek and Roman mythology. She started in on the story of Perseus, the Greek hero who tamed the flying horse Pegasus and slew the horrifying, evil Medusa.

It had been such a long day. All that driving and lifting and walking up and down the stairs. Emma felt her head getting heavier and her eyelids droop. As she read about Perseus' encounter with three strange old women, she thought about the woman down the hall and the apartment with the strange noises. For the first time in days, she was curious to know what her new school was going to be like and if she would make any friends there. She wondered how her father's new job would work out, and how long it would last.

At some point, she must have fallen asleep because when she opened her eyes again, it was very dark, and she found herself in her pajamas in her new bed. She could barely make out the edges of the closet and the door to the hallway. She could see the faint edges of the blind moving gently in the breeze, and she could see a dark patch on the wall near the ceiling, which turned out to be one of those old vents with a decorative metal grill cover. The apartment was very quiet, so quiet she almost forgot she was in the middle of the city.

A cool breeze blew into the room, making the blind shimmy and rattle against the window frame. The air felt good on her skin as it passed over her, taking the edge off the day's heat. A second breeze fluttered past the blinds and felt just as good.

As the breeze picked up, the blind started to dance along with the wind, billowing in when the air pushed into the room, and pressing back into the screen with a little suction–y *pop* when the air retreated back into the night.

Emma allowed her breath to follow along. Inhale. Exhale. *Pop.* Inhale. Exhale. *Pop.* Exhale. Exhale.

Exhale? Emma lifted her head, puzzled. It seemed like the air was pushing from inside the building instead of blowing in from outside. She watched intently. The blinds seemed to be pressing against the screen *harder* each time the outside breeze let up.

That isn't right, she thought. *How can the wind push out? The door is closed. There's no place for the wind to come from in here.*

And then something completely unexpected happened.

The building sneezed.

Emma sat bolt upright and scrambled to the top of her bed, pressed her back against the wall and pulled her cover sheet to her chin with both hands. Everything went quiet, except the sound of her heart pounding in her throat. Then the light came on in the hallway, and she heard footsteps in the hall. A gentle knock at her door sent her heart racing again.

"Emma?"

It was her father, and the sound of his voice brought her heart rate down a notch. He tapped again at the door, then cracked it open.

"Honey, you ok?"

"I heard …," Emma paused, not really knowing how to describe what she heard. Her father entered the room and sat down on the bed next to her. He wrapped his arms around her, and she nestled into the safety of his warmth.

"I'm sorry for all this, Emma." He spoke quietly, and she could hear the sadness in his voice. "I know how hard it has been for you. Always moving. It hasn't been much of a life."

"It's ok, that's not why …"

"They've promised me a six month contract this time. I know it's not much …"

She squeezed him hard, still not knowing what to say. They stayed there for a while, in silence, until Emma forgot the crazy nonsense about the house sneezing. Finally, he got up and tucked her back in. He paused and placed his hand on her cheek. He smiled and closed the door behind himself as he left. A few moments later, the light in the hall went out, and Emma was alone in the darkness again.

Emma peered out from under her worn bed covers into the darkness of her new bedroom. She listened to the rhythmic *whoosh/slap* of the blinds as the breeze passed in and out the way it was supposed to.

Minutes passed, and nothing changed.

She began to feel silly. *What on earth had I been thinking*, she scolded herself. *Houses don't sneeze. It was just the wind.* She was so tired her imagination had gotten the best of her. *Yes, that's right*, she giggled to herself, feeling pretty goofy and tired to the point where silly things seemed hysterically funny. She started to laugh, trying to stay quiet, but she only succeeded in giving herself the hiccups. She tried to stifle it, not wanting to wake her father again, but that only made the giggling and the hiccups worse.

She hiccuped again, then giggled. Then hiccuped, then giggled. Finally, she couldn't control it any more and burst out laughing. She laughed so hard, she didn't notice a sprinkling of dust fall out of the air duct. It caught in her nose, right in the middle of a giggling hiccup, and for one horrible moment she didn't know if she would hiccup, giggle or sneeze.

She sneezed. She sneezed again. Then the house sneezed.

She froze, another monstrous sneeze trapped in her nose. Everything around her seemed to freeze, too. Finally, she couldn't hold it any longer, and she let out the most enormous sneeze she had ever sneezed, and at that same exact moment, the house sneezed too. And before she was able to even wonder what was happening, she heard a sudden clatter, like a bag of marbles rolling down the vent shaft. It clinged, it clanged, it stopped with a hard *thud* and a chorus of very small voiced "*oof*"s.

Just then the wind flung the blind so hard it rolled open all by itself. The city lights lit up the room with a weird glow. Emma looked up fearfully at the iron grate covering the air shaft.

Three sets of tiny, shiny eyes looked back.

Chapter Two: Clangs & Bangs

With the window blind out of the way, the night city filled the room with an eerie light, and the edges of the air vent grate stood out in shiny, sharp relief against the pitch black void behind it. The walls shuddered slightly as details blended together, slipping between the shadows caused by peeling wallpaper and the flicker from the broken street lamp outside.

She relaxed for a moment and told herself she was just imagining things, like the time she thought there was a monster in her closet, but it turned out to be nothing more than a shirt. Then she heard a rustling sound and looked back at the grate. This time there was no denying it. Three sets of eyes glinted back at her and blinked in succession like Christmas lights.

Emma didn't know what to do. She was curious and afraid at the same time, not knowing whether to say something or scream for her father. Maybe it was rats. Rats were ok. She'd seen them before in motels. She'd even befriended one when they lived in a cottage once, near the ocean. She knew not to touch it, in case it had germs, but she'd leave it little bits of peanut butter and cheese, and it would sit in the corner and keep her company when her father was working late. Yes, maybe it was rats. Except rats didn't speak.

"What in Foundation is THAT?" a small voice pierced the silence.

"I'm sure I haven't the faintest foggiest," came another. Both voices were faint and high pitched, making them hard to hear. As far as Emma could think clearly, given the circumstances, it seemed to her that the first voice was female and the second voice possibly male.

"Perhaps it's a dust bunny," a third, even tinier voice chimed in.

"Don't be silly," replied the second voice. "There's no such thing as a dust bunny that big!"

"Well, there COULD be," insisted the tiniest voice. "Just because you've never seen one doesn't mean it doesn't exist, and you don't know everything even if you think you do. Mister Widget says there are all sorts of things in the universe we don't even know about, and he knows everything since the beginning of time, and that's why he's the teacher and you aren't, you know, and anyway that's not the point. The point is Mister Widget says there are eNORmous dust bunnies, and they can be really dangerous, like the killer dust bunny of 1935 –"

"Dust *Bowl*, you parabolic drill bit," hissed the second voice. "Didn't that Mister Widget of yours teach you ANY Upper history?"

"Dust bowl? Who ever heard of a bowl being dangerous? And why would anyone put dust in a bowl on purpose? I'm sure Mister Widget said it was a giant dust bunny."

"Silence, both of you," the first voice cut in. "Whatever it is, it's big, and it's moving, so it's definitely a monster of some sort. And since we don't know yet what sort of monster it is, we must exercise caution. I don't know about you, but I'm not in the mood to be eaten by a monster today!"

"Goodness me," said the second voice. "All this talk of eating and exercise reminds me … I'm famished!"

"Excuse me," Emma said timidly, "I'm really not a monster."

Her announcement was received only with shocked silence. A few seconds passed.

She took a deep breath and spoke again with a stronger voice, "Hello?"

"Did it just speak?" the concerned female voice whispered.

"I think it's safe to say it did.   Or rather, I strongly suspect so. That is –," the male voice rambled nervously.

"There's a talking monster, and you're saying it's safe?" squeaked the tiniest voice. "We don't even know what sort of monster it is!"

"I'm not a monster," Emma said, becoming annoyed. "I'm NOT!"

"By Foundation, I could almost swear the monster was talking to

US!" said the female. There was a murmur of denial and contradiction.

"No, it's not possible!" the little one squeaked.

"Of course not. Indeed! Goodness no!"

"Oh, yes, you're right. How silly of me to think so!"

"Too bad Mister Widget isn't here, 'cause he could tell us exactly what sort of monster it is, 'cause he knows all about all the monsters in the universe, even the ones that no one has seen in eons and eons. I expect this is one of those sorts of monsters. Maybe it's one of those mythological monsters that only exist in story books until you actually see one and discover that they're real. Like a Fussbudget or a Whatchamacallit. Or maybe it's a Human."

"Shush, child! What nonsense are they filling your head with at that school of yours?" the woman chided.

"Of course, if it's a Human, it definitely wouldn't be able to see us," the man's voice piped up. There was a moment of muttering as they each considered this possibility and agreed that it would, in fact, be very nice if the monster in question was a Human and, therefore, unable to see them.

"Yes, well it certainly *could* be a Human. Just look at the size of it and the blank, expressionless face. I wish to Foundation I had my copy of *Mister Widget's Mythological Beasties and Upper Level Monsters* to consult. Or better yet, Mister Widget himself …"

"I'll have words with that Mister Widget as soon as we get back." The female voice was beginning to sound increasingly short tempered. "I think he's been filling your head with a lot of nonsense!"

Emma could not stop herself from giggling, partly because she was relieved to hear that whatever they were, these creatures didn't seem to be dangerous; partly because their conversation sounded just like her own thought process when she was trying to figure out what *they* were; and partly because it was just plain silly to think there were tiny, talking creatures quibbling in the air vent.

"If we get back," the male intoned mournfully.

Emma's giggles and the creatures' chattering were interrupted by another rumbling sound coming from deep inside the air vent. It started faintly, like an empty, grumbling stomach, but got louder and louder, growing into something between a bowling ball and a rolling sack of potatoes. It got louder and closer, amplified by the long, hollow vent shaft until Emma's entire room shook, and she could actually feel the rumbling as her bed started to shudder.

Just then, she heard the smallest of the voices in the shaft say:

"Uh oh."

The thing in the shaft, whatever it was, crashed into the grate with a tremendous *thunk*. The sheer power of it pounded the three creatures, whatever they were, right through the tiny openings in the grate.

Emma saw it all as if it were playing out in slow motion. First, something squished and stretched through one small hole like play dough through a shape mold, long and thin while it passed through the grate and then suddenly puffed out into a round, portly shape as soon as it had cleared the hole. It flew through the air like a tennis ball. Right behind it, another long, narrow thing squished through the grate. It had been flattened in the vent between the round thing and the other mystery object, so when the round creature cleared the grate, the narrow thing shot out like a suddenly released spring. The third creature turned out to be half the size of the narrow second thing and rocketed out past the grate on the narrow one's heels, hanging onto the larger creature's foot and flapping behind like a flag in a storm. All three creatures landed on top of each other on Emma's bed, and for a moment the three of them just lay there in a pile, gasping for breath.

They were definitely small, as Emma had already guessed by their little voices. And, of course, the fact that they'd been able to fit in the air vent and squeeze through the holes in the grate was a pretty good hint, too. Tiny legs and arms branched out from the miniature mountain of bodies, and three distinct heads stuck out, all staring at her with tiny, saucer–shaped eyes.

A moment later, the one on the bottom began to groan, and on this signal, they all shifted and shimmied in a chorus of "*ooof*"s while they untangled from each other. They had landed in an unfortunate order, with the smallest one on the bottom, the tall narrow one next, and the big round one on top.

As they separated themselves, Emma finally had a chance to look at them individually.

The first thought that crossed her mind was that they were larger than she expected, perhaps six inches tall. The largest one appeared to be female, with a wild mane of curly grey hair that half flowed down her back and half clung to the top of her head with a strange looking shiny pin. Her face was a dark brownish red. She was dressed in a brown and grey tunic type dress, which stretched over her round figure and hung down to her knees. It had a grey, fur–like trim around the neck, arms and bottom. She wore brown leggings on her very short legs and tiny, stringy sandals on her stubby red feet.

Next to her was the tall, skinny one, who turned out to be a man, also dressed in a grey–trimmed brown tunic and brown leggings. He had a very long face and a pointy nose, and his skin was also dark red. For every bit that the woman was round, he was angular, from his face to his elbows to his knees. He wore a jaunty brown cap on his head.

The littlest one was neither very big nor very thin, just very little. Emma couldn't tell immediately if it was a he or a she. The creature was also dressed in a tunic, but without the fur lining, and wearing red leggings, instead of brown. The red was nearly the same color as its face and skin.

A deep moan and a rustling sound came from the air vent. Emma had forgotten that something else was in there. Apparently, so had the creatures, and they leapt to attention quickly and began scanning the wall, trying to get a good look at the vent.

"Who do you suppose that is?" whispered the littlest one. Emma was starting to think of it simply as a child.

"Or, more importantly, *what*?" The little man began wringing his hands together anxiously. The woman put her hand on top of his and whispered *hush* in a tone that was intended to be reassuring. Instead, the man grew even more nervous.

"I don't like this place," he muttered. "Too many monsters about. Not enough food."

Another hollow groan echoed from the air vent. The littlest creature shivered and clung to the female, too scared at first to speak. Then words tumbled out so fast Emma could barely follow them.

"Mister Widget says there are twenty seven different species of vent monsters, thirteen duct monsters, ten species of plaster phantoms and fourteen night wraiths, and I wish I could remember which one goes 'cling clang oooo,' but I can't. I don't know why. I'm sure we covered this one in class and let me think, think, thing, thnk, thk, thththththt …" Then the little red–faced creature broke down in a stuttering, crying fit.

At that moment, Emma realized that she wasn't frightened at all, which was strange considering there were three tiny people on her bed and something mysterious banging around in the air vent. Instinctively, she whispered, "Shhhhh, it's ok," to the littlest creature, wanting to help it calm down.

Unfortunately, it had the opposite effect. The tiny thing – Emma still didn't know if it was a boy or a girl – looked up at her and froze with both eyes bugged out so far, Emma wasn't even sure if they were still attached.

"Did it … Did it … didididit …?" the little one stuttered.

"I dare say it did," said the man, his knees starting to shake.

"Would someone *please* get me out of here?" a voice clamored authoritatively from the grate.

The three creatures' heads swung simultaneously toward the grate but almost as quickly swung back to stare at Emma. The grate rattled irately, so they looked back again. Then they remembered Emma, so their heads swiveled back again. Then back to the grate again, then back to Emma again, until they looked like spectators at a high–speed tennis match.

"I say, I say, would you idiots quit sitting there gaping like a city sewer? I've seen more intelligence from a row of coal chutes! Get me out of here!"

The voice's urgency seemed to shake the tall, very thin man out of his stupor. He nudged the woman and whispered, "I dare say, do you think that might be …?"

"Master Tect!" she called out.

Emma wasn't sure if the woman had just finished his sentence, made an announcement, or hailed the creature directly.

"Yes, of course it's me. Who, by Foundation, did you think it was? Who is that down there, anyway? Truss, is that you? And that's Piers wobbling in the breeze as usual, isn't it?"

"Yes, sir, it's me. And him. And little Mat, too," the round woman, who seemed to be named Truss, called up.

Emma decided to keep quiet and pretended to ignore them. They didn't seem to be afraid of her except when she tried to talk.

"Oh, and there's a monster, sir."

"Monster?" the voice echoed back. "Great Crumbling Cinderblock! How horrible. Where is it?"

"There!" said the little one, who appeared to be named Mat, pointing, but not daring to look.

"Goodness Gravel!"

"It seems to know we're here, sir," said the tall, lanky one in a heavy stage whisper.

"Oh my! Oh my, oh my!" the voice in the grate said, terribly flustered. "Has it harmed you in any way? Done bodily harm to your, er, body?"

"No, sir. But it does talk an awful lot," said the little one.

"Oh, well, then I suppose it must be harmless," the voice fretted. "In that case, just leave it alone. Perhaps it will talk itself into a coma."

Emma frowned.

"At any rate, stop sitting there like a lump of wet cement, and get me out of here!" the voice in the grate demanded.

The three creatures sped into a flurry of activity. They began by leaping up and down along the bottom half of the bed, looking in all directions for some way to help, but nothing came into view. They tried to jump even higher, hoping to reach the grate, but they were so very small, and the vent was so very high.

Once they realized that wasn't going to work, they tried a series of acrobatic tricks. The man stood on the woman's shoulders and the little one on his, but altogether they were still less than two feet tall, and clearly, that wasn't going to help.

They all dropped back down onto the bed and went into a huddle, each of them speaking at the same time so that none of them could hear what the other two were saying. The voice in the grate bellowed suggestions and orders, which they dutifully ignored. Finally, the littlest one got the attention of the others and said something very excitedly, pointing and waving his arms. All Emma heard was a high pitched squeal. They broke out of the huddle, and she watched curiously while the man and woman joined hands and squatted. The little one sprang up and balanced on their hands. The man counted down:

"Three ... two ..."

On "one," the man and the woman stood up quickly and flung the third into the air. The little one flew off the bed toward the window, somersaulted once, and by sheer luck managed to grab the cord that hung down from the bottom of the rolled up window blind. The creature swung under the sash toward the screen and then ricocheted back again, this time toward the grate.

Emma held her breath while the streak of red, brown and grey flew toward the vent, arcing through the air, both tiny hands stretching with urgency toward the grate. A larger pair of pudgy red hands stretched out past the ironwork, reaching toward the littlest one. Emma watched entranced as the two sets of hands missed each other by a fraction of an inch, and the would–be acrobat's tiny body bounced off the wall like a rubber band before fluttering back onto the bed like a leaf.

"Great Crackling Spackle!" the voice behind the grate sputtered. The sound of his voice rumbled and thundered in the hollow metal vent. The creatures, even the littlest one still lying in a crumpled heap on the bed, looked up and quivered. Emma couldn't keep sitting there without doing anything, so she spoke up.

"Maybe I can help," she said softly.

The creatures all froze in their tracks, except the littlest one, who just began to quiver more violently.

"What did you say, Truss?" the man whispered hopefully.

"Wasn't me," the woman said. "Mat?"

"Not me, no, ma'am. I didn't say anything. Not a peep," the little one squeaked.

"What, by Foundation, is *that*?" said the voice in the vent.

"It's thuh thuh thuh M–m–m–m–mon–n–n–n–n–st–st–st–ster, sir!" stammered the littlest one.

"I'm not a monster," said Emma. "I'm a girl."

"A ghoul?" said the tall, skinny man.

"Yes, it could be a ghoul," said the little one, chattering nervously. "I've heard of those, and the description fits. Mister Widget said that –"

"I think it said 'gargoyle,'" the woman interrupted quickly.

"Yes, it could also be a gargoyle," the littlest one babbled with increasing courage. "It's certainly ugly enough to be one."

"I am NOT ugly. And I'm not a gargoyle." Emma was becoming indignant. "I'm a girl!"

"What's that it said?" the voice in the vent sputtered.

"It says it's a girl," the man called up.

"A female gargoyle?" the voice asked incredulously. "No such thing!"

"No, I think it means a girl. A human girl."

"Preposterous! Humans can't see us," the voice in the vent bellowed.

"It's not *that* ugly," said the woman, looking at Emma thoughtfully. "I think it's rather nice. A bit on the big side, though. And terribly pale. I wonder if it's sick."

"Yes, I know that," the thin man replied to the voice in the vent, "which is why it must be mistaken."

"I'm not mistaken," Emma insisted. "I'm a girl. A human girl."

She was beginning to feel sorry she'd said anything at all. "Look, if you don't want me to help you, fine, but it doesn't look like you're doing so well on your own."

The creatures on the bed conferred with each other again. After a great deal of whispering, arm flailing, and high pitched squeals, they came to a consensus.

"Fine, fine," said the thin man. "First things first, then. Let's get Master Tect down, and then we'll figure out what the monster wants."

"I'm not a monster," Emma pouted.

The man turned to her and bowed to her with a great flourish of his hand. "Oh, great, monstrous monster!" he shouted at the top of his tiny lungs. "We beseech you to assist us in this, our desperate hour of need!"

Emma looked down at him, wondering why he was suddenly talking to her like that. The creature mistook her pause for lack of understanding and tried again, taking another tack.

"He–llo, mmmmmonnnnnnn–ster," he said, much more loudly and

very, very slowly. "WE," he said, gesturing toward himself and the other tiny beings, "TROUBLE." He brought his hands close together, then moved his fingers around very quickly. "BIG trouble," he repeated, this time spreading his arms far apart before bringing them together and jumbling his fingers again.

"You BIG." He pointed to Emma and then spread his arms far apart again. "Help us. YES?" He pointed to himself and the others and then did something with his hands that Emma could only guess was the gesture for 'help.' Then he nodded his head so hard, Emma feared it might fall off.

Emma sighed and frowned slightly. "I'm not a monster," she said with a pout. She was starting to get bored from repeating it over and over again. "And I'm *certainly* not stupid." She reached down and carefully picked up the little man by the scruff of his neck.

Piers panicked and began kicking and screaming.

"It's going to eat me! Help!" He continued to kick and scream.

Emma lifted him up and brought him very close to her face.

"Play possum!" suggested the voice in the grate to the wriggling little man. The dangling creature somehow managed to combine a resentful glare toward the grate with a look of terror toward Emma, both at the same time. It was a very peculiar expression.

"OK, look here, Mr. Whateveryouare," Emma said. "First of all, I am *not* a monster. Do you understand?"

He managed to blink rapidly and added a nod to his already contorted expression.

"I'm a *girl*. OK? A <u>HUMAN</u> girl. Got that?"

He nodded again.

"OK, so now we're getting somewhere. What are *you*?" she demanded, a little more forcefully than she intended.

Between nodding, shaking in terror and glaring at the voice that was still calling be helpful suggestions from the vent behind him, the creature had become apoplectic. His already dark red skin darkened further, until he looked like a weird, pointy raisin. For a moment, Emma considered shaking him to get him to answer, but he was so little she was afraid she'd hurt him.

"Are you faeries?"

It seemed impossible, but the little man turned an even deeper shade of red, then the purple of a nearly exploding grape, and then started to sputter and cough. Emma put him back on the bed.

"Well?"

None of the creatures responded, so she repeated the question, "Are you? Faeries?"

The man sputtered so hard, Emma was sure he was going to fly right off the bed.

"By Foundation, dearie," said the woman. Emma had been concentrating on the little man so hard she almost forgot about the others. "Of course we're not Faeries. Nasty, tricky critters, those Faeries. We're Basement Brownies."

"Yes, yes, of course we're brownies," Mat, the littlest one, chimed in. "Imagine not recognizing a brownie! Why, it's unheard of! I wonder what Mister Widget would say about a girl human not recognizing a brownie? He'd have such a laugh!"

Emma turned her gaze to the tiny brownie. "But you said that humans can't see brownies, so how can we be expected to know about them? You think you know all about humans, but you didn't know I was one."

"That's true enough, dearie," said the woman, cutting off the little brownie before it could launch into a long–winded defense. "Humans aren't exactly common where we come from."

Emma took this as an apology for the littlest one's behavior.

"And, no, of course Humans aren't supposed to be able to see Underfolk," the little one cut back in. "But just because something is invisible doesn't mean you shouldn't know what it is. Have you ever seen an idea?"

"Well, no. Not exactly, but ..."

"But you do know what one is, don't you?"

"Well, I ..."

"Exactly. So you should at least know about Underfolk, even if you've never seen one," Mat said smugly.

"Underfolk?" asked Emma. She was having trouble keeping up.

"*We* are Underfolk, dearie. Folk who live below the surface, between the cracks," the woman said helpfully.

"Between the cracks of what?" Emma asked, but the answer was lost beneath a loud bellow from the air vent.

"Would someone *please* assist me here?" The voice shook the room.

"Shhhhhh!" Emma was suddenly worried about all the noise waking her father. "Keep still. I'll get you out."

She peered at the grate and quickly discovered it was held in place by four screws with protruding heads. They turned easily beneath her fingertips, and it took just seconds for her to remove the cover. She opened her hand and placed her palm next to the opening.

A little man stepped out onto it, though she immediately realized that *little* was the wrong word altogether. Although he was roughly the same height as the skinny man, he was twice as round as the woman. And where the skinny man weighed nothing, it was everything Emma could do to put this brownie on the bed without dropping him like a stone. His face was dark red, like the other three, but his nose was short and lumpy, and his brow was thick and heavy and half–covered his eyes. They had called him Master Something–or–other, but he didn't look like the master of anything as far as Emma could tell, except that he wore a dark red coat over his tunic and had a large gold medallion around his neck on a wide gold ribbon.

"Right," said the Master, brushing some dust from his sleeve. "So, let's get this show down the tubes. I think perhaps we should begin with a status report. Piers?" He looked at the thin man, who was still flopped on the bedcover, staring nervously at Emma and still quivering.

"AHEM. Piers?"

"Yes, Master Tect?"

The thin man's gaze slowly drifted from Emma's nose, where it had been fixed since she put him down, to the rotund, but highly officious looking Master. He looked stupefied for a moment. The round brownie stared back, with a expectant expression. After a moment's pause, Piers shook off his shock as best he could, scrambled to his feet, and saluted the Master with a great flourish. His knees continued to knock together.

"Piers Rubbletaker at your service, SIR!" He threw out his chest and brought his hand to his forehead with such vigor, Emma was worried he might knock himself over.

"Status report, Mr. Rubbletaker," the Master said in a long–suffering voice.

"Um, yes SIR. Um, well you see, sir …"

"We appear to be Overworld, sir," the little one piped in.

"Yes, I can see that," the Master snapped at Mat, who squealed in fear, ran behind Truss and cowered. The Master turned back to the still quaking Piers.

"Who authorized this … this … excursion?"

"Yes, sir, well you see, sir …"

The tallest brownie's knees seemed to be knocking out some sort of message in Morse code.

"No one?" roared the Master. A delicate sheen of perspiration appeared on his boulder–shaped forehead. "Section 34 of the Basement Brownie Travel Code strictly states that there shall be no travel beyond Under without the authorization of the Travel Authority, the Minister of Granting Travel Permissions, and the seal of approval from the offices of the Grand Poobah of Everything, himself! This is most irregular! We shall have to complete forms TQ–24P in duplicate, submit them to the Office of Transgressive Travel Corrections, apply for twelve separate post–travel permission exemptions, prostrate ourselves in triplicate before the Grand Poobah and beg for forgiveness!"

By now large beads of sweat had begun to pour down his forehead. He pulled a surprisingly delicate white handkerchief from his breast pocket and began to dab at his face. The fabric was drenched quickly.

"It's not that we didn't have permission, sir," the woman jumped in hurriedly. "We were all hand picked by the Grand Poobah himself to seek the Wanderer, by order of the Premonitionary Resolution Control Council. We just weren't given any notice at all. One minute I was in the middle of making a nice plaster stew, and next thing I knew, I was hurtling down that passageway, along with these two." She pointed up to the air vent and toward the other two brownies. "We weren't even given time to pack."

"What's that? Hmmm, sounds like someone in Transimaginative Transportation is sleeping on the job. Come to think of it, that's exactly what happened to me, too. I was working on my weekly top–to–bottom restructuring of the regional governmental infrastructure, when suddenly …" Another torrent of perspiration ran down the Master's face.

"Oh, how humiliating! Hurtled through the air like an inconsequential pixie. Not even enough warning to pack an extra handkerchief. Well, I never!"

All this time, Emma had been trying to speak. She had so many questions. Where was Under? Under what? What does a basement brownie do? Why can't humans see them? Why could she?

She couldn't get a word in edgewise without appearing very rude. She tried coughing politely a few times, but they were so involved in their conversation they simply didn't notice. Their tiny voices droned in a high pitched hum that mixed with the low buzz of the street lights outside.

Emma felt her eyes growing heavy. Her head began to nod. She tried hard to fight it because she was so full of questions and curiosity. The last thing she heard was the voice of little Mat saying something about Mister Widget and then launching into a history lesson filled with names and places that made no sense to Emma at all.

Chapter Three: Snapshots & Shadows

The early morning light crept through the open window and slowly edged across Emma's face, prodding her awake. She resisted at first and rolled over with a heavy sigh. She pulled the bed sheet over her head, but even so, the light seeped through the fabric and continued to nudge at her eyelids. She groaned softly and pushed the heavy coverlets back down.

She opened her eyes with a squint.

A diffuse light filled the room, licking the shabby, crumbling walls and plain furniture. Emma let her eyes wander to the dresser. It had been painted many times, and layers of color streaked the corners and edges where they had worn down.

Something about the colors reminded Emma of something she had seen in her storybook the night before. She reached for the book and began flipping pages until she found it. It was a picture of Perseus in the first chapter, a snapshot of a wall painting from Pompeii, an ancient town in Italy that had disappeared a long, long time ago under the hot ash of a volcanic eruption. A note alongside the image told her how archaeologists discovered the city, and when they dug it out, everything was exactly the way it had been at the moment the town was buried. The wall painting showed Perseus lifting a bag of some sort, and the winged horse Pegasus flying into the air above him.

Emma was fascinated by the image, but it wasn't the flying horse that caught her attention. It was the combination of earthy colors, still bright after all this time. The colors were soaked into the plaster, and a series of dark, wandering cracks divided the painting into a giant puzzle. The lower half of the painting was still buried beneath a sheet of dirt and rubble. It made her wonder what it felt like to break free from the earth and fly.

Her gaze crept from the book to the dresser to the air vent. The grate was back in its place, though she couldn't remember replacing it, and the space behind it was dark and quiet. Then she remembered.

The brownies.

Her early morning drowsiness suddenly gone, she leaped out of bed and started picking through her bed covers, worried that maybe she had rolled over and crushed the little creatures in her sleep.

There was no sign of them anywhere. She pulled all the sheets and covers off the bed and shook them, but there was still nothing there. A horrid thought crossed her mind, but when she checked, no one was smooshed in the space between the mattress and the footboard either. She breathed a sigh of relief.

What was it the little woman said? Something about coming from between the cracks. The cracks of what? She turned the room upside down and checked every crack and crevice she could find, and by the time she flopped back onto the bed, her heart was pounding. Of course, the moment her body hit the mattress she sprang back up again, fearful that maybe she'd accidentally sat on them.

Once she'd convinced herself they really weren't there, she sat down again. On the edge of the bed, of course. And not without checking carefully beforehand.

Maybe I dreamed it, she thought. *I guess I did. They seemed real at the time …*

She admitted to herself that the long trip and the hot sun might have had something to do with it. Maybe the heat baked her brain a bit.

Piano sounds wafted down the hallway. *Dad*, she thought. And just like that, the dream was gone, and reality kicked back in. School Day. Her father wanted to keep her out for an extra day to help her settle in, but she knew his new boss had scheduled a rehearsal at the last minute, and she couldn't stay in a strange apartment in a new town all by herself on the first day. Some rules just couldn't be broken.

She opened the door and padded down the hallway, not paying much attention to the dusty wallpaper that was peeling and bubbling on the dingy walls. The old wood floor was well worn and felt cool and smooth under her feet. A smoky hall light was giving off a dim, sputtering glow, and Emma guessed her father must have been up early, before the dawn. She turned off the light as she passed and then continued down the long hall to the living room. She didn't think the hall was that long and narrow the night before, but then again, she had been so tired she'd dreamed there were faeries in her air vent.

Her father was at the piano, as expected. His fingers ran softly over the keys, playing a song called "Gypsy Girl" that he had written for her mother a long time ago. He smiled at her as she entered and reached his right arm out to her, his left hand still playing. She sat down beside him, and as he wrapped his arm around her, his right hand rejoined the tune. She leaned into the crook of his arm and closed her eyes. He always smelled like soap and aftershave. Sometimes she could also smell her mother, layered somewhere between his scent and the melody.

The tune came to an end too quickly, and the memory slowly faded with the last note.

"Come on, sweetheart," said her father, kissing the top of her head. "Time to get ready for school. Don't want to be late on your first day."

"I can't think of a better time to play hooky. They can't catch me if they don't know what I look like!" she quipped. He laughed and dropped his hand down to tickle her. She screeched and wriggled and, finally, escaped. She stood there panting for a moment, still giggling, and he smiled at her warmly and gestured toward the hall.

"Wash. Dress. School. NOW."

She hung her head in mock humility and shuffled back down the hall. In short time, she was clean, dressed, fed and ready to go. As they reached the front door, she stopped, and leaning against the doorframe said, "Dad, do I *have* to go today?"

"'Fraid so, baby."

"But I can take care of myself. I've been home alone before."

Her father looked down at her and stroked her hair. "Emma honey, you can take care of the both of us with enough left over to handle an army or two. But they're expecting you today, and it won't do to let them think I leave you alone. Sorry, princess. I'd promise to do better next time, but if all goes well at this job …"

He trailed off, but Emma knew what was unspoken. Each time they moved, they always said it would be the last time. Neither of them ever believed it to be true, but this time was a bit different. If they couldn't stay here forever, at least there was a chance she could finish out the school year, and that seemed long enough for both of them for now.

Emma put her hands on her hips and faked a big pout. "But princesses don't have to go to school," she said in a sing song voice. "It says so in the Princess Manual."

"Oh, is that so, your highness? And who wrote this manual?"

"Why, the Official Princess Manual Writer, of course. As dictated by the Princess herself."

He laughed again and reached down, picked her up by the waist and put her back down on the other side of the door.

"The Princess Manual is overruled by the King's Edict. School it is."

"Drat," said Emma with a shrug. She followed her father down the hall, when he suddenly stopped.

"Forgot some sheet music, baby. Stay right here. I'll be back in a sec."

He darted back to the apartment and in a flash was gone.

Emma waited for him for a moment. She looked at the doors to the other apartments and wondered where all the other tenants were. Then she realized she had wandered right up to the door to that horrible woman's apartment. The door with the strange light behind it. It was closed at that moment, so the hallway remained dark, and no sounds came from inside.

What a weird place, Emma thought to herself, looking back down the hall in both directions. First that strange, scary woman and the door with *something* behind it, then that crazy dream about little magic people. She tried not to breathe and turned her head to listen for noise, wondering if anyone was inside. Nothing. She even tried to keep her eyes open, as if blinking might somehow interfere with her hearing, then she held her breath and listened harder. Still nothing.

She stood in the hall for what felt like several minutes and then glanced at the door to their apartment, where her father had disappeared. She wondered what on earth could be taking him so long. The hall was strangely quiet. No light bulbs hissing, no air vents whispering, no creaking doors or footsteps on the stairs.

A song slid its way into her head, and she began shifting from one foot to the other. When it repeated, she started hopping up and down. The song was catchy and easy to dance to, though she couldn't remember where it came from. Before she knew it, she was humming the tune and skipping back and forth in the hall, toward the stairs then back toward the apartment.

Da dum di di dum di dum.

Half way to the apartment door. Stop, jump, turn, jump and skip, then back again.

Da dum di di dum di dum.

Half way to the stairs. Stop, jump, turn, jump and skip, then back again. She skipped back and forth, toward their apartment, then back toward the stairs. On the third time around, she overshot and skipped right to the edge of the staircase. Stop, jump, turn …

Emma found herself nose to nose with the horrible woman, who appeared out of nowhere on the top step.

Every bone in Emma's body wanted to jump back, cringing in surprise and fear. But she found herself unable to move at all. She just stood there with her eyes wide and her mouth open, gaping. The woman had a long, hooked nose and wiry eyebrows that hung heavily over her small black eyes and cast a shadow over them. Her skin was so old and wrinkled, it hung off her face in folds, and she had a curiously shaped wart on the side of her nose. Emma felt she had no choice but to stare at it. The woman seemed to be much uglier that she was when they met on the stairs the day before. The woman squinted and snarled through a curled upper lip.

Just then, the click of a door lock shook Emma out of her freeze, and she leaped back, recoiling from the hissing old woman. The next thing she knew, her father appeared out of nowhere, guided Emma out of the way and apologized profusely to the woman.

"I'm so sorry, ma'am. New place and all. Seems my little girl has forgotten her manners."

He nudged Emma. She didn't know what to do, so she just looked at her feet. It was either that or keep staring at the wart, and she knew that probably wasn't the nicest thing to do.

The woman turned to Emma's father and gave him a long, hard stare. Emma could feel him pull back slightly beside her, which surprised her. As far as she knew, he was never afraid of anything. The woman looked at him as though she was evaluating him, trying to decide something very, very important. After a moment, it appeared she had made up her mind.

The woman's face changed in a flash. She smiled, and all of the wrinkles on her face turned upwards, as though the individual parts of her face were smiling, too. Her black eyes sparkled and shone. She bobbed her head and spread her hands in a gesture of welcome. The overall effect was even more frightening than when she was unfriendly, but Emma said nothing. She stepped back a bit and let her father shield her.

"Such a beautiful little girl," the woman said fawningly. She reached out a bony hand as though she wanted to stroke the child's hair, but Emma pulled back even farther, almost disappearing behind her father's leg. The woman laughed. Emma couldn't help thinking it sounded more like a cackle.

"Don't get a lot of children around here," the woman continued.

"What a lucky father you must be. And the child's mother …?" She paused meaningfully. It wasn't so much a question as a demand for an explanation.

Emma could feel her father stiffen. They didn't talk about her mother. It always made him sad, and that made her sad, even though Emma barely remembered anything about her. She could remember her mother's smile, and the way her laugh tinkled in concert with her father's booming guffaw. She remembered the way her mother's hair fell across her face when she leaned over to tuck Emma in. And then her mother got sick. Emma remembered the laughter fading and her mother's hair disappearing behind an old handkerchief she wore wrapped around her head. She remembered being sad, very sad. But that was such a long time ago.

Her father paused for a moment before replying.

"It's just the two of us, I'm afraid."

The woman's eyes lit up as though they were on fire as she stared at Emma, or at least, Emma thought she could feel the woman's eyes burning her right through her father's torso.

"Oh, dearie, dearie me. What a tragic shame. A girl needs a woman to show her the ways of the world. Yes, she does indeed." The woman turned her gaze back to the father.

"Name's Madge, by the way, Madge Terrabane. That's Mrs. Terrabane to you, dearie," she added with another gleeful cackle, wagging a finger in Emma's direction.

"Ben Sheridan, ma'am. And this is my daughter, Emma."

"You must let me know if you ever need any help. Must be good neighbours, indeed we must. I may be old, but I've still got a few tricks up my sleeve, yes indeed, I do."

Emma had no doubt that she did.

"That's very kind of you, ma'am," he said. "We're both much obliged. Now, if you don't mind, I must get this one off to school."

"Yes, yes, of course you do. I'll wager she's a clever one, too, aren't you, my dearie?"

Emma wondered how she could be so clever when yesterday the woman was calling them both idiots.

"I don't know what I'd do without her," Emma's father replied truthfully and ushered his still trembling daughter down the stairs and out to the car.

"Well, that was unexpected," he said, as she climbed into the front seat. "She seemed a bit dodgy when we saw her yesterday. Just goes to show, you can't judge a book by its cover."

Emma looked at her father and furrowed her brow. Sometimes she worried about the way he trusted people, but then again, it was that same trust and optimism that helped them both when things got tough, which happened a lot. The image of the woman's beady black eyes flashed in her mind, and she could feel them burning into her skull as if they were still watching her. She shuddered. Her father looked down at her and smiled.

"Give it some time, Emma. Things often seem more frightening when they're new, but when you actually get to know them, they turn out just fine indeed."

He reached down and turned the key in the ignition. The car coughed a few times, grumbled a bit, but didn't start. He tried again. Still no luck. On the third try, the car coughed, grumbled and hummed, but still refused to start. He released the key and slumped back in his seat, then looked at Emma with a weak smile.

"Sorry, honeybunches. Looks like the chariot isn't cooperating today." A troubled look of defeat crossed his face.

Emma tried to think of something encouraging to say, but the sun was starting to bake the streets, and she found herself fixating on the shimmer rising off the pavement instead. She looked back up at the apartment building and wondered why it looked like a face to her yesterday. Today it was just an old brick façade with rows of windows and a slightly lopsided entrance way. A curtain moved on the top floor, and Emma remembered feeling like she was being watched the day before, when they first arrived. That feeling was the only thing that hadn't changed.

"Emma?"

Her father was reaching for the door handle.

"Got to make tracks, sweetie," he said. "I've got rehearsal in an hour, and we still have to walk over and get you registered."

Emma let herself out of the car and waited for her father to come around before they crossed the street together. She couldn't shake the feeling that they were being watched. Once they reached the sidewalk on the other side of the road, she looked back at the window. There was nothing there. She still felt a pair of eyes burning into the back of her head as they walked down the street.

She reached up and took her father's hand. He looked down at her and smiled, but for once, she didn't feel any better.

Soon enough, they reached the corner and turned to walk down the busy commercial road. It was bustling with cars, trucks making deliveries and shopkeepers hosing down the pavement in front of their stores. The early morning heat quickly turned the water into steam, and for a moment Emma felt like she was walking on a cloud.

A few blocks later, they approached the school, a formidable old stone building with a paved yard surrounded entirely by a chain link fence. A throng of children, some older than Emma, most younger, pushed and shoved their way through the gate into the yard. About half a block away, Emma felt her father's hand on her shoulder.

"Feels like déjà vu, doesn't it, honey," her father said.

"You can say that again," she replied.

"Feels like déjà vu ..."

She punched him playfully in the arm. He laughed. "Ok, sweetie. You know the ropes. Be good. Be safe, k?"

He made a fist with his right hand and presented it to her. She suddenly felt very nervous and afraid, but she was also grateful that he kept their private conversations away from the main gate. She smiled as brightly as she could, made a fist and tapped his knuckles with her own. Then they hooked their fingers together, shook their clasped hands three times, then each made a fist and tapped them together again.

They walked into the schoolyard through the crowd of children, identical to every other first day crowd of school children she had seen. Many stopped to stare at her, as they always did. She could hear them whispering as she passed.

No matter how many times she started at a new school, she just couldn't get used to the first few days. A couple of girls passed by, and one of them hit Emma with her shoulder. Emma stumbled so hard she would have fallen over, but her father tightened his grasp and steadied her. Two more girls joined the first pair, and their harsh laughter struck Emma almost as hard as the first girl's shoulder.

Oh, Emma thought to herself. *It's going to be one of* those *schools*.

They found the office, and Emma sat on a chair while her father spoke with an officious looking woman behind the desk. Emma studied a poster on the wall. Her feet couldn't quite touch the floor, so they swung loosely under the chair while she waited. By the time her father finished his conversation, Emma knew the *School Behavior Standards* by heart. The woman came around the counter, and Emma's father squatted down in front of Emma and put his hand on her shoulder.

"Ok, princess, this is the principal, Madame LaRoche."

A girl passed by the door just at that moment, and Emma could see her mouth the word *princess* with a snicker.

"She's going to show you to your class. I'll see you right after school."

Emma nodded. In reality, he would be in rehearsal until late, so she would have to fend for herself until then.

He turned to the heavyset woman and shook her hand. "Thank you, Principal LaRoche, ma'am. The secretary has my work number, yes? Good. Thanks again."

Madame LaRoche smiled back at him, all doe–eyed and giggling. She did not look like she giggled often. The act of smiling was so unnatural that the muscles in her face quivered in protest. Emma rolled her eyes. Women always acted weird around her dad. He shook the principal's hand again, smiled once more at Emma and was gone.

Madame LaRoche folded her arms, looked down at Emma, and frowned. The woman was undeniably solid, and her expression quickly turned hard as a rock. The walls and furniture in the room her seemed to bend toward her where she stood, like she had her own gravitational pull. Her skin had a strange, bluish hue, and the light glinted off her nose, which stuck out just enough to look like an arrow, pointing wherever the principal turned. Then she smiled again, but this time the result was something less of a horrifying smile and more of a horrifying sneer. Emma cringed.

"RRReady, grrl? You'rrr alrrready tarrrdy." When she spoke her voice grumbled deeply, reminding Emma of a rock quarry they had once visited while they were traveling, between one of her father's jobs and another. She slid off the chair and followed the woman down the hall.

"RRRegisterrr forrr sporrrts, did you, girl?" the large woman grumbled.

"Um … no, ma'am."

"Team needs a strrrong arm. State champ, I was, back in the day."

Emma tried to look sincere while she declined, but the truth was they'd never stayed anywhere long enough for Emma to join a team.

The four girls who had run into her earlier were still in the hallway, clustered around a locker. The one who bumped her shoulder was in the center of the group. They all stopped, turned and stared at Emma and the principal, and the ringleader's mouth formed the word *princess* again as they passed. The other girls waited until Madame LaRoche walked by before they started to snigger.

Madame LaRoche's heavy head immediately swung around, and they cowered under her unwavering stare.

"Shouldn't you girrrrls be in a classrrrooom?" Her voice rumbled so deeply the locker doors shook, and the hair on the back of Emma's neck stood on end.

The girls froze in their tracks until the commanding voice finished resonating through the hall, and then they sprang into action, closing the locker door and slithering away down the hall, muttering excuses and apologies under their breath.

Madame LaRoche watched them vanish into a classroom, then cast a withering expression at Emma. Then she turned abruptly and stomped down the hall in the opposite direction. Although the principal was solid and heavy looking, she was surprisingly quick, and she was several yards away before Emma realized she was to follow. She scurried to catch up.

Madame LaRoche stopped in front of a door marked 2B. She knocked heavily. The rapping sound echoed down the hall in both directions. The door swung open and a tired looking Polynesian woman pushed her head out.

"Yes?" the woman sighed heavily.

"New rrregistrrrant, Mrs. Pheegee."

Without even glancing at Emma, Mrs. Pheegee pushed the door open. She sighed again. "Well?"

Emma stepped into the room.

She had been through this so many times that she could do it on auto–repeat: the humiliation of standing in front of the class while she was being introduced, the awkward moments when she was forced to say something about herself, and the painful walk to the desk assigned to her. All the time with the judgmental eyes of her new classmates trying to size her up.

Knowing what would happen didn't make it any easier.

Emma dealt with this by doing what she normally did: stay quiet, keep to herself and try not to get in anyone's way. Her mother used to read her an old fable about a willow tree that was stronger than a mighty oak. The willow could bend in the wind and survive in a terrible storm, while the oak tree would not budge and got blown over. The story made sense to her. There was almost always a way to get by without being noticed, she reasoned. Bend like the wind. Slip through the cracks. It was a lonely way to be in the world, but Emma was used to being alone, and it was always much safer to be lonely and ignored.

Sometimes she got lucky, and a new school was easy to settle into. This wasn't one of those schools. And it kept getting worse. Some of the teachers made a point of asking her questions she couldn't answer because she was new to the class, and they thought they could make an example of her. The other students hid behind their books and laughed at her.

Then there were the classes where Emma seemed to know too much, and then the students looked at her with resentment, even if she tried to downplay her answers. She just couldn't win, especially not in math, which not only had a teacher who seemed to delight in pointing out that she hadn't done last night's homework, but which also had all four of the nasty girls from the hallway seated right behind her. By the end of class, Emma knew she was sunk.

At lunch, the four girls threw pieces of food at her and laughed when they got something gooey stuck in her hair. Emma wondered if the girls knew they were just like all the others, but she suspected it wouldn't make a difference. All the while, Emma could see Madame LaRoche watching her from the cafeteria window. The principal's face was impassive, and she made no attempt to make the girls stop.

As soon as school was out, Emma headed straight for her locker to gather her things. The girls were waiting for her. They were all heart–stoppingly perfect a creepy sort of way, like the porcelain dolls in her book, the ones that came to life and did terrible things at night. Emma was starting to think of them as the Gorgeous Gang, though their behavior was anything but.

"Hey, look, it's *Daddy's* little *Princess*," the leader called out. Emma knew from class that the girl's name was Thena. The girl had a very pretty face and strawberry blonde curls. At the moment, however, her mouth was twisted in a mean smile and her eyes squinted at Emma in a very ugly way. The three other girls positioned themselves behind her. They were also too pretty, each in their own way. Emma noticed that the girls spoke and moved mostly in unison.

"*Daddy's* little *Princess*," they echoed. Emma could barely glimpse her locker behind them. She made a move toward it, but they blocked her.

"Where's your daddy, *Princess*? Huh?" Thena stepped forward, making it impossible for Emma to pass. There was no place for Emma to go.

"She doesn't look like much of a princess, does she?" she sniffed at Emma and looked down her pert little nose at Emma's thrift store clothes. The three girls tittered behind her. "Where's your tiara, *Princess*? Does your precious mommy, the *Queen*, have it?"

A sudden well of tears rose up inside Emma, and it was all she could do to keep it down. She could take a lot, but talk about her mother always got to her, and this was the second time someone had mentioned her that day. She looked up at the golden haired girl standing menacingly in front of her. Thena looked even more horrible as she screwed up her face again to laugh. But then she froze with her face all twisted, and her eyes drifted to the side.

"What is going on herrre?" an unmistakable voice grumbled behind Emma. The four girls snapped into poses of feigned innocence.

"Nothing, Madame LaRoche," Thena said, staring hard at Emma. "Absolutely nothing." Then the girls vanished so quickly, Emma thought Madame LaRoche had vaporized them.

She turned around slowly and was startled by how close the principal was standing behind her. She looked up to see the woman smiling down at her with the same tight, unnatural smile she'd seen that morning.

"Thank you," Emma said, timidly. Madame LaRoche frowned, harrumphed, then turned and clomped noisily back down the corridor.

Emma collected her things from her locker and ran back down the busy commercial street, past the grocery store, down the street to the apartment building they now called home. She was so intent on getting inside, she did not notice the eyes watching her from the upstairs window, and by the time she climbed all the stairs, her own eyes were so full of tears she did not see that the old woman's door was open again, just a crack, just as it had been the night before. Nor did she notice the bright light coming from inside, spilling into the hallway. She ran straight to the door of their new apartment, fumbled for her key, let herself in and locked the door.

Then she put her books down, ran into the living room, crawled under the upright piano's keyboard, curled up with her arms around her legs, the piano pedals pressing into her back, and cried until she fell asleep.

Chapter Four: Explaining & Complaining

Emma was dreaming. She was running up an endless staircase, panting for breath. The stairs looked exactly like the ones in their new building, but they kept repeating on themselves, over and over again, with no end in sight, and she was getting very, very tired. She wanted to stop, but as she slowed down, she realized there was someone else on the stairs, much lower down. A pale hand and a dark sleeve were on the banister many floors below her, moving toward her with considerable speed. She didn't know who or what it was, but she was suddenly terribly afraid. She started to run, but she was already so tired. She could feel her legs buckling. Looking down, she could see the figure behind her. It was closer. She grabbed onto the banister and tried pulling herself up the stairs, but her hands were sweaty and slippery, and she couldn't get a grip. Her lungs hurt. She wanted to stop, but the thing was getting closer. She ran harder, faster. The steps began to blur under her feet as she spiraled up, higher and higher. Whoever or whatever was down below was getting closer and closer.

Something appeared up ahead. It was a door, slightly open, with a brilliant light streaming out of it, pouring down the stairs like a warm welcome mat calling her home. She found a burst of speed, but even as she did so, she could feel the thing behind her closing in on her. She was gasping for air, her lungs tight in her chest, her legs screaming and wobbling as they hit each step faster and faster, but still the thing got closer. She could feel its hot breath. The hairs on the back of her neck shivered. The door was so close, she could almost reach it, but as her hand stretched out for the knob, she knew the thing behind her was also reaching out a long, claw–like hand toward her. Sharp nails grazed her shoulder. At the same time, the door flew open, and another figure stepped into the light. It was draped in long, white cloth, and the light shone behind it like a halo. Emma was certain it was an angel.

A deep, resonant musical chord echoed in the hall.

The angel leaned down and offered its hand to the girl. Emma reached out with all her remaining power and caught its fingertip with the tips of her own. She could feel herself being whisked into the air, and the long white fabric of the angel's dress wrapped around her like cocoon. The creature behind her let out a horrific screech. Emma turned her head and saw a monstrous creature with its face contorted. It seemed to be in rage, but it might have been laughter.

The angel's sleeve fell over Emma's face. Just before it cut off her sight, she realized that the creature behind her was, in fact, the old woman from the apartment down the hall. She was laughing and pointing at her, like the kids had done in the hallway at school. Emma started to scream, but then she was bathed in white and floating, and the fear melted away.

She was happy, peaceful, safe.

The fabric of the angel's dress fell across her face again, and she brushed it away. It fluttered back down again. She brushed it away again, but down it came again. And again. Emma became annoyed. Soon, she was flailing her arms in front of her face like she was trying to shoo away a particularly persistent fly. She waved her arms harder and harder until finally, she woke up.

She was still waving her arms in front of her face, and it took a moment before she realized that a pile of sheet music had tipped over on the piano, and sheets of paper were falling off the keyboard and onto her face. The room was dark. The street lamp outside the window shone directly in her face and cast a long rectangular patch of light onto the living room floor. The heavy window curtains flapped wildly in the wind, sometimes waving directly in front of the light and causing it to blink, sometimes flapping so hard it sounded like thunder cracking.

The dream lingered as she continued to rub the sleep from her eyes, and for a while it seemed like the dream was more real than the room she woke up in. Just then, another pile of sheet music slid off the top of the piano onto the keys, and the crash made Emma nearly jump out of her skin. A second later, a single note rang out.

D sharp, she thought, instinctively. She wondered why the piano lid was up. Then a C note rang out, then a crashing chord that sounded something like a C major.

Something small and heavy fell over with the papers, she told herself. But then something happened that seemed far less likely: the first nine notes of the song "Heart and Soul" rang out, clear as day.

Emma wondered if she was still asleep.

Another flurry of papers fell off the piano, striking a few more random notes.

"OUCH!" a tiny voice rang out. "By Foundation, that HURT!"

"Best watch out for that falling paper," another vaguely familiar voice responded. The tiny voice belonged to a deep–throated woman. Emma only knew one woman's voice that was so earthy and yet so tiny.

"I said, pay attention," the voice insisted. "BIG paper. LITTLE brownies. I'd hate to have to be the one to report *that* paper cut to the Poobah!"

It was definitely Truss.

An even smaller voice giggled and was immediately hushed. It had to be Mat, Emma realized. Her eyes widened at the thought that perhaps she hadn't dreamed them up after all.

Emma crawled out and peered over the keyboard. Sitting sideways and cross–legged across the middle B and C keys was Piers, the tallest, thinnest brownie from the night before. Truss spread heavily across the center F and G keys, facing Piers. She was leaning back casually with her arm slung over the black D sharp, which depressed slightly under her shoulder weight. The littlest one, Mat, sat behind Piers on the lower D, dangling both red clad legs over the edge and swinging them merrily. The creature was so small the key didn't indent even a tiny bit.

Since the other two were deep in conversation, Mat was the first to notice Emma's face rising above the keyboard. The little brownie froze, blinked twice, pointed right at the tip of Emma's nose, then started to stammer.

"Ummmm…mm…mm…m…mon…st…st…st…er…! It's baaaack!"

The other two swiveled around and were so startled by Emma's looming face that all three screamed simultaneously. Emma couldn't help but notice that they screamed in perfect harmony, with Mat taking the high notes, Piers a fine tenor, and Truss a deep alto that was nearly a bass.

It was all just too bizarre for Emma. She was so confused. Was she still dreaming? Then there was her frustration from school, her fear of the old woman down the hall. And on top of it all, she was still disoriented by that other strange dream. Everything bubbled up at the same time.

She started to cry. It was a heartbreaking sound, and as she wept her tears splashed on the piano and soaked the brownies, who looked up at her, astonished and dumbfounded.

"I don't *want* to be a monster," Emma wailed. The brownies threw their hands to their pointed ears and grimaced like their heads were about to explode. The force of her exhalation caused their hair and the skin on their cheeks to blow backwards as if they were in a hurricane.

As she ran out of energy, Emma sank to the floor, nearly curled up in a ball, and continued to weep softly.

The three brownies were understandably surprised but also curious, so they gradually inched to the edge of the piano, which made a tinkling sound as they shifted forward on the keys. They leaned over the edge in unison, peering down at the girl and her quivering back.

"Oh, this will never do," said Truss in a motherly tone. "Come, come, child. We'll get this all sorted out."

Mat looked up with wide eyes.

"How can it be a child if it's so BIG?" the brownie whispered in awe. The relatively tall, lanky Piers screwed up his mouth, confusion and shock on his face. Then he broke into a fit of uncontrollable giggles. Mat looked at Piers in surprise and started to giggle too, until Truss turned angrily and pinched both of their noses simultaneously.

Mat squealed and fell back onto the piano keys with a plink, and Piers rubbed his nose, which was rapidly turning an even darker shade of red. Truss shot them another warning look, then turned to address Emma again.

"Now, now, dearie. It can't be as bad as all that."

Emma looked up tearfully, her damp hair half plastered to her face. The three brownies were all peering down at her in a row: Truss' round red face and wild hair, Piers' face so long and pointy she could not tell which was pointier, his nose or his chin, and little Mat's impossibly tiny one. All three of them were peeking over the edge, blinking at her with concern, curiosity and suspicion, respectively.

There are brownies on the piano, she thought to herself. *And they're real.* It was all perfectly ridiculous. Her sobs were now turning into giggles, causing the brownies to start giggling again too. *Maybe my brain is broken*, she thought. The next thing she knew she was laughing so hard her sides hurt, and she curled up in a ball again, her back still heaving, but this time in laughter instead of tears.

The brownies' expressions quickly turned back to alarm, and they began to back away again in fear.

"Do you think it's broken?" Piers asked, deeply concerned. Emma laughed even harder to hear her own thoughts echoed by this strange creature.

"Must be defective," Mat agreed.

"Let's figure this all out together, shall we?" Truss said to Emma, while she shot a warning glance at the other brownies. They had certainly never seen anything like this before.

"Why don't we all start at the beginning. Child? What are you?" Truss prodded gently.

"I told you yesterday. I'm a human," Emma hiccuped.

"Impossible!" Mat howled in a voice much too large for such a little body. "Humans can't see brownies. It's a fact. Mister Widget says so, and it's written in the Blue Scrolls and cross–referenced in the Purple Parchments. Humans are big, stupid creatures and blind to brownie blood. This creature is certainly big, and undoubtedly stupid, but it can clearly see us. It's impossible!"

By now, Emma was getting tired of being called a monster and big and stupid, especially by this tiny little creature. Her eyes narrowed, her face flushed, and she brought her nose up to the keyboard so she was staring at the little brownie eye to enormous eye.

Mat froze.

Then the tiny creature's teeth began to clack together, quietly at first, but loudly enough that Emma could hear the sound clearly. Another banging noise joined the clacking, and it took Emma a few moments to realize that Piers, the tall brownie, was cowering on another key not far away, his knees knocking together again as well. She suddenly felt badly about using her size to frighten the little creatures, even if the littlest brownie was rather nasty.

"Well, I think she does *look* like a human," said Truss.

Piers pulled his eyes off the human's horribly enormous face. This was the second time he'd gotten so close to her, and it still frightened him. With a great deal of effort, he turned to look at Truss.

"Goodness me, are you sure?" he chattered. "Have you ever *seen* a real human? I didn't know there were any brownies who had lived to tell of it."

"No, by Foundation, I haven't," she replied.

Mat quickly interrupted.

"But there *are* stories, and the Blue Scrolls are very specific about what a Human is and how they behave. There are the hominus giganti snorasaurus, who sleep all night long; the hominus colossi munchasaurus, who eat all day long; and the mysterious hominus hush–upicus–catatonicus, who do nothing but sit all day and stare at a mystical, flickering light source." The little brownie grew increasingly agitated and high pitched and finally collapsed, gasping for air, on the nearest piano key.

E, Emma noted.

"They are a strange breed, to be sure," Truss added casually, ignoring Mat completely. Then she turned to Emma, tilted her head, and asked, "Which sort are you, dearie?"

Emma wasn't really sure what either brownie meant by all that, so she just shrugged. "Just a plain old regular human," she said.

"Plane–owld–re–gyu–lore human," all three brownies repeated. They looked at each other, shook their heads and shrugged. "Never heard of it."

"How very strange," nodded Truss, like a doctor analyzing a patient's symptoms. She turned back to Emma. "Where did you come from, child?"

"I moved here yesterday with my father."

"And your mother?"

"My mother is gone. We lost her when I was five."

The brownies gasped in horror.

"Lost your mother? Lost your mother? How is that possible?" Mat cried out. "Where in Foundation could you have left her?"

"Did you check under the sofa cushions before you left?" Piers suggested, trying to be helpful. Truss pinched the lanky fellow and whispered heavily in his ear.

"Not that, you gravel–for–brains. She means lost as in…" She looked at Piers meaningfully. A questioning expression crossed his face, then he furrowed his brow and scratched his head. Then, suddenly, his eyes widened and Truss nodded at him. His eyes widened even more, and he dropped his head, clasping and twisting his hat in his hands.

"O, dearie, dearie. So sorry. So sorry to hear it." The other brownies nodded in agreement. "I say," continued Piers, who was struck suddenly with an idea. "Do you suppose *she* might be –?"

"Impossible!" Mat jumped in. "We're looking for the savior of our realm. This creature never even heard of us!"

"Well, perhaps it's not … er … finished, yet," Piers replied with a shrug.

"Not finished? How can it not be finished?" Mat was growing increasingly high pitched again. The little brownie seemed to be highly excitable.

"I don't know, exactly. Maybe it's missing some of its parts," Piers said, scratching his chin thoughtfully.

"I'm starting to think you may be right," said Truss, thoughtfully. "The other criteria do seem to fit."

The littlest brownie considered the facts for a moment, but didn't seem able to let go of the idea that Emma was clearly some sort of monster, and an undeniably stupid one at that.

"We're basement brownies!" the tiny creature announced, having decided that Emma was feeble–minded and needed lots of reinforcement.

"Yes, I know," said Emma. Mat squinted and frowned. This was clearly not the reply the little brownie expected. Emma added gently, "You told me so yesterday, but I thought it was a dream."

"Well, you're not supposed to see us," said Mat. "Mister Widget says humans can't see brownies. It's in the blood, you know. Human blood is so thin and weak. Too much oxygen, they say, but of course, that's still just a theory. Leads to feeble eyesight, linear thinking and poor digestion. Oxygen, that is, not theories. Mister Widget says humans can't even digest gravel. Imagine that!" The little brownie tried to imagine it and made a horrible face. Piers recoiled in horror at the idea of not being able to eat such basic foods.

Truss ignored the others and continued her questioning. "Where did you come from, child? Where were you before this?"

"Many places. Small towns in the prairies before this. Another city before that. We were by the seaside for a while; I really liked it there. And before that there were other cities. Lots of them. We go wherever dad finds work."

The brownies gasped again and quickly huddled together, whispering softly. As they broke apart and turned to face Emma again, she could hear Truss saying, "By Foundation, you were right, Piers! It all makes sense now. The child IS the Wanderer."

"I still don't understand how this can be a child," said Mat, a bit crossly. "I mean, look at the size of the thing. Can you imagine how big the father must be?"

Mat shivered, and then squealed as though pinched from behind. Emma chose to ignore this rudeness.

"What do you mean?" she said to Truss. "What is a Wanderer?"

"A Wanderer is a creature that travels restlessly across the world, carrying its uneasy energy from place to place. None of us has ever seen a real one before. We've only heard about them in stories told by the ancients."

"So Wanderers are human?" Emma asked, still confused.

Truss shook her head. "Not always. Wanderers come in many forms, but they are very rare, no matter what the species. These are uneasy times, child. The building is dying. It must have called you to help, and when you arrived, it summoned us and pulled us topside to help bring you Under."

"I was enjoying a nice breakfast of gravel and pegs when it happened," Piers grumbled. His stomach grumbled too. "It was so very nice and delicious."

"I don't understand," said Emma.

"Gravel and pegs," said Piers. "Breakfast. First food of the day.

Delicious."

"No, I mean I don't understand about the building. We came here because my father got a job here, so if anyone summoned us, it was dad's boss, not the house. And anyway, how could a building summon anyone? Houses aren't alive."

"Not alive? What sort of nonsense do they feed you humans? Of course they're alive," said Mat, truly horrified that she didn't know this.

The brownies chattered all at once.

"Then why haven't any people seen one sneeze before? I mean, that's pretty strange," Emma persisted.

Little Mat sighed heavily and loudly. Piers shook his head sadly. The two brownies rolled their eyes at each other. Truss turned around quickly and shot them both warning glances, but as she turned, they both looked upwards and tipped their heads back, as though the ceiling contained something fascinating.

"Oh, dearie, dearie me," Truss shook her head and furrowed her brow. The stout brownie sighed heavily with a strange sound, like a cross between "Ahem" and an odd grumbling noise in her throat. Then she nodded her head decisively and turned back to Emma, gesturing to her to come closer and sit down. Emma did.

"Pay them no mind, child," the woman began, shaking her head toward the other two brownies, who were now whispering to each other down in the piano's lower register. "Of course you wouldn't know about buildings. It's true humans build buildings, but the life of a home comes from a different place altogether. It's a place humans know nothing about. And not all buildings are lucky enough to experience the life force necessary for them to take root."

"Take root? But how?"

"Let me explain it to you this way, child. Buildings are born from ideas. Human ideas. Once the building is created out of brick, cement, wood and stone, the ideas themselves take root beneath the foundations and connect to the underworld, where magic lies. Then the building begins to absorb bits of life and history into its bricks, and the roots grow slowly, over time. Eventually, the building begins to breathe. Human life generates its life–force; history, its blood–force.

"Not every house on a street is alive, of course. Not every building will be lucky enough to experience the right combination of magic, history and life energy. But the ones that come to life have the power to change the lives of everyone and everything connected to it, including the people inside it and the underfolk beneath and within it.

"Haven't you noticed that buildings are often the passageway to magic worlds in the stories your father reads to you at night? It depends on where their roots grow, of course. Dorothy flew away in her house in a tornado. Peter Pan found Wendy and her brothers in their bedroom and whisked them away to Neverland. No wonder his shadow was attracted to the room, it was so full of life–force from those children. The White Rabbit's hole rests right over the spot where the roots of Alice's house enter Wonderland. The children of Narnia snuck through the wardrobe. That magician boy and his friends get to school by crossing through the magic wall at the train station."

"But those are all make believe stories," interrupted Emma.

"Not make believe, child. Architecture and magic are irreversibly linked to each other. Architecture is one of the forms magic takes. The building contains life just as form and structure contain magic. And just as magic without laws and form is dangerous and deadly, life without shelter is feral and frightening."

Emma was having trouble understanding, but she kept quiet while Truss continued.

"You can tell a living house because it seems to wrap itself around you when you enter. It supports you and makes you feel instantly like you're at home. Of course, a living house can also get old or ill if it's not cared for, and then just being inside it can make you sad.

Haven't you ever noticed that some places just make you happy, while others stifle you and make you feel like the walls are squeezing in on you, trying to suffocate you? That is an unhappy house. Its heart shrinks, and it cannot breathe, and everything that lives in it will feel its pain. A home is more than shelter, you know. When it's filled with love, there's simply nothing more magical in the universe."

Truss fell quiet, and a sigh came from a lower register on the piano. It was Piers. He sighed again, and in a melancholy voice said softly, "Of course, there haven't been any new living buildings in many years. No place for them to grow, you know, no land for them to take root in."

"I'm sorry I made the house sneeze you up," said Emma.

"What are we going to do now?" Piers wailed, great droplets of tears welling up in his eyes. "I want … I want … I want my breakfast!"

"Hush. You and your breakfast," Truss said crossly. "But you're right, we must find a way to get back home."

"And find a way to put things right again," said Mat. "If we don't fix it soon, Mister Widget says all of Under may be in danger, not just the brownie burrows. And if we don't do something soon, the house will be dragging up underfolk left, right and center, and what a mess that will be!"

"What can I do to help?" said Emma.

"You've done quite enough, I should think," muttered Mat, apparently still feeling a bit disgruntled about getting so close to the giant and then witnessing the monster going quite insane.

"Mat, what do the Blue Scrolls say about getting home?" said Truss, trying to help restore Mat's confidence.

"Nothing. Nothing that I've ever heard or read. Nothing that Mister Widget has ever taught us, I'm sure of it," Mat replied.

"No one has ever been actually summoned by a house before, so there's no record of anyone ever getting back. Of course, if we make a mistake, it means the future of the burrow will be – " The little brownie lifted both hands to face level and shook them, "Kablooey!"

"Not good, not good," muttered Piers. "Everything rumbling and grumbling, just like my tummy. So hungry!"

"Can't you get back through the air vent?" Emma suggested helpfully.

"The what?" said Piers, momentarily distracted from his hunger.

"The air vent. The way you came in."

"No, child, it doesn't work like that. We need to find an open portal to Under, a place where the roots meet the foundation. The way we came in isn't the way back. It's like a breathing valve. It only opens one way. The return path will be trickier to find without the house to guide us."

"Well, then why don't we just ask the house to open one up the other way?" Emma wasn't about to give up.

"Ask the house? Are you completely daft? You can't ask a house to do anything. They're not sentient, you know. At least, not in the way we are." Mat's voice began to rise again.

"Well, it sounds like we should check the basement for a portal, then," said Emma. The three brownies scratched their chins, tilted their heads and considered this for a moment.

"I say, I say, the creature may be onto something," said Piers.

"Let's go now!" Emma was starting to get excited by the possibility of adventure, though the memory of her dream and the creature chasing her up the stairs made her shudder inwardly at the thought of wandering around the halls without her father.

"Wait a moment," said Truss, "I have the strangest feeling we've forgotten something." She sat back down on the D sharp, sending a clear *plink* into the air.

"Forgotten something?" asked Mat. Piers scratched his head, and continued to rub his empty tummy at the same time. Emma looked around, but all three of the brownies were there. They hadn't arrived with anything, so nothing seemed to be missing. Then she realized they weren't missing a *what*, but rather a *who*.

"Where is the other guy? The, um, Master Something–or–other."

The brownies looked at her, then looked at each other. Then they freaked out. Master Tect was missing, and no one had the slightest clue where he had gone.

Emma was starting to think that basement brownies weren't very bright.

Chapter Five: The Missing Master
& Other Mysteries

It was pretty clear that none of the brownies had given a second thought to Master Tect either. They all looked up at Emma, as if they had been bonked on the head simultaneously with big rubber mallets. Mat looked at Piers and then at Truss. Piers looked at Truss and then at Mat. Truss looked at Mat and then at Piers. Then they all leapt to attention and began running up and down the keyboard, looking for the missing brownie. The piano tinkled under their tiny feet. It sounded a bit like a Scott Joplin rag.

"Goodness Gravel! We've lost the Master Surveyor!" Piers wrung his hands as he plinked and plunked up and down along the keyboard.

"The Grand Poobah will never forgive us!" wailed Mat. "We'll be ground into bits and turned into stucco!"

Emma barely felt a tiny tug at her sleeve. She looked down to see Piers holding her cuff button and leaping up and down like a Mexican jumping bean.

"Please, you must help us!" he cried. "We must find him!"

"Maybe the monster sat on him," suggested Mat helpfully. Emma squinted and was about to say something mean in return, but Piers tugged at her button again and pleaded with her again to help.

She did.

They looked everywhere, searching every inch of the room, under all the papers and sheet music and in all the boxes, but there was no sign of the little round Master Tect anywhere.

They collapsed after about an hour of searching, exhausted and disheveled, back at the piano where they started. Piers slumped against the upright lid at the back of the keyboard with a mournful expression that made his long, narrow face look even longer and more narrow. Mat crumpled in a heap of despair in the far corner and started to cry. Truss plunked herself down in front of Emma and wrung her hands with a very worried expression on her face.

Emma suddenly realized she was very, very tired and wondered what time it was and why her father wasn't home yet. Mat was still crying, and somewhere in the middle of her other musings, Emma wondered idly how so much water could come from such a little creature. Then she wondered if the puddle forming around the brownie would be bad for the piano, and she furrowed her brow in concern. Truss mistook the frown, thinking Emma was sad for the missing Master.

"There, there, now dearie. No sense in fretting about it. There's only so much we can do. I'm sure he'll turn up soon, if he hasn't been smooshed, or eaten by something horrific," Truss said, trying to sound reassuring. Emma paused for a moment, trying to figure out how to explain that she was actually worried about the piano, but without sounding like she didn't care about their missing friend.

Just then, a deep and horrible groan shook the room.

It was a low, rumbling moan that shook the windows in their frames and sent a shiver through Emma's bones. Piers and Mat nearly vibrated right off the piano until the sound stopped abruptly. The room fell terribly silent. A beat passed. The silence hung over their heads like a water droplet waiting to drop.

The silence was shattered by another groan that rocked the piano, sending Mat right over the edge, where the little brownie scrambled for dear life in an attempt to hang onto the lip of the F key. A pile of papers shook and shifted on the top of the piano and sent another flurry of sheets cascading downward.

A third groan filled the room, and this time Emma noticed that the vibrations around the papers on top of the piano were especially strong. She reached up and pushed the papers aside.

"Aha!" she cried out, triumphantly.

Master Tect lay on his back, sleeping, with his head tilted to one side.

An empty soda bottle had fallen over such that his mouth was right near the opening of the bottle. The Master inhaled deeply, then exhaled with another deep groan. The bottle amplified the sound and vibrated beneath the papers on the piano.

"What is it?" asked Mat, trying to clamber back onto the keyboard and see what was happening on top of the piano at the same time. "Is it another monster?"

Emma reached out a finger and gently poked the enormously round brownie. He snorted, rolled over and wrapped his arms around her finger and leaned his head against it like a pillow. Try as she might, she couldn't pry him off. She shook her finger gently, but he just snuggled in tighter. He was drooling a bit, too, blubbering like a baby. She lifted her entire hand and raised him right into the air, dangling upside down from her pointer finger. He snored, loudly.

By now the other brownies were jumping up and down, at first curious to see what Emma had found, then impatient and finally with urgency as they realized it was, in fact, their lost companion. All this jumping and leaping on the piano keys made a horrible racket. Mat was pogo–ing up and down on the lower octave G, while Piers leapt slowly and gracefully on the E. The two of them together approximated the opening notes of Beethoven's Fifth Symphony.

The cacophony finally caused the Master to stir, and he half cracked open an eye. Emma could only imagine what went through his head as he processed the scene. The room was upside–down because he was still dangling from Emma's finger with his head pointing toward the floor. Down below (or rather, up above, from his perspective), the other brownies were leaping about waving their arms and shouting things he could not hear due to the plinking piano keys. Somewhere in the same picture, an enormous, upside–down human girl's face peered at him. He took a few moments to assimilate all this. He blinked, then blinked again, then paused.

A moment later, his eyes shot wide open, and he let out a terrified *eeeeeeeeeeek.* As he did so, he loosened his grasp on Emma's finger but instantly realized he was upside–down and that gravity was not his friend, and so he grabbed it again, scrambling for his life to hang on. Emma reached over with her other hand and plucked him off by the back of his collar and carefully placed him on the piano. The other brownies scrambled to his side and began to fuss over him.

"I say, I say, I say," the portly red gentleman sputtered. His face was particularly red from being held upside–down.

"Archibald Tect, you gave us such a scare!" Truss scolded.

"What in Foundation is going on?" the round brownie blurted, still disoriented and blushing to hear Truss call him by his proper name.

The brownies began speaking in rapid succession.

"The monster from yesterday, we've determined without question that it can see us," Piers chattered.

"Yes, I know that, but …," the Master sputtered.

"It's not a monster, it's a human," Truss interrupted.

"Well, humans *are* monsters," Mat clarified.

"No, they aren't," Truss contradicted.

"Yes, they are."

"No, they aren't."

"Yes, they are."

"No, they aren't."

"Yes, they are, and this one is super monstrous 'cause it can see us," Mat said with a pout.

"Yes, we established that yesterday, but," Master Tect tried to get a word in edgewise. "Humans can't see Underfolk," he finished, surprised to have gotten it all out without interruption.

"That's what I said," Mat affirmed.

"Well, this one can," Piers asserted.

"Very strange," Master Tect muttered.

"Strange indeed," Truss agreed.

"And there's more," Piers added.

"More?" Master Tect asked.

"More," Piers said, nodding. At this point, the conversation began to unravel.

"Well, what is it?" the Master sputtered.

"What is what?"

"What more is there?" The Master was beginning to grow impatient.

"Oh, *that* more. The monster …"

"You mean the human?"

"Yes, the human–monster. It can see us."

"Yes, I got that part."

"Well, there's more."

"So you said. What's more?"

"More what?"

This particular portion of the chatter looped around several times before it finally got back on track.

"The monster, the human–monster. It's the Wanderer," Piers finally declared triumphantly.

"By Foundation, no!" cried Master Tect.

"Yes!" the brownies replied in unison.

"Seems the house summoned it," said Truss.

"By Foundation, no!" Master Tect repeated.

"Yes!" replied Piers.

"And we must find a way to take the monster back with us, before our entire burrow is destroyed. According to Mister Widget – "

"Oh, my breakfast. Will it be destroyed too? My beautiful breakfast!"

moaned Piers.

"By Foundation, no!" The Master appeared to be in a prolonged state of shock.

"Yes! It was a beautiful breakfast!"

"I mean, no, we can't let that happen!" the Master sputtered.

"Indeed, but it's probably cold by now," Piers said, mournfully.

"The burrow is cold?" said the Master, confused.

"No, my breakfast."

"The burrow! The burrow! We can't let anything happen to our beautiful home!" The brownies all chimed in, then started to run around in an insane frenzy.

"Or my breakfast."

"Blast your breakfast! There are more important things concerning us now!" The Master had begun to sweat profusely again. He pulled the handkerchief out of his pocket, only to discover it was still soggy from his last bout of distress. He made a face and poked it, disdainfully, back into his pocket.

"Probably cold, anyway."

"The burrow?"

"No, my breakfast!"

"Arrrgh!"

"The monster ..." Mat started to say.

"It's not a monster. It's a human," Truss chastised the small brownie.

"The human–monster ...," Mat corrected.

"I'm not a monster," Emma frowned.

"What about it?" said the Master, still confused.

"It said it would help," Piers said.

"Help? How? Why?" Master Tect sputtered.

"Well, it's the reason everything's downside up to begin with," Mat added, grumpily.

"But I didn't mean to …"

"All that wanderer spirit coming in here and making the house act all strange …"

"Mat, do behave. It's not like that at all. The house clearly summoned her here. It's not her fault," Truss reprimanded the little brownie.

"Summoned who?" Mat replied, peevishly.

"The human," Truss said, starting to lose her temper.

"Oh, you mean the *monster*?"

"I'm *NOT* a monster. And I'm not an *IT*, either." Emma was not liking the direction this conversation was heading.

"Only proper that it should help put things right. After all, that's why we're here," said Mat.

"And I want my breakfast," Piers piped in.

"I'm a *girl*. A human girl. That makes me a *she* not an *it*."

"It's also very opinionated."

Already confused and tired and increasingly grumpy, Emma turned to confront the littlest brownie. As her body moved, a shaft of pale light pushed through the window and struck the piano over her shoulder.

It was dawn.

How can it be dawn already? Emma wondered, while the brownies all ran around in a panic. Had she been awake all night? Where was her father? Piers was clawing at the piano lid, trying to leverage himself to the top. Why hadn't her father come home? She was very confused. Mat ran to the end of the piano … *plink, plink, plink* … and tried to hide in the shadow of one of the black keys. What was she going to do about school? The brownies began scurrying back and forth, making her dizzy. The room began to spin. She tried very hard to concentrate on the brownies, to see what they were doing, but her mind was still wondering where her father was and why he hadn't come home. The brownies sprang about the room, screeching about the light and begging her to protect them. The room became brighter as the sun grew stronger, and the light spread across the room, until all she could see was the light and nothing else. She still felt like she was spinning, or rather, it felt as through she were pinned in one place while the room spun around her. She was so tired. The brownies were in some sort of trouble. They needed help. But she was tired. So tired. She just needed to close her eyes … for a moment …

Emma was floating in a big black sea. She could almost hear the waves lapping at the side of her bed, or the boat, or whatever it was she was lying in. It sounded like the boat was singing to her, trying to tell her to be calm.

Shhhhhhhhh, it sang. *Shhhhhhhhhhhhh.*

Then she slept.

After what seemed like a very long time, Emma cracked open her left eye. She was in her room. She opened her right eye. Yes, definitely back in her bed. She could see the window and the old, tattered dresser and the air vent with its rusty, decorative iron cover.

She glanced at the old wind–up clock on the dresser. It was her regular time to wake up for school. She sat up slowly, expecting to be exhausted from staying up all night, but to her surprise she felt like she'd just slept for a very long time and was totally rested. She slid into her slippers and opened her bedroom door.

The hallway was quiet. She tiptoed down to her father's room and stood by the door for a moment, listening. It was strangely quiet. She remembered she hadn't seen him come home, and she started worry. She reached up to the doorknob, turned it and slowly pushed the door open.

The light from the hall cast a long, rectangular box of light across the floor, and Emma could see her own silhouette outlined perfectly in the middle of the box. She looked across the floor to the foot of the bed, then across the bed itself. A large body loomed in the dim light. Emma could see it moving up and down, slowly, like the body of a large man sleeping and breathing heavily. She breathed a sigh of relief, backed out of the room and closed the door.

The house was still eerily silent as Emma got ready for school. She scribbled out a note telling her father she'd gone to school on her own. She paused again in the hallway, listening for signs that he was awake, but the apartment was so quiet she could hear her own heart beating. Her face creased into a worried frown. She knew her father was exhausted from the drive and the move and from worrying about her all the time. *He probably just needed to sleep*, she told herself. She listened once more to be sure, then turned and stepped out of the apartment.

The door closed behind her with a clack, and she looked down the hall. It extended like a dark, dank gullet in front of her, longer and darker than ever before. Around the halfway point, she could finally make out the stair landing and the dim light signaling the way out.

She took a deep breath and stepped forward. She was ready for anything: bright lights, loud noises; anything at all.

Nothing happened.

She took another step. Still nothing. Cautiously, she crept her way down the hall toward the stairs. Her heart sped up as she passed the old woman's apartment, but the door was closed, and there was no sound from inside. There was no hint of the bright light inside, either. She tiptoed quickly past the door to the landing and ran down the stairs as quickly as she could.

When she burst out the front door into the morning air, the bright sun and warm morning air made her gasp. She stood there stunned for a moment while she tried to adjust, then looked both ways to make sure the street was safe. There was not a soul to be seen anywhere, except three old women on the stoop in front of an old, dilapidated house about halfway down the block. They were hunched together, whispering something, and one of them had something small in her hand, which she carefully passed to her neighbour soundlessly. They looked up when Emma came into sight and watched her intently until she passed. Emma quickened her step, anxious to be somewhere else, anywhere else, as quickly as possible.

She hurried along the block, feeling the three sets of eyes boring into her back. At least the feeling that someone was watching her from the apartment was gone, but oddly enough, the absence felt even stranger than the fact that the trees weren't rustling and there were no sounds of televisions, radios or people shouting at each other. Finally, she reached the corner and turned onto the main street.

The silence broke the moment she stepped off her block. Car horns and motors, grumbling trucks and growling motorcycles, the chatter of people came at her from all angles. Radios and sirens assaulted her from every side.

Within a half a block, she was starting to feel more or less normal, or as normal as she could manage when walking down an unfamiliar street, alone in a new city on her way to a new school. She thought about the brownies and the things they had told her about buildings having roots stretching down to some sort of faeryland. The whole thing seemed absurd. Really, it did seem like nonsense. But then again, she never would have believed that brownies were any more than the figment of someone's overactive imagination either. She had read lots of faerytale books and enjoyed a good story like anyone else, but she always knew the difference between the magical world in her mind and the hard reality of her day to day life. But now, it felt like the line between those two worlds was gone, and she really didn't know what to do about it.

Just then, a passing woman brushed up against Emma's shoulder, and the jolt woke her out of her reverie. She had been thinking so hard she had just walked and walked, and she'd completely forgotten where she was going. She stepped over to the corner of an apartment building and looked around, chastising herself for not being more careful. It was risky enough being out in a strange city by herself, whether her father needed the rest or not, but to wander off like this without paying attention was really dumb.

I'm not lost. I'm not lost. I'm not lost.

She figured she couldn't be more than a few blocks off course, so she backtracked to the last corner and looked down the cross street in both directions and then glanced back down the street she just came from. Nothing looked even remotely familiar. She walked another block. Same thing. She was starting to get nervous but decided to go one more block before asking for directions.

I am so lost, she thought with a sinking heart.

She went one block and then one more, but she still couldn't recognize anything around her. She was just about to give up when she noticed a grocery store on her left side. She remembered passing a grocery store that looked a lot like it on her way to school the day before, but she was pretty certain they'd passed that one on the right. She was either very confused, or the buildings had switched sides in the middle of the night. At any other time in her life, the suggestion would have been a joke, but lately all bets were off, as her dad's friends sometimes said.

The grocer himself stood in front of the small shop, just as he had the day before. And, just like yesterday, he was hosing down the sidewalk. The cold water turned to steam when it met the hot pavement. He was old and shriveled on the outside, his skin dark with age. Emma wasn't immediately sure what nationality he was, maybe Asian, maybe Middle Eastern, maybe even a deeply tanned, leathery Caucasian. It was impossible to tell. He was incredibly wrinkled and terribly thin underneath, as if his skin were made for a much larger man. Despite this, he seemed to be surprisingly strong and spry, and his eyes glistened and sparkled at Emma as she passed by.

"Whaztsssa matter, gurrrrr–lie?"

When he spoke, his lips flapped together and his voice grumbled in a raspy manner. It came out sounding like a combination of the putt–putt sound people make when they're imitating a running motor and the squishing sound boots make in the mud. Emma was a bit taken aback and not a little grossed out.

"Nothing … I …," she paused, trying to figure out how to finish the sentence. She did need help, but one always had to be careful when dealing with strangers.

"Whaztsssa matter," he repeated. "Buildings got you all knodder blodder?"

Emma had no idea what he meant by knodder blodder, and she stepped back, as much in surprise and confusion as to avoid the sudden rain shower that accompanied his pronunciation of so many b's and d's through those incredibly flappy lips.

"Thumthhhhhhing's goin' on bu–bu–bu–basement–way," he added, leaning forward conspiratorially and pointing to the ground with a wink. She still couldn't help cringing a little at the long th's and staccato b's. Mostly, though, she was very surprised to hear him mention basements.

"Excuse me?" she asked, with as much courage as she could muster. She leaned in to hear better and was rewarded with another spray–filled response.

"I thththaid, whu–whut's wrrrrong, litul girrrrl, loooooze yore way?"

By now, Emma was even more confused, but confused was starting to feel like normal since they moved to this place. She could feel the dampness rising off the sidewalk and seeping inside her as well as all around her. A fog, both literally and mentally. The water hose was still gurgling away, slicking down the pavement as the man held the nozzle in his hand, half forgotten. Steam rose from the sidewalk and surrounded them, and his speech was undeniably – *soggy*. Emma could feel her hair starting to curl.

"School's ththhthataway, girrrrlie," he raspberried suddenly, and just as suddenly the cloud of mist disappeared and the city came back into full view. Emma looked as he pointed across the street. Of course, she thought. That's exactly where it was supposed to be. She'd gotten turned around somehow, and everything looked wrong. That's all.

She backed up a few steps, mumbled heartfelt thanks and ran full tilt to the corner and across the street. The cross light turned to "walk" almost as if it was waiting for her. She wasn't sure, but she thought she could hear the strange old man behind her, laughing in a strange, gurgling way. She didn't stop to look.

Sooner than she liked, the school loomed down at her from the top of the dead–end street, waiting for her to enter. She hadn't really looked at it the day before, but now that she was alone, she could see it spread out across the end of the street like a giant bat, its gaping entrance wide open and swallowing school children as they streamed up the stairs.

The east and west wings spread out in opposite directions, and she suddenly realized exactly *why* they were called wings. Two flagpoles over the central entrance bore flags that waved crazily like hair, or antennae, or pointy ears. There was a second floor bay window above the entrance doors, making it look like a strange, multifaceted Cyclops' eye, or maybe like an insect instead of a bat. Or maybe it was a cross between the two, she wasn't really sure. All she knew was that the school building definitely had roots, and it was alive, just like the brownies described. She wondered why she'd never looked at buildings like that before, and why she'd never noticed them looking back at her.

It took every ounce of courage she had to walk up to the gates and go inside.

"*Princess.*"

Not two steps in the gate, she found herself face to face, or rather, face to faces, with the Gorgeous Gang. She'd almost forgotten about the horrible girls who had tormented her the day before. It was almost as though they had been standing there, waiting just for her. The ringleader Thena stood in front, her golden curls bounced and glistened in the morning sun, so perfect and so lively they appeared to have a life of their own.

Emma shuddered.

Meanwhile, bits of her storybook seemed to be stuck in Emma's head:

Perseus swam up the rocky shore on the island of Medusa, a sorceress and a monster, a beautiful woman with snakes on her head instead of hair. She was so horrible to look upon that anyone who looked at her turned to stone, and the island was covered in hundreds of statues, the frozen remains of visitors who came before him.

"Look, girls. Princess is ignoring us. Maybe she thinks she's too good for us."

Emma realized she had to concentrate. Things were going to get out of control very soon. She could feel it. She looked at Thena and tried to focus, but she just couldn't keep her mind in one place, and she just kept thinking about Medusa. Emma wasn't sure this girl could turn a person to stone just by looking at them, but her sneer sure was petrifying.

There was something different about these girls, too. She didn't like them. They were far too pretty. Their skin was too perfect, their hair too curly, their clothes too trendy. When they moved, it was in a pack like a multi–headed animal.

The next thing she knew, her mind was wandering off again, digging up old memories. She could almost hear her mother's voice reading from her storybook: *and so, the mighty Hercules, strongest man in the world, fought the Hydra, a horrible, snake–like creature with many heads. And each time he cut off one head, two more grew back in its place …*

"… *Princess?*" Thena's voice cut menacingly through her thoughts, and her heart started beating faster again. The girl was standing with her leg thrown forward, her fists on her hips and her head thrust forward in a mean grimace. Emma wondered how anyone so perfectly pretty could look so horrifyingly horrible.

The girls advanced slowly, menacingly. Emma knew she should hold her ground. She was on their turf, and they would do anything to defend it. She knew that if she gave in, even an inch, it would be all over for her, at least until her father found a new job somewhere else. And since his current job looked like it was going to last at least a little while, she had to make a stance right here, right now. Instead, she looked around for something to distract them long enough for her to slip away.

"You know, if you scrunch up your face like that, it will stick there eventually." Emma could hear the words coming out of her own mouth, as if she was powerless to stop them. "But I suppose in your case that would be an improvement."

Emma's heart skipped a beat while the girls allowed the words to sink in.

Wow, that was stupid, Emma thought in a panic. *Why did I say that?* Clearly, they were not accustomed to being challenged. *Stupid. So very, very stupid.*

Thena's face scrunched up further in fury.

I am so dead, Emma thought as she braced herself for the inevitable. But even as she did so, Emma could see that the girl was hesitating, clearly calculating the chances of her face actually getting stuck.

"What'z going on here, girrrlz?"

All four of the nasty girls broke into innocent, relaxed poses and their faces transformed into warm, friendly expressions. Almost in unison, they chimed: "Why, hello, Madame LaRoche."

Emma hadn't heard the solid woman's deep, rumbling voice so much as feel it rattling her bones, but she had her way out. She breathed a quiet sigh of relief.

"Absolutely nothing," purred the Gorgeous Gang. "We're just trying to talk our new friend here into joining the softball team."

Thena slid forward and draped an arm oh–so–casually over Emma's shoulder, and turned to face the principal. The ponderous woman loomed over them like a massive cliff. She directed her impassive expression toward the girls, first at one, then another, assessing the situation. Her eyes evaluated each one and finally landed heavily on Emma. Her stare was so penetrating, Emma could almost feel the woman walking through her brain, inspecting it. Her thoughts may as well have been a pile of apples at the grocery store. Thena's hand tightened around Emma's shoulder, and her painted fingernails dug under Emma's skin.

They're afraid of Madame LaRoche, Emma realized. But then again, so was she, but at least they were afraid of something.

"Yes, that's right," Emma stammered. The steel grip on her shoulder relaxed, and Emma tried not to wince. Madame LaRoche continued to stand there, immobile, looking at Emma for what seemed to be an eternity. Finally, her expression relaxed, or softened ever so slightly, though Emma could barely detect the change.

Just then the bell rang.

"Well now, get yourrrrrr–selves to home–rrrrrrooom," Madame LaRoche rasped.

"Come with us, *Princess.*"

The golden–haired Thena spun around, whipping Emma around with her, and guided her forcibly up the stairs and down the hall toward their homeroom. The three others followed close behind. Other students scurried out of their path the way iron shavings do near the wrong end of a magnet. Emma couldn't see her, but sensed that Madame LaRoche was looming somewhere behind them, watching their progress from a distance.

As they neared the homeroom door, Thena leaned her head toward Emma in a movement that could have easily been mistaken for a friendly gesture of camaraderie. Her face still radiated innocent purity, but under her breath she hissed, "We'll see you later, *Princess.*"

She released Emma from her constricting clutch and slid gracefully into her seat. The rest of the posse did the same, like synchronized swimmers gliding through water. The classroom filled up quickly, leaving only one seat in the very front, opposite the teacher's desk.

As Emma sat down, she caught a glimpse of Thena, who was still staring at her darkly. Her eyes seemed to burn into Emma's skin. The rest of the girls were draped decoratively across their desks, whispering to each other. As she arranged her books and settled into her chair, Emma could hear the words *Princess* and *Daddy's little girl*, followed by snorts and giggles. She wondered if her father was all right, and if he'd gotten up in time to get to work.

Emma could still feel the stares burning into the back of her head as the teacher walked into the room. And for every minute of the rest of the day, Emma knew without question that she was being watched.

Chapter Six: This Is Not a Pipe

By the time Emma turned back down the street toward home, she was cranky and exhausted. She had made it through her second day without crying though, and that was something, considering the kind of day it had been. The Gorgeous Gang had followed her around most of the day, hovering in the shadows, whispering and pointing, sometimes talking about her in voices that were deliberately too loud so everyone could hear.

They found it particularly funny to huddle together and speak in exaggerated whispers, telling secrets that everyone could hear. Most of their chatter was punctuated with one of them saying *"Princess"* a little too loudly, at which point they would all freeze up, look around in pretend embarrassment and then break into hysterical giggles. Even though Emma knew not to take any of this personally, it was starting to wear her down.

Then there were the bumps. The girls kept their distance most of the day, but they took every opportunity they could find to bump into her. Passing in the halls, passing to and from her desk, in the cafeteria when she had her hands full with her lunch tray. They were usually stealth bumps, when she was least expecting it. The other students kept their heads down and pretended it wasn't happening. Emma guessed they had seen it happen often enough that they knew not to attract undue attention from the girls, lest they become a target themselves.

Somehow, though, she made it through the day. It certainly didn't hurt that Madame LaRoche always seemed to pass by whenever the girls were acting particularly badly. Maybe it was just coincidence, but Emma was beginning to feel rather grateful for the large, lumbering woman and her unpredictable schedule.

Exhausted by the day's events, Emma felt herself tense up as she turned the corner back toward the tree–lined street where she now lived. There were so many things she couldn't explain since they moved here, and she was so tired. The idea of another strange thing happening now made her cringe in trepidation. The street was perfectly peaceful, however, and the apartment building sat quietly at the end of the row, almost romantic in that old, broken things way. A cool breeze rustled through the trees, and, for the first time in days, Emma felt herself starting to relax.

The street unfolded in front of her. It was paved with very old cobblestones, worn so flat with age and use that Emma hadn't even realized until now that it wasn't blacktop. The gutters formed an uneven U–shaped groove, hanging off the sidewalks like an elongated magazine rack. Surprisingly, the gutters were sparkling clean without a single leaf in sight, which was odd considering it was early autumn and the breeze continuous. The sidewalks, by contrast, were rough and uneven, with stones poking up as if they were trying to trip up passersby on purpose. Odd bits of grass sprouted up between the cracks, determined to grab hold wherever they could.

The homes were mostly old brick townhouses that had been converted to multifamily duplexes and triplexes. They had worn out stone steps with old, fractured lions perched on top. As she walked by, she could see that many of them had once been grand old homes that had clearly seen much better days. Now mostly low–income housing with four or five families in each, they still bore traces of their once glorious past: little bits of iron work around the windows that had not yet been sold off and replaced with plain iron security bars; little ornamental details above a window; an elegant stone medallion that managed to survive tucked under the eaves; random gargoyles and dragon heads, most of them missing their mates.

Emma had never really paid that much attention to buildings before. She hadn't realized the details and variations that made each one unique. Before, she would have looked at this street and seen a row of identical brick townhouses. Now she saw them as individuals, each with its own personality, history and residual life. All of the lives that had passed through each building, filled with childbirth and marriage and death, had left their mark. Where before she would have seen sad, old walls and windows, she now saw traces of a much richer and more elegant past. She saw that some houses were truly happier than others. Some of them still radiated hope and happiness, under the heavy façade of wear and tear. Others were dark and forbidding, hollow shells containing nothing but despair, dooming anyone whom dared enter. And then there was the odd wooden Victorian tucked in between: short, squat, sagging, but still painted gaily in pretty pastels and bright blues, greens and shocking pink. These and other buildings on the block seemed to seethe with life. The life was in their bricks, their bones.

She looked again at the building that was now her home. It was so quiet. Not a sound came from the windows or from inside. She looked up at the place where she'd felt someone watching her the day before, but the window was still closed, and everything inside was perfectly still.

She looked again at the apartment building, scrutinizing it closely. It was quiet, peaceful, but it did not have any signs of life that she could see. The sun cut down the street and glinted off the windows. The trees rustled softly. There wasn't a single sign of humans around or hints of the strange upheavals of the past two nights. She never would have guessed the place was alive, with roots that reached down into the earth and touched another world. Assuming, of course, that the brownies were telling the truth, and it wasn't some kind of trick. And, of course, that the whole thing was really real in the first place, because right now Emma was feeling more or less normal for the first time in days.

A sliver of doubt crept back into her head.

It was only natural that she should have strange dreams when she was so very tired from moving and driving and packing and unpacking. And sure, she'd moved around a lot before and was an old pro at it, but that didn't change the fact that it was still an exhausting process, no matter how good and efficient she was.

Another cool breeze brushed across her face and she realized her face was starting to burn in the hot sun. She quickly shook off her reverie and ran up the steps into the dark, cool lobby. She paused for a moment to listen, heard nothing, then ran up the stairs as fast as she could. By the time she reached the top, her chest hurt, and she was gasping, but the exercise made her feel much, much better. She stood at the top landing and leaned against the wall, panting heavily. The only sound she could hear was her breath scraping in her ears. The hallway was perfectly still. The strange door was shut. Everything was normal.

She stepped into the apartment and shut the door behind her. The lock tumbled closed with a heavy click that echoed in the hall, followed by a heavy silence. Her father did not appear to be home. She kicked off her shoes and put down her school bag and padded down the hall to his bedroom. The door was slightly ajar.

She called out, tentatively.

"Dad?"

There was no response, so she pushed the door open. There was no one there. It looked like he'd done some unpacking, but hadn't finished. Some of his clothes had been hung up, but the rest were scattered about the room, some left in piles on a chair and strewn across his suitcase. He had probably left for work in a hurry. His bed wasn't made yet. She padded back to the living room and found a note on the table.

Early rehearsal, Em. Back late.
Food in fridge.

Emma sighed. He never had been much of a writer; the only kind of notes he dealt with were the musical kind. She sat down in the chair and looked around. She was exhausted, but there was homework to do, and there was still so much to unpack. She sighed heavily, then laughed inwardly as she realized she sounded like an old woman. She pushed herself off the chair and started to unpack.

She was sorting through her father's sheet music, trying to straighten up the pile that fell off the piano the previous night. Everything was out of order, and she wanted to fix it before her father needed them for practice. She was in the middle of sorting and reorganizing when she was startled by the sound of scratching at the front door.

She stopped for a moment to listen.

She heard nothing for a moment, but then it was there again, barely audible, a soft scratching and rustling sound at the front door. Emma froze, not quite sure what to do. She waited for a knock, but none came. She wouldn't have answered the door anyway, not with her dad gone, but a knock would have made her feel better, if only because it was the normal thing. Instead, the scratching continued for what seemed like forever.

Scratch. Scratch. Scratch.

Suddenly, something white and rectangular shot under the door into the apartment. The scratching stopped abruptly. By the time Emma started breathing again, the apartment had fallen silent again.

Carefully, slowly and ever so quietly, she put down the sheet music that was in her hand and picked up her storybook. She held the book in front of her like a shield as she crept across the floor, trying to see what was there.

It was a postcard with a picture of a pipe on it. It was the old fashioned sort of pipe, the sort that old men sometimes used to smoke. The one on the postcard was painted against a plain beige background. Underneath it read:

Ceci n'est pas un pipe.

She had no idea what that meant.

She flipped it over. In the corner, some small text informed her that the card was a reproduction of a painting by some French artist named Henri Magritte, and the painting was named "This is not a pipe." Emma flipped the card over again, confused. It certainly was a picture of a pipe, so what on earth could it mean? How could a pipe not be a pipe?

She flipped the card over again and noticed something scratched near the edge. It was very hard to read. The letters were all pointy and long and overlapped each other. She picked up the card and looked at it more closely, tilting the card one way and then the other, hoping the angles might make it easier to decipher. Giving up, she carried the card back to the kitchen table and put it down.

The word jumped up at her as if by magic. Someone had scrawled a message into the cardboard with something sharp. There was no ink, but with the light reflecting at just the right angle, the words stood out clear as day. It read, simply:

Help.

Help, she thought. *Help whom?* She tiptoed back to the door and peered out the peephole. The hall was empty. She put her ear to the door and listened. Nothing. She reached a hand forward to unlock the door and realized she was shaking.

Very carefully, she turned the lock. It clicked loudly, and she winced. She turned the doorknob with the same amount of care, trying to be as quiet as possible. If there was something out there, she didn't want to scare it, or even worse, let whatever was outside know she was inside, in case it meant to attack her. Sure, the card asked for help, but it could just as easily be some sort of trick.

She eased the door open a crack, ready to throw her body against it if something tried to come in. Nothing. She opened it a bit more, and by now could see well into the hall.

Nothing.

Finally, she opened it far enough to step out, which she did, still holding the book in front of her, peering over the top of it to the left and right.

Still nothing.

Then she looked farther down the hall and saw the door to the crazy old woman's apartment. It was open a crack, and the light was streaming out across the floor, like a bright scar.

Without warning, the door shut with a click, and the light vanished.

Emma paused. Her mind was racing. She waited for another moment to see if anything else would happen, but nothing did. She slowly backed into the apartment and closed the door behind her. Her hand quivered as she turned the lock, and she suddenly realized she was having trouble standing because her legs were knocking together so hard they made her feet slip across the hardwood floor. She sank to the ground and wrapped her arms around her knees. She even tried to force them to stop shaking by pressing the book against her calves, but that didn't work, either.

Part of her desperately wanted to go back outside and see if she could discover more. She could get up, walk down the hall, knock on the door and just ask. She could find out what was going on and see who needed help. Sure, that would all be easy enough if her knees weren't knocking together. Besides, she told herself, it could be very dangerous, and she would never go knocking on strangers' doors without her father.

She thought very hard, trying to piece together what she knew. First, there was a witch in that apartment. Well, ok, so maybe it wasn't nice to call the old woman a witch, but she was scary and creepy enough, and she did look like one, that was certain. Second, there was someone inside who needed her help. Maybe. Or it could be a trick by the horrible old woman to get her into the apartment so she could eat her, or whatever it is that witches do. Third, there was a strange light in that apartment. What was it? Somehow she doubted it was the sun.

Finally, Emma's curiosity got the better of her. She got back up again, holding the book out in front of her with both hands once again, as if it offered some sort of protection. Then she opened the door with as much resolve as she could muster and marched down the hall until she was right in front of the strange door. She took a deep breath and raised her fist, ready to knock.

The door flew open, and the horrible old woman thrust her face out with a scowl. The woman was hunched over, their noses almost touching. Emma could feel the hair on the old woman's chin tickling her own. It was not a pleasant feeling.

"What do you want, child?" croaked the woman. Emma simply froze. She hadn't expected this at all. She did the only thing she could think to do. She ran.

She ran down the hall, back into her apartment, slammed the door behind her, sprinted down the hall to her father's empty bedroom and dove under the bed. As she ran, she thought she could hear the woman laughing with that grating, croaky cackle. She cowered under the bed, visions of the old woman's face flashing in her mind, and she shivered uncontrollably. She kept seeing that crooked nose and hairy chin. She could still feel the woman's hot breath on her face. It was so, so horrible.

But as she cowered under the bed, she remembered that she had seen something else inside the apartment when the woman opened the door. She wasn't really sure, here in relative safety under the bed, but she thought what she had seen was a boy. A young boy about her own age.

He was peering around a doorframe inside the apartment. The room behind him had been uncommonly bright. But the light hadn't come from inside the room; it was more that the light came from the boy himself. Yes, she was sure of it. The boy had been glowing with the most beautiful white light she had ever seen.

Many hours later, still crouched beneath her father's bed in fear and still clutching her book tightly against her chest, the thought of this light comforted her as she slowly, imperceptibly, fell asleep.

When she opened her eyes, she was surrounded by that same light, almost as though she were bathing in it or floating in the mist that came off the sidewalk down by the grocer's in the morning. She even thought she could see the strange old shopkeeper standing off to the side, hose in hand, cold water pouring out like a waterfall and turning to steam and bubbling foam as it struck the warm ground, somewhere far below. The steam rose thickly, but this time it lifted her right off the ground, suspending her in the warm mist while the strange light cut through, diffused by the steam, so the light seemed to come from everywhere at once.

As she floated there suspended, she found it odd that she was not in the least bit afraid. It occurred to her that she should be concerned, or at least curious about this turn of events, but it was so peaceful, and she felt so safe, that the thought just melted into the mist and was gone. Instead, she found herself starting to hum.

She didn't recognize it at first, but it was the same tune she had stuck in her head the day before, when she was in the hallway waiting for her father. She hummed it several times, playing with the melody, improvising a bit, until she realized what it was.

It was an old song, one her mother used to sing to her, and she felt the notes reverberating in her chest, filling her with warmth from the inside out, until her body felt warmer than the mist around her. As she sang, the memory of her mother grew stronger, too, and as her memory grew, the song grew louder and her body warmer. By the third verse, Emma could picture her mother in perfect detail, with her hair pulled back in an old handkerchief, leaning forward to stroke Emma's hair as she lay in bed, singing the song to her. By the fourth verse, the mist around her had grown brighter, and by the fifth verse, she realized the source of the glow was herself.

As she grew warmer, the image of her mother became even clearer, until Emma was almost certain she could touch her.

Momma, she thought as she reached her arm out. But she was just out of reach, never quite solid or close enough. Emma began to strive harder, reaching as far as she could. Her mother seemed to be hovering just past her reach, the fabric of her white dress lightly brushing Emma's fingertips, never close enough to allow her to grasp it.

The song rang in her chest until her whole body began to vibrate. She was so hot and bright, she was sure she would explode, but she couldn't stop. Not when her mother was so close. Hotter and hotter, her whole body vibrated with the song, and she reached even farther still. But, just as she could feel her fingers catch the cloth, a flash of light blinded her and sent her flying backward, head over heels. She felt the fabric catch between her fingers. And then it was gone.

She started to fall.

"Momma!" she cried out. She fell, as if down an elevator shaft, through the mist into nothingness. Soon, the apartment building came into view far below, and she continued to fall toward it. She approached the roof and instinctively threw her hands in front of her face to protect herself.

She shut her eyes, expecting impact. None came. Instead, she passed straight through the roof as if it didn't exist. She passed through the roof into the attic, which was more of a crawlspace and storage area, filled with cobwebs and insulation, old boxes and mysterious pipes interwoven with each other and leading whom knows where. She passed through the floor into her own apartment, where her father sat at the kitchen table, looking very sad, with boxes and furniture tossed everywhere and some abandoned sheet music littering the table and floor. She called out for him as she fell, and he looked up as if he heard her, but it was clear he could not see her as his eyes glazed over again, and he dropped his head again in sadness.

Papa! she called out again as she continued to fall, though now she felt herself being yanked sideways, flying through the walls and apartments toward the old woman's place.

Once there, she passed through the side room, which was filled with light, just as she thought it would be. Inside, the room was sparsely furnished, with only a bed and a small trunk and no windows that she could see. The young boy sat on a plain bed. His skin was white as bleached paper, his hair was almost transparent in its whiteness, and his eyes blacker than hers. He sat perfectly still on the bed. So still she could not tell if he was even alive, until he turned his eyes slowly and looked directly at her. He looked terribly sad and alone. Before she could respond, she was pulled through the wall, into the kitchen where the old woman stood at the stove, stirring something foul, bubbling and seething in a big metal pot. As Emma sped by, the woman stopped, looked up, and laughed, with her hand still resting on the old wooden spoon. She said something, though Emma was moving so quickly she couldn't make out the sounds, but she was pretty sure the woman's curled lips had formed the word *princess*. The woman laughed again and pointed at Emma with the end of the spoon. Something foul dripped and oozed.

Emma dropped through the floor, through many floors, into the dark, damp basement. Before her eyes had time to adapt, she looked down in horror to see the furnace open its hungry metal door, ready to devour her. The heat was unbearable. She kicked and flailed her arms and legs, trying to grab onto something, anything to save her, but the force was too strong and pulled her toward the furnace. It seemed to be alive.

She shut her eyes as tight as she could and tried to scream, but she heard the sound before she made it. She screamed again, or rather heard a scream that sounded as though it came from her, but her mouth was still closed. And she wasn't burning up at all. Then she started to shake, but she wasn't making it happen. Something or someone was shaking her.

She was so confused.

She cracked open an eye to see the brownies assembled on her chest and face. Little Mat was holding onto the edge of her nostril, leaning toward her ear as far as possible, screaming, "Wake up! Wake up, Monster!"

The other brownies were clutching parts of her clothing and tugging furiously and jumping up and down on the book, which still lay resting on her chest. Master Tect was pounding on the cover as if it were a door knocker.

"It's awake!" shouted Piers, pointing at her one open eye.

"Oh, thank Foundation!" Truss gasped, sinking heavily to her knees in exhausted relief.

"I ... what ... ?" Emma was still not sure if she was awake or dreaming. Suddenly, the floor began to shake, Emma and the brownies along with it. The brownies each clung to her for fear of being thrown off, and Mat's grip on her nostril caused her to yelp. The front door began to shake. Someone was trying to get in.

"She's coming!" the Master wailed.

"Save us!" Mat screeched in her ear. Emma winced. Then the door rattled harder, and they could hear the sound of wood cracking.

"She's coming through!" Truss shouted, tugging at Emma's hair. "Get up, girl! We've got to get out of here!"

"Go where?" Emma said, still confused and disoriented. The floor continued to shake.

"The building … she's trying to kill it!" Piers shouted.

"And us, too!" cried Mat, in a panic.

"By Foundation! The Underworld! It will all be destroyed!" Truss cried.

She turned to Emma again. "Please, save us!"

"Oh, my beautiful breakfast!" wailed Piers, sinking to his knees and weeping uncontrollably.

"Blast your breakfast with a double stick of dynamite!" the Master exploded. He turned back to Emma and screeched, "Please! You must get us out of here!"

Emma could hear things falling all over the apartment. The walls shook. She was glad she was still under the bed.

Just then the front door smashed open. Heavy footsteps thundered down the hall. Emma was truly afraid.

The steps grew louder, until they were right outside the door. The brownies clung to Emma, shivering in fear.

"What do I do?" Emma whispered, the words sticking in her throat. The brownies looked around. Truss tugged at her shirt frantically and pointed.

"There!" she gasped. Emma followed her arm, which pointed toward the wall.

"There's nothing there. Just a wall."

"Not the wall. The vent," Piers cried out, clutching her collar. "Down there, along the baseboards."

"But I can't fit in there," Emma whispered urgently. "I'm too big!" Just then the doorknob rattled.

"GO!" the brownies screamed in unison as the knob turned and the door began to creak open.

Emma didn't know what else to do, so she scooted out from under the bed and ran toward the air vent. The brownies clung to her, grabbing her ears, her nose and even the edges of the book, hanging on for dear life.

"Jump!" Mat screamed in her ear.

"I can't."

"There's no time! Jump! Jump NOW!"

She was so afraid, she couldn't even think straight.

"Jump NOW!" Piers shouted.

"Slip through! You can do it!" a voice echoed in her ears. She did not know if it was one of them shouting or herself.

"Slip through!"

"JUMP!"

"NOW!"

Emma took a deep breath and looked once more toward the bedroom door. It rattled and shook, and the doorknob started to turn. She turned back to the wall and looked at the tiny vent near the floorboards. Then she did something she never thought she would do.

She jumped.

She flew through the air, hurtling herself toward the air vent. She flew for what seemed to be an impossible length of time, arcing through the air in a perfect dive. The brownies all clung to her, the air blowing their hair and cheeks back like parachutes. She kept expecting to crash into the air vent on the wall, but it didn't happen. Instead, she flew through the tiny spaces in the iron grate and into the vent, then tumbled several times before landing on her behind. She sat, stunned and disoriented.

Something grasped her hand and tugged. It was large and solid. She looked down. There was a large red hand in hers. She followed the hand along the grey clad arm to a fur lined shoulder, then up to the large, round face of Truss, who, strangely, was looking down at her.

"Come, child, it's still not safe. We must run."

Why are the brownies so huge, she asked herself. *No, wait. I'm in the air vent, so I must have shrunk.*

The walls started to shake again. She looked out of the vent and saw a large, dark figure looming out there. It was rapidly approaching the iron grate. The brownies screamed again and all five of them – Emma and the four brownies – began to run. Emma struggled to catch up, amazed at how nimble the brownies were. They vaulted over openings and slid down various vents, following some impossible maze she did not understand.

Finally, they came to a small opening in the side of the tunnel, and the brownies scrambled through the gap. It was an impossibly small opening, so Emma froze, not sure what to do. A moment later, Truss' head popped out.

"Come on, child. It's not much further now," she said, coaxing Emma into the hole.

Emma looked over her shoulder, toward the labyrinth of air vents and ducts, then back at Truss and the tiny space. She decided the only course was to keep going forward. She took a deep breath and dove into the opening. The next thing she knew, she was inside an even smaller pipe, slipping and sliding down into the dark, still clutching her book, with the voices of the brownies echoing in her ears.

Chapter Seven: A Long Way Down

Emma felt herself slip–sliding down the narrow pipe. It was pitch dark. All she could hear was the swooshing sound of five bodies moving rapidly down a metal slide. Occasionally, someone would hit a snag and yelp, so the swooshing was punctuated by hollers and moans. Every so often, her own bottom would make contact with a thick seam or a mineral growth on the pipe, and she would cry out in surprise and pain, too.

They continued to slide.

Swish swish OWW *swish* ACK

Swish swish swish OOF URG OUCH!

They slipped and slid for ages, until Emma could no longer tell where they were relative to her father's bedroom. She began to wonder again what the postcard meant. *This is not a pipe.* Except the tobacco pipe in the picture definitely was one. Now here she was, hurtling through the dark, down a different kind of pipe. How could a pipe not be a pipe? A pipe is a pipe is a pipe. *Isn't it?*

She couldn't even tell which way was up anymore. The brownies seemed comfortable enough, or at least she assumed so based on their conversation.

"Wheeee!" came a smallish voice. Emma assumed it was Mat.

"OOF!" This one was deeper, huskier. Probably Master Tect.

"OOF!" *Squish.* Heavy *thud.* "OOOF!"

Yes, it was definitely the Master.

Swish, swish, THUMP, OOF.

"By Foundation! This route is much bumpier than it was on the way up," Truss' husky voice floated along the pipe.

"Great *OOF* Galloping Gr*AH*vity!" Piers exclaimed. "Well, it's *OOF* a long way down, isn't *ACK* it?" *Thump.* "OOOF!* I say, do you suppose my breakfast *OOF* gravel will still be hot?" His voice sounded as wistful as it could sound, given the bumpy circumstances.

"You're assuming we're going to get through the *AGGH* gate. Mister *OOF* Widget says the *OOF* odds of the gate being *ARGH* open at just the right *OOF* time are infinitesimally *OOF* slim. According to Mister Widget's *OOF* Theorem of Pr*ACK*tical Urgency, the odds *OOF* are inversely *ACK* proportional to our need to *OOF* pass thro*OOF* the gate, you *OOF* know," Mat said with as much authority as one can muster while bumping along down a pipe in the dark.

"But my *OOF* need IS enorm*OOF*!" wailed Piers. "I do *OOF* so need my breakfast!"

"Thank Found–*AH*–tion we have the Wanderer with us," chipped in Truss. "I think that evens our *OOF* odds considerably."

"If you *OOF* ask me, that monster is *ACK* more odd than evens," replied Mat in the darkness. "It's certainl–*OOF* a random force OOF of nature. That's for certa*AAGH*n. What happens OOF when random meets improbable, well —"

Big *THUMP*.

Pier's voice echoed in the darkness, "*ACK!*"

"I would really appreci–*OOF* it if you would stop speaking about me like I'm not here," Emma asserted herself as forcefully as she could muster, considering she was hurtling down a tiny, dark pipe the size of her wrist, or rather, the size her wrist used to be.

"Do you think it will be?" Mat's voice flitted up the pipe, warbling with anxiety.

"Do I OOF think what will be what?" Truss' voice replied in the darkness.

"The gate. *OOF*. OH!pen, I mean …," Mat sounded terribly nervous, which in turn was making Emma nervous, too.

"Eh, what's that? The gate?" The Master sounded startled, as if he'd just woken up. Emma wondered how he could sleep through all the bumping and sliding. Then again, even she had become comfortable enough that she barely noticed all the *OOF*s and *ACK*s anymore.

"Will the gate be open, do you think?" Mat repeated.

"How by Foundation should I know?" sputtered Master Tect with a yawn.

"I wasn't asking you!" Mat shouted back in frustration. "OW!"

There was something different about that *OW*, as if something other than bumping along the pipe had caused it.

"I mean, thank you, sir, for your input, sir!" A moment later, Mat whined contritely, "OW! You didn't need to pinch so hard!"

"I rather think I did!" replied Truss, disapprovingly.

"What if it isn't?" Piers' voice floated mournfully through the pipe.

"Isn't what?"

"Open," Piers replied. His voice echoed in the hollow pipe, so what Emma heard was: "Oooooooooooooooo–pen."

"What gate? Where does it lead?" Emma interrupted, curious to know where they were headed.

"What's that? Did *it* speak?" Mat called out peevishly.

"Mat, my little bricklet, do stop referring to the human child as *it*. It's really not very nice."

"Oh, I totally agree with you there. It's not a nice monster at all. Not nice at all," Mat agreed.

"No, that's not what I meant. It is a *very* nice monster. I meant it isn't nice to call it an *it*," Truss replied. "And stop calling it a monster!"

"But it's true. Did you hear the way it snarled at me? I'm quite sure it's trying to kill me." The little brownie was growing hysterical.

"I'm sure you're mistaken, Mat, but be that as it may, it's our only hope of getting us through the gate. Oh, look, now you've got me calling it *it*, too."

"Excuse me," Emma interrupted. "What gate?"

"What's that, child? Oh, pardon us. We're talking about the Over Gate."

"Over? Over what?"

"Over Gate. It's a gate. Over is the name of the gate," said Piers with a melancholy sniffle.

"Oh, I see," Emma said, furrowing her brow. "Well, then what is it over?"

"It's not over anything, silly. It's a gate, not a bridge," Mat said smugly.

"Well, then if it's a gate, it must lead somewhere. Where does it go?"

"Under," said Piers, matter-of-factly.

"Really not very bright at all, this one," Mat muttered. "Are all humans this stupid, or did we just get a particularly daft one?"

"I am *not* stupid. I just haven't even heard of Under or Over or any of this before, except in stories, but they're not supposed to be real."

Swish swish. *Thump.* The brownies were so shocked by Emma's statement they didn't even *OOF* on the *THUMP.*

"How could you not know?" Mat gasped.

"Not real, dearie?" Truss tsk–ed.

"By Foundation, how odd!" the Master muttered.

"I want my breakfast!" Piers grumbled.

The brownies chattered simultaneously.

"Don't they teach you *anything* in human schools?" Mat sounded genuinely shocked.

"Well, I've read stories about brownies, but I never knew they were real. And I never heard of them living in basements before."

"Not *in* basements, child. *Under,*" Piers said. Emma noticed he sounded a lot less frightened of her now that they were the same size.

She wished Mat felt the same way.

"Under the basement? But there's nothing under the basement besides dirt and rocks."

Mat sighed so heavily, Emma thought she could hear the little brownie's eyes rolling in the darkness.

"And besides, it's not like you lot know the first thing about humans, either," she said, shortly.

"Well, I'm sure Mister Widget's research is infallible," Mat huffed.

"Then why do you keep calling me a monster? Humans aren't monsters. We're not! Seems to me your Mister Widget is more like the Wizard of Oz to me," Emma shot back.

Mat's insulted gasp filled the dark pipe with such force, the entire pipe rang and shook. Apparently the little brownie was very certain about everything, and the very suggestion that a known fact might be wrong had deeply, deeply offended the creature.

She immediately felt badly for hurting Mat's feelings, misguided though they were. Come to think of it, she supposed it really wasn't fair of her to be so upset, considering she still didn't really know anything about Mat either. She didn't even know if Mat was a boy or a girl brownie. Perhaps it would be easier to tell now that they were roughly the same size, but she hadn't had a chance to really look while they were fleeing from the old woman, and now it just wasn't convenient, what with all this hurtling down dark pipes and all. Besides, she reflected, she really had no idea if brownies were like humans at all in that respect, and it seemed unlikely she could find out without being terribly rude. Perhaps she could find a moment to ask Truss discretely. Truss seemed nice enough.

The pipe rumbled and shook slightly.

"Great Grumbling Cement Trucks! What was *that*?" Piers' voice wavered. He sounded terribly worried.

"I don't know," said Emma.

"No, you wouldn't, now, would you?" Mat whined petulantly.

"I do hope it's not …" Truss' voice trailed off.

The pipe rumbled again.

"I say, I say, I say," Master Tect muttered as he woke up and tried to assess the situation. Then, after a moment's pause, he cried out.

"NO!"

The sound of fear in his voice was more terrifying to Emma than the distant rumble in the pipes.

The pipe rumbled yet again, this time more loudly, and the walls shook so hard that Emma began to bounce. She hit her head against the side wall.

"Ouch!" she cried out.

"OOF!" echoed the brownies.

"Hold on, dearie!" shouted Truss.

"To what?" Emma couldn't imagine what there was to hold on to.

The pipe took a sudden turn and Emma found herself freefalling. The rumbling grew louder still, and Emma became aware that part of the sound came not from the pipes shaking, but from a deep throated screech. It grew louder.

"IT'S HER!" wailed Piers and the Master together.

"The gate! We're approaching the gate!" yelled Mat.

"Do you think we'll make it?" Piers moaned. He didn't sound very optimistic.

"You're going to have to get us through, dearie!" Truss shouted over the growing din.

"But how? What gate? I don't understand!" Emma was terrified. It was as if she had only just then realized she was falling down a pipe into the dark with four brownies and a horrible screeching creature chasing them. Panic set in.

"There, there, dearie. Please. You must concentrate," Truss pressed with growing urgency.

"But how? What do I do?" Emma began flailing her arms and legs, half trying to find something to hold onto so she could stop falling, and half trying to hasten her way downward and away from the horrible thing behind them. She started to cry.

"Dearie, shush. Listen to me. You are the Wanderer. You have the power to take us through."

"But I …"

"Close your eyes. Think. Trust yourself."

Emma couldn't think over the sound of the rumbling pipes, no matter how hard she tried. The screeching grew closer, louder, like the sound of metal scraping against metal or the sound of a heavy wind tearing through a narrow tunnel. Emma threw her hands to her ears, trying to drown it out.

Instinctively, she clamped her eyes shut too, as if closing them would help block out the sound. She felt her body falling faster and faster downward, her eyes shut against the darkness. The echo of the approaching creature started to fade away.

Emma gradually became aware that she wasn't falling as quickly. Instead, she seemed to be buoyed up, as if on a cloud. She felt herself surrounded by light. Soft, white light wrapped around her like a cotton blanket, just as it had in her dream. All she could see was light. Her eyes were still closed.

Then she felt something brush against her fingertips.

No! she cried out, recoiling her hand in fear.

She felt it again. This time she looked up, but when she opened her eyes, she saw only darkness. The noise thundered in her ears. She closed her eyes once more, and light and quiet surrounded her again. The thing brushed against her fingers yet again, and this time it slipped between her fingers and clasped them together. She turned her head upwards.

This time, she kept her eyes closed.

"Momma?" Emma whispered, almost afraid that saying it would make her disappear. The cloud of light shifted and grew brighter in a spot where, if the thing holding onto her was a hand, the face belonging to that hand would be.

"Shush, child."

The soft, sing–song voice didn't speak to her so much as fill her with sound. It rang so clearly through her bones, Emma felt like a tuning fork, with its perfect pitch reverberating through her entire body.

"Momma," Emma half spoke, half whispered to the light. "Momma, I'm lost. I don't know what is happening, and I don't know what to do."

"Child, you're not lost. You've got wandering blood in you. Wanderers can't get lost. They are simply on their way."

"On their way to what?"

"None of us know that, child, until we arrive at our destination."

"I don't understand. If I don't know what my destination is, how can I not be lost?"

"Be true to your path, and you will understand in time, child."

"But Momma ..."

"Trust yourself. The Gate is approaching. You must find your way through."

"But how?"

"Trust yourself. The key is within you. Look inside yourself, and you'll find the answer."

The light began to fade.

"Momma!" Emma reached upwards even as she fell, but the grasp in her hand grew lighter, and then slipped away entirely.

She began to plummet down again. Soon she was enveloped in darkness again, whether her eyes were open or shut. She was falling again, faster and faster. The pipe walls were shaking violently, and the screeching sound was right above her.

"The gate! The gate!" the brownies cried out, but only Master Tect had a voice deep and loud enough to carry over the screeching. She felt something grasp one of her feet, and then the other one, and in a moment she realized it was the brownies, now clinging to her arms and legs for dear life. She had no idea what to do.

The pipe took another sharp turn, so instead of plunging straight down, they were skidding forward on their bottoms again, flying forward at an alarming pace.

"Ow!" "Oof!" "Ugh!" they each cried out as they sped forward in the dark. Then, without warning, they cleared the pipe.

Emma barely had any time to assess the situation as they rocketed through the air. They were in a room. It was also very dark, but since they had been falling through total darkness for so long, her eyes were hypersensitive, so even the slightest bit of light showed detail in the dark. She saw pipes twisting this way and that, a monstrous metal knitting project gone horribly wrong. The walls glistened in the dim light with some sort of indefinable moisture.

She quickly scanned the room for the light source and then realized they were heading straight toward it. It was the furnace, looming like a big, hungry beast in the darkness. The fire inside flared and crackled, sending flickers of light through the heavy plated door slats. It was just like her dream.

Just as she realized all this, the heavy furnace door swung open, and a blast of heat whipped her cheeks and blew her hair back. The brownies screamed and clung to her and to each other. As if in response, another horrible screech echoed back at them, this time from the pipe. The brownies screamed louder and clung to Emma even tighter. Emma could barely make out Truss' voice over the clamor.

"Do something, child! The key! The key!" the brownie shouted.

There was no time to think. Out of the corner of her eye, she saw a sliver of light cutting through the floor in the darkest corner. It wasn't coming from the furnace, but from something below.

The Gate, she thought. *That is the Gate.* She had no idea how she knew this or if it was even true.

As they flew across the room, barely grazing the ceiling, Emma caught sight of a bare light bulb, just out of reach ahead of them. Below it hung a single, frayed string tied to a short chain. She reached out her hand and twisted her body as hard as she could without shaking the brownies off. At the last instant, her fingers closed around the string.

Suddenly, they weren't flying forward anymore, but whipping in circles around and around the light bulb, which kept turning on and off. The brownies clung to her as they swung around, their legs flapping outward like a bizarre pinwheel.

"Do it, child. Do it now."

Emma heard the voice in her head and could not tell if it was Truss or her mother or if she was just plain loopy from all the spinning. But she obeyed.

She released her grip on the string, and they flew through the air, not toward the furnace, but past it, toward the corner and the light coming through the floor. Just then, a dark creature flew out of the pipe, filling the room with black rage and horrible, scraping screams. Emma felt her heart ride into her throat. She held her breath.

The crack in the floor, she thought. *That is the gate. The key is in me. What does that mean? What do I do? The gate. It's too small. I'm too big. I can't. I can't.*

And then she remembered her day at school. She remembered her own rules for surviving in so many schools before: *keep your head down, bend with the wind. I am the willow, not the oak. Just slip through the cracks.*

Yes, she could slip through.

Emma smiled, and the crack in the floor burst open in a flash of blinding light. The room filled with a horrible scream as the dark creature was thrown back against the far wall and shattered into dust.

Emma and the brownies sailed safely through the light, which closed up behind them, leaving the room as through nothing had happened, except for the light bulb string, which swayed gently in the darkness.

The old woman picked herself off the floor, muttering and cursing. She crossed to the crack in the floor and scraped at it with a long, gnarly fingernail, but all she disturbed was some dust.

Cursing once again, she stood up and slowly mounted the stairs to the lobby, all the while shaking her head and muttering terrible things under her breath.

Chapter Eight: On Top of Ol' Under

"Did we make it?" a small voice echoed in the darkness.

Emma felt dizzy, as if she had just stepped back on land after a long boat or amusement park ride. She put a hand out to steady herself and realized that they weren't moving. Finally.

Master Tect groaned heavily.

"Looks like we all made it, safe–sound. And oh! What a beautiful day it is, too!" Piers' voice declared. He sounded different. More confident.

Emma was confused. *Day? What was that brownie thinking? How could it be day when it was so dark?* Then Emma realized her eyes were still clamped shut, and her other hand was still covering her face. Slowly, carefully, she peeled her fingers away and cracked open her left eye.

A deep red and yellow glare nearly blinded her, and she was forced to shut her eye again. A dark shadow fell over her eyelids. She opened them both, but just a crack. A figure was looming over her, a dark silhouette surrounded by a brilliant red and yellow aura.

Oh, no, she thought. *What now?* She was still clutching her storybook to her chest, and she was prepared to use it as a shield if necessary.

The figure leaned forward and obliterated the light. Emma caught her breath. Then it poked her.

"Psst, monster, are you ok?"

It was Mat.

Emma sighed. Looking around, she noted that she was sitting on the ground and was leaning against a large rock. She put her book down next to the rock and climbed to her feet. She might have shrunk proportionately to match the brownies, but she was now about the same height as Truss, which meant she was still bigger than Mat. She leaned over the little brownie and tried to look menacing.

"Who are you calling a monster?" she growled. She'd just shrunk down to a fraction of her original size, hurtled down a very lumpy pipe and had a very sore bottom. She was not in a very good mood. Mat yelped, then scuttled off, cringing behind Truss, who was still dusting herself off.

Truss looked at Emma and shrugged apologetically. Too late, Emma realized that Mat had actually been expressing concern. A lump of remorse settled in her chest.

"Where are we?" Emma asked, taking in her surroundings for the first time.

"Why, home, of course," Master Tect said grandly, waving a pudgy arm toward the light. "Level 24, Tier 12, Quadrant 19, South–south–west Corner, Fourth Passageway counter–clockwise from the Keystone. In other words, I guess you could say we're over Under. Welcome!"

Emma followed his hand with her eyes. She gasped.

They were certainly Under, that much was clear. What exactly they were under was less clear. She followed the outcropping with her eyes and discovered they were lodged in a smallish cave. The walls were made of densely packed rock and soil, crammed between two enormous, spindly pillars, but instead of reaching up to support the ceiling, these pillars seemed to push downward. They twisted and spiraled from somewhere above the ceiling and pushed down into the earth, along the walls of the cave and down through the floor.

She had never seen anything like them. They seemed to be made from an odd combination of materials, not quite organic, not quite stone and not quite metal, but a combination of all three. It was as if metal had grown organically like a plant, but cross–pollinated with softly luminescent stone. There were places where the pale sheen gave way to large grey patches. They seemed to be spreading like some sort of rash, making the surface crumble and disintegrate in patches. Emma didn't know why, but when she saw them, a terrible feeling of sadness crept under her skin and spread like an infection toward her heart.

Meanwhile the Master, oblivious to the shabby surroundings, was suddenly overflowing with excitement at being home.

"Well, ceiling joists and concrete blocks, but it's good to be back! I daresay the office will be a shambles by now. They never could manage without me, not even for a day. I'm sure there will be piles of forms to fill out, papers to file and edicts to ratify. Oh my!" His eyes gleamed in anticipation for a full half a minute, after which he announced he was exhausted and plopped back down in a corner to take yet another nap.

Emma looked out past the edge of the cave, toward the light. The ledge overlooked a much larger central cavern that vanished into a wide and bottomless abyss. The light came from someplace deep down below and filled the cavern with an intense red and orange, but the actual fire source was too far away to see. She tried to follow the pillars with her eyes to see where they went, but they quickly splintered and began to twist, less like pillars and more like interwoven fingers, weaving and prying down into the depths of the cavern in a convoluted pattern that made her feel dizzy.

She reached out a hand and grabbed the pillar closest to her, but to her surprise, it contracted and shuddered at her touch. Startled, she immediately let go. The pillar was breathing. Then she realized it wasn't a pillar at all. It was a root. A living root.

The entire cavern began to shake as the root convulsed. Bits of stone and dirt crumbled from the walls and ceiling and fell like rain.

"Woah there, girlie," said Piers, reaching out a long, gangly arm to snag her dress collar and yank her back onto the ledge.

Emma regained her balance and took a deep breath.

"Did I do that?" She looked up wide–eyed at Piers.

"No, child. The roots are dying; the witch is trying to get in," Piers replied.

"It's so much worse than when we left," Mat said in a hushed voice.

"Much worse," Piers agreed. "She's grown stronger than we

expected."

Emma jumped in fear and prepared to run.

"Shush, child. She's close, but she can't harm you here," Truss said tenderly. Emma wondered how this could be true, for there were signs of the witch's devastation everywhere.

Beyond the ledge, the warm glow filled the cavern and seemed to drop forever below them. The dark walls were supported by more enormous roots, which grew out of various points in the ceiling like the inside of a bizarrely imagined gothic cathedral. Brown and grey slabs of stone and earth cast shadows that danced weirdly at various points along the wall.

The root system spread out below like a giant net, which in turn supported a series of burrows, built deep into the earth, but with openings and entrances all along the cavern center. What appeared to be random pockmarks and gaping holes were actually a beehive of homes, markets and offices. Great stone and earthen parapets pressed into the cave walls, held in place by the monstrous roots, which flanked and supported the complicated brickwork, holding it all in place. But signs of the grey blight were everywhere, leaving behind crumbling surfaces as far as she could see.

Emma's eyes continued to adjust to the light, and soon she could see a series of fires and torches dotting the little nooks and ledges which lined the cavern. Then she realized that many of the tiny fires were actually large bonfires, but they were so far away they appeared to be the size of match flames.

Some movement around one of the flames caught her eye, and she turned to see a group of brownies in a nearby nook, several of them frozen in surprise. They appeared to be refugees, dressed like her friends, but in tattered tunics, many with bare feet. Bundles and wooden crates were piled up around them. Some of them were cooking over an open flame, while others huddled near the fire to keep warm.

Toward her right, Emma could see a momma brownie in a faded

kerchief putting a baby to sleep in a little makeshift cradle made from a hollowed out stone, frozen in mid–rock. Beyond them, a large family of brownies sat frozen, mid–bite around a dinner table, waiting to see what Emma would do.

Further along, yet another brownie, this one dressed in a chef's hat, stood in front of an enormous cauldron with a very big spoon, mid–stir. He had been sampling the stew when Emma had appeared on the ledge, and a very big drop of something steaming hot plopped on his foot as he looked up. His yelp echoed through the chamber. No one else moved, but from somewhere deep below, a softer version of the yelp echoed back.

Everything she could see was very simple, bare and worn out, as though it had all been used longer than it was designed for. In spite of this, the brownies kept a cheerful look about them and seemed to be making the best of a very hard situation. The result was a place that felt like home but which seemed sad around the edges, like her father's eyes when he smiled.

"Wow," said Emma. Her voice carried clear as a bell through the cavern, bounced off the unseen bottom, and ricocheted back as clearly as she had whispered it.

"Wow," said the echo.

"Go on, say something to them," Piers nudged her.

"Say something?" Emma didn't have any idea what was expected of her. "Say what?"

"Go on, say something to them," the echo whispered back. After a brief pause, the echo added with unexpected urgency, "Say *something*!"

"Are you sure she's the Wanderer? I mean really," muttered Mat, apparently still peeved from Emma's earlier snide remarks. "We really scooped us a clever one, didn't we. We're doomed. All of us!"

"*Dooooooooomed!*" the echo called back.

"Look, you can't expect me to know what to do if I have no idea why

I'm here, or even where here really is," Emma replied smartly.

"*Here really is,*" the echo called back.

"This is an awful lot to assimilate all at once."

"*Assimi–what?*" the echo replied.

Piers leaned over and whispered something in Master Tect's ear. The Master sat up, startled to have been asked anything at all. Then, realizing that no one was paying any attention to him, he shrugged and nodded off again in the corner.

"They're not quite sure what to make of you, dear," said Truss. "They've never seen a Wanderer before, or a topsider, for that matter. We don't get many magic folk around here." Emma wanted to say she wasn't magic, *they* were, and she wondered if *magic folk* was just a nicer way to say *monster*.

The brownie smiled and patted her arm.

"Just say something nice, so they know you're friendly."

"Oh, I see," Emma replied. She didn't see at all, but she figured her best bet was to play along. After all, she was on a ledge at the top of a bottomless pit, somewhere deep underground, surrounded by basement brownies. At this point, it certainly wouldn't hurt to try, though she felt a bit as though she'd been picked to give a class presentation but missed the class when the assignment was handed out. Fortunately, this wasn't the first time she'd had to improvise, though never before under such unusual circumstances.

She stepped up to the ledge, as close as she could without getting dizzy.

"Ahem," she cleared her throat. The cavern remained absolutely silent and still except for the flicker of torches and the random curl of steam lifting off a well–cooked pot of stone stew.

"*Ahem,*" the cave echoed back.

"*Ahem,*" the brownies responded loudly and in unison. Apparently, they thought *Ahem* was a greeting of some sort.

"Um, hello, everyone. My name is Emma. I don't want to hurt anyone …"

"*GASP!*" the entire cavern cried in unison.

"Er, I mean … I'm not here to make trouble."

"*Ah!*" they sighed in relief.

"So, um, well, I mean, I'm not really sure why I'm here, actually."

"*Huuuuh?*" The crowd scratched their heads and looked questioningly at each other.

Mat nudged her shoulder, a bit harder than Emma thought was necessary. She was terribly flustered.

"So, um, they tell me I'm a, um, Wanderer."

"*Ooooooooo!*"

"And that all you brownies are in trouble."

"*Awwwwwww!*"

"Well, I, um, don't really know what I can do to help."

Cries of "Oh no!" and "We're doooooooomed!" overlapped each other. The cave walls shivered.

"*Doooooooomed!*" wept the Echo. Master Tect awoke with a start.

"But I'll certainly do my best."

"*Huzzah!*" the crowd roared.

Emma remembered some things the emcees sometimes said at her father's shows, and without really thinking about it, they all just tumbled out.

"So, thank you for coming, Ladies and Gentlemen. Really. Truly. I mean it from the bottom of my heart. You've been a wonderful audience. If I could take you all home with me, I surely would. You're all great! Be well, drive safely, and see you next time!"

Emma's voice filled the cavern, echoed back and then faded into silence. Emma looked at Truss, who shrugged. Then Truss looked at

Piers, and he shrugged. Master Tect and Mat looked at each other, and they both shrugged, too. Emma looked back at the cavern and stared into the thousands of flickering lights that blinked back at her in the darkness.

Silence.

Suddenly, the entire cavern erupted into applause. Piers, Truss and Master Tect all sighed heavily and looked very relieved. Emma did the only thing that seemed appropriate; she bowed repeatedly, slowly backing up on the ledge until she was hidden from view.

"Well, that went as well as could be expected," muttered Mat.

"You did fine, child," Truss said reassuringly. The block has approved you. We can move on now." The brownie heaved herself onto her feet and prepared to hike down the cliff.

"No, wait," Emma said. "I'm not going a step further until you tell me what's going on. I'm very far from home, and my father has no idea where I am, and I'm pretty sure he won't think of looking for me here, wherever here is. He's going to be worried sick. And YOU," she turned to Mat angrily, "YOU have been nothing but nasty to me since we met. It's not polite to ask someone for help and then get angry at them when they don't have any idea what you need. It's just not nice."

The brownies were silent.

Piers looked at his feet as though there was something very interesting on the ground right where he was digging his left toe into the dirt. Master Tect nudged Mat, who stumbled forward from the force. Suddenly flustered, the smaller brownie tried to retaliate by nudging back, but the Master was three times larger, mostly width–wise, so it was rather like trying to nudge an enormous block of cement.

The Master nudged Mat again, and this time the little one sighed heavily, eyes rolling like a tennis ball in the dryer, and stepped toward Emma as though invisible forces were dragging the brownie forward forcibly.

"I'm sorry," Mat mumbled. The Master nudged again.

"It won't happen again." Another nudge from the Master knocked the little brownie completely off balance.

"I *promise*," Mat said, mostly through clenched teeth.

"It's ok," said Emma grudgingly. Satisfied, the Master trudged over to a corner, plopped down and promptly fell asleep.

"Mat, why don't you show our guest the History? Maybe that will help her understand," Truss suggested gently.

"OK!" Mat said, brightly. "Let's go to the Academy! I can cross–reference the History with the Time–Line and triangulate with the apocryphal sub–fictions!" This was the first time Emma had seen Mat appear genuinely enthusiastic about anything, but she remained adamant.

"No, please, I want to know now, before we go further."

The little brownie shrugged and reached deep into a tiny vest pocket, rummaged around for a bit, then pulled out a book. It was impossibly large and just kept getting bigger as Mat lifted it from the vest. In the end, the book was nearly twice the size of the brownie, who teetered left, then right, then staggered forward and back, then finally managed to guide it to the ground with a thunderous thud.

"Oh, goody!" Piers declared. "I do so love a good story."

Emma wondered how something so big could fit in such a small pocket. She glanced toward her own book, which was still sitting undisturbed in the shadows, next to the rock where she had placed it. It seemed so worn and battered by comparison.

"Yes, you see, this is how *real* knowledge is stored," a smug Mat said with a nod toward the larger book. *Can't judge a book by its cover*, Emma thought to herself. It took all of her power to keep from saying it out loud.

Still, she had to admit that Mat's book was far more spectacular than hers. It was naturally big and heavy, with a large cover studded with beautiful blue stones and metals that glittered in colors Emma had never seen before. The edges were painted gold, and the spine arched perfectly, except where strange geometric designs were embossed in the thick and ancient leather. On the cover, Emma could see a title:

Mister Wallter Widget's
Wonderful World of Under Wonders

In smaller cursive text below was written:

by Mister Wallter Widget

Mat lifted the cover with both hands, grunting and groaning under the weight. After heaving the cover high enough, the brownie was able to ram a shoulder underneath, and with pure brute force and a deep–throated grunt, pushed the cover up, higher and higher until it was vertical.

"I say, would you like a hand with that?" Piers inquired politely.

"NO!" Mat huffed. "*I* am the Book's Keeper and Protector! Mister Widget said so. No one touches it but *ME*!"

The brownie pushed once more with a grunt, and then jumped out of the way as the enormous panel careened to the earth and landed with a satisfying thud. Two clouds of dust, one from the earth and one from the pages of the book, burst into the air.

Once the dust had settled and Emma and the brownies had stopped coughing, Emma leaned in to take a look. The inner pages were thick and yellowing, each page ridged with texture, like a unique, bubbly fingerprint. The paper made Emma want to reach out and touch it. The text was printed in a deep, rich black ink, with a kaleidoscope of colors and ornaments filling the borders and sometimes tripping into the text itself. It was a crazy dance of color and exotic patterns.

Emma looked back again at her own storybook. Where Mat's book was edged in gold, hers was dark from dirt and fingerprints. The illustrations in the brownie's book nearly jumped right off the page, while hers were faded and worn. Nevertheless, the storybook had been her mother's, and now it was hers, and she wouldn't trade it for the world.

"Let me see, let me see. What page did Mister Widget say that was?" Mat seized an armful of pages and flipped them over, though not without a great deal of effort, groaning and complaining. Emma could tell, however, that the brownie was clearly excited and more than ready to dive in.

"Ah, here it is, *Chapter 946*."

Another cloud of dust filled the air, and Emma found herself breathing into the sleeve of her dress. Mat coughed politely and began to read aloud.

"*Chapter 946: The Creation of Under.*" The brownie announced the title with an air of majesty.

"It takes nine hundred and forty six chapters just to get to the beginning?" Emma asked Truss.

Mat looked up sharply. "Do you mind?"

"Sorry," Emma said with genuine contrition.

"I can start at the very beginning, if you'd like," Mat said, still a bit peevishly. "There are the tales of the creation of Creation, and the creation of the Creator. There's a great passage somewhere around Chapter 473 that goes into great detail on the atmospheric qualities of the Creator's left nostril."

"Um, thanks. I'll pass."

"Suit yourself. Now, where was I? Ah, yes," Mat coughed once more, then went back to reading:

"'In the beginning, the beginning of Under, that is, which is not the beginning of Everything since Everything comes from Something.'"

"Is it all this long–winded?" whispered Emma to Truss.

"Ahem," Mat said, looking up with a raised eyebrow.

"Sorry. Again."

"Where was I?"

"'Since Everything comes from Something.' Where does the something come from?" Emma couldn't help asking.

"What something?" Mat said with a start.

"The something that everything comes from."

"Well, I, er… something *else*. Obviously. May I continue?"

"Oh, yes, please."

"'Since Everything comes from Something,'" Mat repeated. The brownie paused significantly, as if daring Emma to interrupt again.

"Why don't you just skip to the prophecy, Mat. Elsewise we'll be here until Foundation falls," Truss suggested.

Mat was clearly prepared to be interrupted again by Emma, but not by Truss. Emma thought she could see steam starting to rise off Mat's wiry little neck, which was quickly turning a deep, dark shade of red. A little higher up, the brownie's lips clamped tightly together and started to turn white, which created an odd candy cane effect against the brownie's red skin. A strange sound that might have been rocks grinding together seemed to be coming from Mat's throat, too.

"Easy there, young 'un," cooed Piers from his perch on a tall rock in the shadows. "Let's just get this tale told."

"Fine," hissed Mat, taking a deep breath and gradually regaining a natural tone of red. Mat muttered quietly while skimming the text, looking for the appropriate spot. "The first foundations … the cosmic notion of basements … Over … Under … In Between … AHA! Here it is," the brownie finally continued.

"'Thus, Under came to be, and, yea verily, the basement brownies were at one with the world, and the world was at one with the brownies. And the magic that brought the brownies into being infused the rock and the stones so that when the humans came into Over, these rocks and stones made their way into the humans' homes. And when the humans were in harmony with the world, the stones and the magic grew like wildflowers, until they grew into the earth and took hold, like the roots of a mighty tree. And when the humans began to hate each other and learned to fight, the roots shivered and shriveled and died. And when this happened, the brownies, who made their home among the roots, were cast from their homes and abandoned in the cold and the darkness as the brownie strongholds fell one by one.'"

"There are other strongholds? Like this one?" Emma asked.

"Not anymore, child," Truss whispered back. "There used to be burrows all under the world. But ours is the last, and now our burrow is dying, too," Truss whispered back.

Emma looked out into the crumbling cavern, and her eyes filled with tears. Master Tect snored obliviously in a dark corner of the cave.

"'The brownies began to despair as their homes began to crumble. A group of sturdy brownies was dispatched to Over to try to talk to the humans and explain to them what was happening to the brownie homes, but they discovered that humans had changed so much and become so twisted and blind with greed and hate, they could no longer see the creatures of Under. Worst of all, the humans' hatred had become so strong, part of the magic of Over became sick, and from this dark magic an evil witch was born.

"'There is only one creature in Over capable of defeating the witch and restoring health to Under and happiness to the humans: a young boy known as the Prince of the Elementals. This child has the power to pull magic from all of the elements, a combination more powerful than any single magic on its own. One day, the witch captured the Prince using the darkest magic in the universe, and many brownie trackers died trying to help him escape.'"

"I've seen him," Emma whispered with a gasp.

"Who?" Truss whispered back.

"The Prince. I think I know where he is."

"Shhhhhhh!" Piers hushed at them crossly. "You're interrupting the story again!"

Mat continued:

"'Discouraged, the remaining members of the resolute Trackers returned to Under and a Great Council was called. The brownies debated and discussed the matter for days. No solution could be found. They consulted with root specialists and spiritualists, politicians, poets and pragmatists. The Great Architects of Under assembled, but they too could find no way to save Under.

"'The brownies asked for help from a great sorceress, the Earth goddess Ceres, or Demeter as she was known to some. Ceres was powerless against the witch, who knew a dark magic that hurt the earth, but she told the council there is one way to release the Prince. They would have to seek out the Wanderer, a being who has no home and no roots and who can see things that belong to other worlds beyond their own. The Wanderer does not obey the rules of nature and can manipulate them. Only the Wanderer has the ability to break the four magic locks that bind the prince.

"And so the brownies chose four new bands of Trackers to search for the Wanderer in each of the four corners of the earth, to no avail. Meanwhile, the witch began destroying each of the remaining brownie burrows, one by one, by locating each human house from which the roots had grown. She took possession of the house and spread her darkness until the roots below shrivelled and died, taking the life–force of the burrow along with it. And when all was dead, she destroyed the human house, leaving ugly scars and deep holes all over the land. All of Under lived in fear of what was to come. Burrow after burrow was destroyed.

"Then, one day, a strange thing happened. The witch located the last human house and began to destroy its magic in the same way she had destroyed the others. But the power of Under was strong, and the struggle to survive was long and slow and horribly painful to the creatures above and below. Fearful of losing her advantage, the witch brought the Prince of the Elementals from the prison where she kept him and held him captive in Over, stealing his Under magic to strengthen her own. The burrow below began to shake and shrivel and die like the others.

"Finally, one autumn afternoon, the last survivors in the last surviving brownie burrow assembled and called out for help. The Wanderer heeded their call. Sensing her approach, the house seethed with renewed energy and began to fight back. The witch did everything in her power to suppress the house, and she nearly succeeded, but the house, in a final attempt to save itself, opened a tiny passageway and pulled four Trackers from the brownie burrow into Over, summoned by the magic of the house to bring the Wanderer back to help them.'"

"I say, is that what happened?" Piers piped in.

"It is until the book says otherwise," the Master mumbled. He stretched and yawned, waking from his nice, long nap.

"Fascinating," Truss added.

"Yes, yes, wonderfully fascinating. May I continue?" said Mat crossly.

"Oh, yes, of course," the other brownies chimed in.

"It says I'm 'special,'" Piers chirped, swinging his legs in glee.

"'When they came face to face with the Wanderer, who was in her night dress at the time of this auspicious meeting …'"

"Um, I think that's where I came in," Emma piped in, trying to be helpful, but mostly just excited to find herself in the story.

"Oh, yes, quite right," piped in Piers and Master Tect at the same time. Mat was growing increasingly agitated.

"I don't understand. How does it know about me already? How does it know what only just happened?" Emma was curious to know. "Who could have written it?"

"The book writes itself as things occur," Truss told her. "It's a Truth Book. It only reports the truth, as we know it."

"As you know it? Isn't truth always the truth?"

"Oh no, child. Truth is only as true as the information that makes it true."

"I don't understand."

"Well, a few days ago, you didn't know that brownies existed. If someone had come to you last week and told you there were basement brownies living under your house, what would you have said?"

"Well, I guess I would have said it wasn't true."

"And now?"

"Well, I … I see what you mean. Does that mean that anything I believe is also true?"

"No, of course not, girlie. They're only true if facts make them so. You can believe in green–faced googily bears all you want, but they aren't real, not here or anywhere. Wanting something to be true only makes it real if it was already meant to be."

"Green–faced googily bears aren't real?" Mat exclaimed. The little brownie's eyes widened and filled with tears.

"Sorry, kiddo. They're just a story," said Truss. Mat sat heavily on the edge of the book, clearly upset.

"I say, I say, I'm rather anxious to see if my breakfast is still on the table," said Piers.

Truss turned to Emma with a serious expression on her face.

"Well, child? Will you follow us?"

"Do I have a choice?" Emma asked.

"We do need your help, but you must decide if you will come with us or not," said Truss.

"And if I don't want to, can I go home?" The brownies all looked rather uncomfortable at this question.

"Well, er, actually … um, no," said the Master abashedly. "I'm afraid we have no idea how to get you back."

"But I'm sure that Mister Widget will," Truss said quickly, noting the look of alarm on Emma's face.

"Well then, I suppose we have no choice but to keep moving forward," said Emma, as bravely as she could. Then, more tentatively, she added, "So, where are we going then?"

"To see Mister Widget," said Truss. "He maintains a vast repository of knowledge and wisdom at the Academy."

"I'll need some time to stop by the administration offices," Master Tect added.

"Well then, shall we?" Piers leaped up, eager to eat.

Emma nodded, suddenly feeling very, very tired.

"Don't forget your things, girlie," Piers added, pointing to her tattered old storybook, which still lay on the floor of the cave. Emma took it in her hands and wondered when it got to be so very heavy.

The brownies started down a narrow path that led from the back of the ledge down into the cave. She followed behind, not knowing what else to do, while Piers chatted merrily about being reunited with his breakfast.

Chapter Nine: Bits of Brownie Business

"Come along now, quickly," the Master said, twiddling his medallion between his fingers and looking very pleased to have something officious to do at last. "If we hurry, we can file our reports today, while the Official Officer's off–site office still offers its official off–hours."

"Of course," Mat said blandly.

"Do you suppose we'll have a chance to see the Grand Poobah, himself?" Piers chattered nervously. Distressing signs of the blight grew worse with each step.

"The Grand Poobah? Oh, I doubt it very much. The Grand Poobah doesn't see *anyone*, as you well know," the Master replied haughtily. "And *certainly* not before the proper forms have been filled out. Come along, come along," he continued. "We must keep to the schedule."

Emma followed the four brownies down a short path that twisted along the cliffside, quickly turned into a narrow staircase, and then suddenly vanished into an arched opening in the wall. Emma followed the brownies inside. The staircase continued to wind around in circles, spiraling downward with a single, solid root at its core. Miniature torches were affixed to the walls at regular intervals, held in place by intertwining vines that grew off the root. Each torch held a single flaming rock, which cast a soft light throughout. Even so, Emma found it very difficult to see. She nearly missed a step and stumbled forward.

"Watch it there, girlie," Piers called out. Luckily, the wall was rough and full of stones and vines, and her hand found something long and narrow to grab onto. It felt like a root, and it gave slightly as she pulled on it. But at least she regained her balance.

"OW!" Mat yelped. "That's my arm!"

"I'm so sorry," Emma gasped and tried to catch her breath.

"Mat, behave. We're almost there," said Truss. Her large frame filled most of the stairwell and darkened the torches below. Emma squinted in the dim light. It was hard enough finding her way, without Mat grumbling at her every time she stumbled.

"Ah, here we are now," Truss said, stepping out of the stairwell. Emma found herself blinded again by the reddish orange light which filled the center cavern from below.

They seemed to be on yet another landing, directly below the smaller ledge where they had first arrived in the burrow. She could see the same family of brownies she had seen from the ledge earlier, but now they were directly to her right. The chef with his bubbling pot was now just across the way, close enough now that Emma could see the steam rising off the top of his gurgling stew and the flames licking at the pot's underbelly.

Her gaze dropped back down to the deep red glow at the bottom of the seemingly endless cavern. Once more, Emma found herself nearly overcome with vertigo from the sheer drop.

"Come along, dearie. Easy does it," Truss whispered.

"Oh, what is it now?" Mat grumbled impatiently.

"Shh, child," Piers said to Emma. "Breathe. Breathe again." He laid a long, lanky hand on her shoulder, but seeing her turn an even darker shade of green, he immediately pulled it away again.

"Poor child. So much to take in, wot?" the Master declared. "I should think we were all due for a nice bit of a rest, don't you think? I certainly wouldn't say no to a nice little nap right about now." He yawned and patted the tip of his bulbous nose with his very sorry–looking handkerchief.

Emma could barely hear what they were saying.

"Where are we?" she whispered hoarsely.

To their right, a vast cavern cut deeply into the earth, seemingly without end. Tattered banners with frayed, tasselled fringe hung on metal rods throughout the cave, attached by invisible means to the ceiling, such as it was. The floor below was littered with hundreds of dilapidated carts, wheelbarrows and makeshift stalls, each displaying a modest pile of odd looking goods. As far as Emma could see, hundreds and hundreds of brick red faces surrounded the stalls and filled the cave with blinking eyes.

A moment passed before it occurred to Emma that the faces must belong to people. *Not people,* she corrected herself. *Brownies.*

A sad and mournful moan turned Emma's attention back to her friends. Truss had her hands clasped over her mouth in shock. Piers was staring slack–jawed and amazed, with his long, lanky hands slapped against either side of his face. Master Tect looked like he was going to cry at any moment. Mat was doing a very bad impression of someone who couldn't care less.

"By Foundation! What, under Earth, has happened here?" Truss gasped.

"It's horrible! Horrible!" Piers shook his head in disbelief.

"What's wrong?" Emma was still whispering, though she wasn't quite sure why. "Where are we?" she repeated. The brownies paused, each trying to recover enough to respond.

"Central Market, dearie," Truss replied.

"Goodness Gravel! It was starting to turn when we left," Master Tect said, the horror rising in his voice as he spoke. "I can't even begin to imagine the paperwork this situation has created."

"It's grown so much worse," Piers moaned.

"She's coming far more quickly than we ever imagined," Truss spoke nearly at a whisper.

Piers suddenly blanched, which for a brownie meant turning somewhat pink.

"Truss ... do you suppose ... mother ...?"

Truss shuddered and a look of desperate worry crossed her face.

"Quickly," she said breathlessly, "we must go to her." She took off at a gallop toward the center of the crowd that was forming around them. Piers followed close behind, and the others scrambled into action, doing their best to keep up. The crowd parted in waves.

Emma struggled to keep up, astonished again at how quickly the brownies could hustle when they wanted to. They passed through the labyrinth of stalls, wagons and hung blankets with their odd displays of colored sands, stones and thingamabobs, and arrived at a stall somewhere in the market, though by the time they arrived, Emma was completely turned around and had no idea which way was which.

The stall was slightly larger than the others, but in a desperate state of disrepair. Its roof was propped up with broom handles and bits of found wood and scrap metal. The walls were patched in so many places, Emma wondered why it didn't all come tumbling down.

"Ant–y Truss! Unk–y Piers!" A set of tiny voices broke the silence. The voices were joined by the flutter of tiny feet, and a dozen tiny brownies flew out of the stall and leaped onto Piers, knocking him to the ground.

"You're back!" one of them squeaked, bouncing on his chest.

"We missed you sooooo much!" another chimed in, its arms and legs wrapped around Pier's calf and hugging tightly.

"Didja find it? Didja find the Over–Monster?" yet another dropped down to sit on Piers' chest and started rocking back and forth excitedly.

"Yes! Didya? Didja, Unk–y Piers?" a fourth brownie giggled, struggling to hang on as Piers wriggled about, struggling to get back on his feet. Piers looked both pleased and embarrassed by the sudden flurry of attention.

"Come now, children, let your Uncle catch his breath." An elderly brownie in a headscarf stepped gingerly out of the stall, holding a big mixing spoon in her hand. Piers sniffed the air and his eyes lit up.

A large group of brownies began to stream out of the stall and fussed over Truss and Piers. There were so many of them, Emma couldn't help but think of circus clowns coming out of a tiny car.

"Momma!" Truss said. "Are you alright? What happened here?"

"We're all fine, my precious pebble. We're managing as best as we can. We lost the West Branch, and the whole burrow is pressed for space, so the immediate family is all staying here for now"

"But what happened?" Piers said, still shocked to see the way the blight affected his entire family. "It wasn't this bad when we left. Not nearly this bad."

"She's coming, my darling bricklet. The council is at wit's end. And then you two disappearing without notice. Others were worried, but I knew, in my heart of hearts, that you had been called up. And here you are again, safe–sound, just like I told them you would be." The elderly brownie sighed and appeared to deflate. It was only then that Emma could see just how old and worn out she really was.

"So, Unk–y, didja? Didja find it? Didja find the Over–monster?" Piers' nephews and nieces continued to climb his lanky legs and dangled from his arms. Emma couldn't take it anymore.

"I'm not a monster," Emma said firmly.

The children spun around, saw Emma for the first time, froze and fell to the ground in shock.

"M–m–m–m–m–onnnn–stt–t–t–er!"

They pointed at Emma and began to wail.

"I'm so sorry," Truss said to Emma, looking quite embarrassed and trying to hush the children.

"It's not a monster. It's a human," Mat remarked snidely. "The plane–owld–re–gyu–lore variety, it says. New genus. Definitely *not* a genius."

"Hush. I'm afraid our little ones have no manners at all," Truss said. Emma was not sure if she was apologizing for Mat or for the children.

"Won't you come in?" Truss and Piers' mother said as she turned to

Emma. "There's hot stew on the fire. It's not much, but we're always glad to share what we have."

"We can't, momma," Truss replied.

"Stew?" Piers said with wide and hungry eyes. Then he looked down at the two little brownies that were cowering behind his leg and sighed. "Feed the little ones, Mother. We have to deliver the Wanderer to Widget."

"Yes, momma. We really have to go," Truss added, softly. "But we'll be back as soon as we can."

Their mother smiled softly. "There's always plenty of stew for you, Piers. It will be waiting for you when you get back."

Piers smiled broadly, and after several minutes of hugs and crying and reassurances, Emma and the brownies headed back across the Market.

Emma would have been more than happy to slink through the crowd, remaining low key, but that was not to be. Instead, she and her four companions began to march across the market place to the drumbeat of brownie whispers.

Overling! *Wanderer*! *Monster*! *Human*! And every so often, comments like *Awfully pale, don't you think?* and *Do you suppose it's ill?* punctuated the murmuring hum. It seemed to take forever to cross the market, and Emma felt herself growing increasingly self–conscious.

Their path ended abruptly at the back wall of the cavern. The largest door Emma had ever seen loomed directly in front of them. It seemed to be made of the same material as the massive roots: part metal, part stone, part plant. An ornate archway composed of more intertwining vines and roots framed the door, above which spread a carving of a large, bare tree with outstretched branches. Unlike the great pillars and intertwining vines, the material in the door pulsed with a faint glow.

"Where are we?" Emma whispered once again, this time to no one in particular.

CLANG!

The great doors began to swing inward. A shaft of faint pearly light cut into the cavern for a moment before the doors swung open into a full curtain of cascading light.

"Well, child? Come along, I say!" The Master had grown increasingly twitchy as they crossed the Market. Emma couldn't tell whether this was due to nerves or excitement or his lack of naps in the past thirty minutes.

"Yes, do hurry. Some of us have important work to do," Mat added with a huff.

"Come along, I say," the Master repeated. This time he placed one hand on Emma's arm and the other on her back and gently pressed her forward. Unfortunately, he underestimated his own strength once again, and before she could protest, Emma flew forward, passed head first through the light and landed flat on her belly on the other side.

It took a moment for the dust to settle and a few moments more for Emma to finish coughing, look up, gasp in astonishment, inhale some more dust, and then stop coughing again.

She was in a courtyard, surrounded on three sides by rows and rows of walkways stacked one on top of another until they disappeared somewhere toward infinity.

More peculiar than the style, which was as ornate as a Tibetan mandala, was the fact that the building did not seem to have been built so much as cultivated. Every inch of the walls and walkways were part of a single glowing root system that hung from above like a chandelier. The roots stretched out across the open air to the walls, where they shot up and down in the form of pillars, then splintered off into delicate vines and tendrils, creating intricate designs over the columns and walls. The result was a single organic structure, all made from the same central root, yet interwoven with a complexity beyond Emma's comprehension.

As she lay there on the floor, a single thought crossed her mind. The building was alive. Every inch of it.

Each of the four walls had a large, central door. The two to her left and right were slightly smaller and less ornate, like the door to the Central Market, but the one directly in front of her dwarfed all three and glowed with a stronger, pulsing light that reminded Emma of a heartbeat.

She had barely enough time to get her bearings before the light dimmed and the wall vanished behind a pair of very dirty brick red feet in a pair of stringy sandals.

Emma tilted her head upward. The feet were connected to a pair of knobbly legs to the neatly patched hem of a longish tunic. She looked further up, past a simple rope belt, past the fur–like neckline trim, past a scrawny, knotty–looking neck, to the face of a pointy–faced, elderly brownie.

"I say, I say, I say, I say," the brownie said in a nasal tone. "No need to stand on such ceremony. Not that you're standing, of course. I meant to say so meta*phosphor*ically." He continued with a flourish, "Save it for his Wholiness, the Grand Poobah. When you see him, that is."

This last bit struck the creature as ridiculously funny for some reason, and he pursed his lips in an attempt to keep from belting out laughing. It didn't work, and an unfortunate snort came out instead.

"I say, I say, we're so dreadfully sorry, sir!" Master Tect's voice boomed from behind. Emma looked over her shoulder and saw her companions pass through the curtain of light and approach quickly.

"Well, I say, I say, I say," the elder brownie said with a squint. "Archibald Tect, is that you?"

Master Tect hurried forward.

"I daresay it is, honorable Managementor."

"I say, I say, this is fortuitous, indeed. I've been meaning to book an appointment with you to discuss a suitable meeting time to review an apparent administrative anomaly in sector 4976K dash Q. Seems there were several unauthorized travellers into Over recently. Most distressing."

"Why yes, sir, that's true sir," the Master had begun to sweat profusely again, and his handkerchief was worse for it. "I say, how about a spot of tea first, since I require a request for a requisition for the requisite forms, and we'll get right to the root of the matter, sir?"

"And I say, Master Tect," the elderly brownie continued, ignoring Tect completely, "What's all this I've been hearing about a supposed Wanderer entering Under? Where on earth is it? And where is its paperwork?"

"I say, sir. This is it, sir," Master Tect croaked. He nodded anxiously toward Emma, who was just sitting up and starting to brush herself off.

"This? This is the Wanderer? Or is this the paperwork? It doesn't resemble the current paperwork format, I must say. Did Head Office change filing procedures again?" The elder brownie inspected Emma with a wince. "How, erm, unusual. Why is it so pale? Is it sick?"

Mat chortled unkindly.

"I say, I say," the elder brownie continued to analyze her thoughtfully, "I was led to believe it would be, erm, larger, I suppose. And not quite so ghastly pale."

"Hearsay, sir," Master Tect said, trying to regain an air of authority. "See for yourself."

"I daresay. Are you sure?"

"I say, sir. Sure as soot."

"Well, I say, I say."

The two brownies continued to mutter *I says* at each other until the elder seemed to accept the Master's say so.

"I see," the elder said ceremoniously.

"You see, as I said, sir," Master Tect stuttered nervously.

Meanwhile, Mat was looking wistfully at the large door to the right of the courtyard.

"Can we get on with it, please?" the little brownie whined.

"I say, I say, I suppose we must," Master Tect nodded agreeably. "Sir, do you suppose we might …," he nodded emphatically toward the largest door, directly across the courtyard.

The elder was clearly shocked at the suggestion and burst out into another long string of *I say, I says* before finally collecting himself enough to respond.

"Absolutely out of the question. Preposterous! His Wholiness is exceptionally busy. You'll just have to submit your *T478b – Plan to Rescue All of Under From Total Annihilation Form*, in triplicate via the regular channels!"

"I say, sir, do you mean I should submit a three–fold plan once, or a single Plan–To–Prevent–Triple–Annihilation?" the Master asked.

"Or perhaps he means you should triplicate your single plan and only submit it once?" Mat suggested mischievously.

"Yes … er, NO … er … Submit *that* question in writing to my under under secretary, and we'll take it under advisement. Yes, indeed," the elder replied with finality.

The two brownies simply stared at each other uncomfortably, seemingly out of *I see*s. Emma took advantage of the pause.

"I say," she interrupted, then stopped herself. "I mean, excuse me. But weren't we supposed to see Mister Widget?"

"Yes, yes, of course, child," the Master said, flying into action again. "But I've got paperwork to do, so off you go then."

"Go where?"

"To Widget's. Didn't you just say you have urgent business with him?"

Emma looked at the Master as if he were completely off his rocker.

Maybe he's just confused, she thought. *Sleeping through half the action will do that to a person.*

"But I don't know Mister Widget or how to find him," she reminded him.

The Master blinked at her uncomprehendingly but noticed that his Managementor seemed to be taking mental notes and was evaluating his answer, quite possibly in triplicate. He began to perspire.

"Er, not quite finished this one, it seems. Hoping the ol' Widget might have a go at her and fix all the broken bits."

"Ah," said the elder brownie with a sage nod. "That probably explains the extreme paleness, too."

"AHEM!" Emma coughed loudly and stared at Master Tect hard enough to burn holes in his thick skull.

"Why don't *I* take it to Mister Widget, since I'm going that way, myself?" Mat announced. Master Tect's face lit up, and he gratefully accepted. The elder turned with a whoosh and a wobble and set off toward the large door to the left. Master Tect shot Emma a nervous smile, turned and ran after him, spewing *I says* as he went.

"Oh, my," Truss suddenly exclaimed. "I really should get back to check on Mum."

"And I really should check to see if there's any breakfast left," said Piers. "I wonder if she made it with quartz dust, the way I like it."

"But I was going to show you the lilac scroll translation I've been working on," the little brownie said to Truss and Piers, as they scurried away.

"I'm translating it into sasquatch and then back again. Mister Widget says the work is quite –," Mat broke off sadly. They vanished from sight.

"– skillful."

Piers and Truss were gone. Emma looked at Mat, who didn't seem terribly thrilled to be left alone with the monster. The brownie looked glumly at the glowing door and witheringly at Emma in turns. Finally, after a deep sigh meant to convey ultimate suffering, the little one pronounced: "Fine."

It was clear the situation was anything but.

"Well? Are you coming or what?" Mat glowered at Emma and scurried away toward the large door on the right. Emma scrambled to her feet and ran as fast as she could, trying to catch up.

She only narrowly missed flattening Mat completely when the brownie came to an abrupt stop, thrust a hand into a gap in the intricately woven tendrils that covered the door, felt around for a clasp or lever of some sort and pulled. Emma heard a small click, followed by a ringing noise somewhere deep within. The door swung open noiselessly.

"Wait! Where did Master Tect go?" she cried out. She had barely begun to absorb the sights at the Central Market, let alone the courtyard. Things were moving too quickly. She was terribly lost.

"Administration Offices, of course. Come along!" Mat snipped.

"But ... the other door ... where does *that* go?" Emma persisted.

"To the Poobah's Palace, naturally. Are you quite done? I've never heard of a Wanderer ask so many questions!"

"And exactly how many Wanderers do you know personally, little Mat Pantograph?" a haunting voice filled the dark hallway.

Emma looked up, startled. She couldn't see much in the light that spilled in from the courtyard. They seemed to be in a large hall, though she could only see the barest hint of walls and a small patch of oddly–tiled floor before it all disappeared into blackness.

Mat's arrogance vanished too, and the little brownie was transformed into an insecure schoolchild.

"Sir! I ... yes ... I mean ... no ... I mean ...," the little brownie began to stammer. "But the scrolls said ..."

"And what did I tell you about the power of the written word?" the voice echoed.

"That books contain all the wisdom of the ages, sir!" Mat announced with glee.

"And?"

"And all the folly, too, sir." The brownie trembled.

"And how can we tell them apart?"

"Um … other books, sir?"

"Tsk." A dark, sinister–looking figure stepped into the edges of the faint light. Emma detected a long coat with a large hood, but little else.

"Come now, Mat. Try again."

"Experience, sir?"

"Very good, child. You must excuse our little ambassador," the figure continued, turning to Emma. "Mat has always been one of our most enthusiastic students. Shows great promise, that one,"

Mat practically glowed in the dark from blushing.

"But still has many important lessons to learn, experience and etiquette being foremost on the list." The hooded figure wagged a finger at the suddenly crestfallen brownie. "But where are my manners? There can be no enlightenment without light. Lights!" The dark figure clapped his hands together, and the entire hall lit up in a flash of brilliant light. The mysterious figure threw off his hood.

Emma was half expecting a storybook wizard in horn–rimmed glasses and patches on the elbow of a purple, star–speckled cape, but Mister Widget turned out to be short, stout, and exceedingly jolly.

"I love it when he does that," Mat giggled. "Mister Widget possesses deep magic. Deep magic indeed."

"I say, I say," Emma replied thoughtfully. "Er … I mean, I see."

To her surprise, Mister Widget glance furtively at the ceiling and winked at her. He then pantomimed clapping his hands twice. Mat remained oblivious. Curious, Emma raised her own hands and clapped twice. The light in the great hall flicked off in an instant.

Mat's attitude toward her changed in an instant. "I … but … you … how?" the little brownie stuttered. Another thunderous clap rang out, and the lights came back on. Emma looked up to see Mister Widget wink at her again with an amused grin.

"Seems our little Wanderer has more power than you imagined," Mister Widget admonished Mat. "There is a lesson to be learned here, little one. Can you tell me what it is?"

Mat thought carefully before responding. "The hall lights are malfunctioning?"

Emma and Mister Widget both sighed heavily.

"Our little one is most impetuous and stubborn. I'm afraid someday that hard-headedness will cause a rift so great that no amount of diplomacy will ever heal it," Mister Widget said to Emma, and he looked directly at her for the first time. "Oh, my! By Foundation, but you're pale."

He peered into her eyes, as though searching for something. "How odd. Not what I expected, no indeed. I always thought the Wanderer would be more … more …"

"More impressive? Less monster-like?" Mat piped in helpfully. Mister Widget sighed and tsked.

"But come. Our hospitality has been lacking. It has been many years since we have had a guest, and certainly none so illustrious as you."

Emma tried to protest, but Mister Widget raised a hand and motioned her to stop. "Please, come. These are hard times indeed, but what little we have we will gladly share. I imagine you are tired and full of questions."

"Oh yes, it's full of questions alright," Mat piped in. "More questions than answers, in fact."

"Then let us see if we can shift the balance," Mister Widget said grandly. "Come!"

The old academic started down the great hall, but stopped for a moment and took Emma aside.

"I don't suppose you happen to have brought any spare Over

batteries, by any chance? I'm especially keen on some new double A's," he whispered. Emma shook her head. "What a shame. I've salvaged an old remote control car from one of the access tunnels, you see. I was hoping to convert it into a leisure vehicle someday," he sighed and started to walk down the very long hall.

They walked for a very long time. Every so often, they would pass a set of large doors, some open, some closed. Emma could see signs on some:

Prof. Nutsnbolts
Office Hrs. Every 5th Wednes–
Day at 10:12, SHARP

and

Passage to Permanent Pass–holder's Parking

One door simply read *Food Hall*, and another was marked *Seedling Laboratory*, and every so often a small door oddly marked *Boom Closet*.

"Definitely must get that buggy working," Mister Widget muttered. "Getting too old and arthritic for these long halls, yes, indeed."

The hall was cloaked in silence for the most part, except for the flip flop of their feet on the floor. Sometimes a faint murmur could be heard behind one door or another, a strange *fizz!–crack!–creak*! behind the door to the Seedling Laboratory and the occasional sound of something mysterious exploding in a Boom Closet or two. Emma was surprised, therefore, when a faint roar in the distance grew into a moderate roar, and finally into an ear–splitting one. Mat's excitement grew proportionately.

Mister Widget came to a stop in front of a room with a large set of double doors that were flung wide open. The sign above simply read: *Translations*.

The roar was deafening.

"Sir, do you think I might –," Mat pleaded earnestly, tugging repeatedly at Mister Widget's sleeve. Mister Widget looked down and smiled.

"Of course, child. Your desk awaits you."

Mat scampered off like a four–year–old who had just discovered where the cookie jar was hidden.

"An exceptional student, our Mat, but still inexperienced in the ways of the world. We selected the original team of Trackers based on their unique abilities, but we were all surprised when the house chose Mat. The little one has an insatiable thirst for information but has yet to learn the difference between information and wisdom."

Emma was only half listening. She had watched Mat run into the large, clamorous room, where the little brownie's arrival caused quite a stir, but Emma was not paying attention to the brownie.

The Translations Room was an enormous cavern somewhat reminiscent of a medieval monastery. The floor was lined with row after row of tiny desks at which sat hundreds of tiny, Mat–sized brownies, each scribbling away furiously on parchment–like scrolls, except in the vicinity of Mat's desk, where a small, excited crowd had begun to form.

Ghostlike apparitions formed above each desk, playing out scenes from the text that was being written on the scroll below. At a nearby desk, Emma saw a silver and gold griffin taking flight. Above the next desk, a boy's angry mother threw some beans out the window, where they quickly took root and began to grow. Further down the aisle, witches and monkeys flew through the air, alongside a castle made of ice to the left and a meeting of ancient spirits and sprites in a primordial forest of talking trees on the right.

Emma looked back at the small crowd gathered around Mat, who was bent over a scroll, scribbling furiously. She could see a distinct cloud, filled with familiar images: her apartment, the view of her bedroom as seen from inside the vent, and a terribly unflattering image of herself. She wondered if she really was so big and clumsy looking. She was certain she didn't look quite so ghostly pale.

The scrolls themselves were locked in place at the top and bottom of each desk and moved forward by a crank that the brownies turned constantly with one hand while writing with the other. As soon as the parchment was finished, the brownie would unhook the scroll, wave it in the air, and call out.

Instantly, a member of yet another group of brownies snatched up the scroll. These individuals rode on the backs of field mice, and they rushed the scroll to a center console station to be sorted, labelled and filed. As soon as one scroll was dispatched, the riders spun their mounts in a glorious pirouette, and dashed off again to retrieve the next one.

Emma did a double take.

Field mice?

The mice wore saddles made of thick, brilliantly coloured silk and carried large baskets on either side of their plump, sleek bodies. They ran and leapt down the rows, barely missing each other, somehow surprisingly nimble in spite of their width. As they neared the desk of a ready brownie, the mice ducked their heads and began to skid. Then, suddenly, they leapt into the air in a graceful arc, just as its rider grabbed the scroll and flung it into the basket. The scene was thrilling, chaotic and incredibly exciting.

"Ah, to be young and spry and handy with the reins again," Mister Widget said with a melancholy smile. "They are an enterprising bunch, to be sure." He looked at Emma and his wistfulness quickly turned to alarm.

"Oh, my, but you must be tired, hungry, confused and disoriented!"

"No … I …," Emma tried to protest, but she was truly all of those things, though not necessarily in that order.

"Come," Mister Widget said kindly. "My quarters are quite near. I'll have Missus Styrene cook you up something appropriate."

He ushered her back down the hall a short way to yet another door. He opened it, waved her in, and called out.

"Polly! Polly?"

A female brownie in overalls came bustling into the atrium. She was very short and very stout, even by brownie standards. Her face was smudged with black grease, and she wiped her hands on a grimy towel that may have been a color other than grey at one time.

"Well, Wally, that's the carburetor taken care of. I don't suppose you managed to unearth any working batteries, did you?" She looked up, saw Emma and froze in her tracks.

"A guest? A guest! Oh, and the house is such a shambles, too. Really, Wally, you could give a gal a tad more warning, you know, and –." She stopped mid–sentence, now realizing who Emma was. "Oh, my goodness! Goodness gravel indeed! Why, it's … it's …"

"Polly, meet Emma, our Wanderer from Over. Emma, Missus Polly Styrene. My groundkeeper."

Missus Styrene quickly shook off her astonishment and stumbled forward with her still greasy hand outstretched. "Oh my goodness gravel, indeed. This is an honor. My, but you're sickly pale. Must be nearly dead with hunger, I imagine. Come in, come in, child. We'll have you right as roots in no time."

Emma followed the headmaster's groundkeeper obediently into the apartment. They passed down a short hall into a potato–shaped sitting room. The far side of the cave opened up into the same echoing abyss that had greeted Emma when she first arrived in Under, and the red orange light that filled the central cavern lit up the sitting room, as well. Additional torches placed in sconces in the bare stone walls helped brighten the place.

There was an enormous circular sofa in the center of the room, which gave it a rather cozy feeling, and a series of bookshelves filled to overflowing with the most peculiar collection of doodads Emma had ever seen. One shelf contained a pile of enormous bolts and screws the size of automobile tires. There were bits of twine and a couple of enormous nine–volt batteries acting like workhorses, with a shelf strung up between them. The shelf itself was barely visible beneath a pile of giant buttons and a wire sculpture that she soon recognized as a large, twisted paperclip.

"Here we are now, piping hot and fresh as pebbles in a pond," Missus Styrene came bustling back in, wearing a clean tunic, her face scrubbed so hard it sparkled. She pulled a cart so overloaded with steaming hot platters the wheels creaked.

"I've just made a fresh batch of stone soup, and there's a nice gravel loaf from Miss Quickset Cement's Stone Oven Bakery, too." She looked up and saw the look of alarm creeping across Emma's face. She smiled.

"Worry not, overling. I've got some nice root stew for you, too. Made 'special," she added as she ladled a dollop of thick, dark slop into a bowl and passed it to Emma, who wondered how anyone could make stew so quickly for an unexpected guest. "Here you go, dearie."

"Thank you," Emma said. "You really didn't need to go to so much trouble."

"P'saw," Missus Styrene replied. "We can't have you falling over from hunger, and I understand you overfolk aren't too keen on stones and rocks. Unless Mister Widget here has done some seriously faulty research, that is. And Mister Widget's research is never wrong." Mister Widget flushed happily. "I can't imagine where you get sufficient minerals from, though."

Emma looked down at the mound of brown slop in front of her. It smelled vaguely like grass; not an unpleasant smell, but not necessarily the sort of smell she normally associated with food. She picked up the spoon and skimmed a small amount from the top. She lifted it to her mouth and noticed that both Mister Widget and Missus Styrene were both trying very hard not to stare. She tasted the stew.

"Mmmmmm," Emma said. "It's delicious."

It really wasn't half bad: surprisingly sweet like cooked yams, but heavier feeling. The brownies breathed sighs of relief and dug into their own meals. No one spoke as Emma slurped and the brownies crunched. Finally, Mister Widget pushed his plate away with a satisfied sigh.

"First rate cooking there, Missus S.," he said. "And now, child, let's figure out what to do with you, shall we?"

"Sir, I've been wondering … how will I get home?" Emma asked. The question had been nagging at her since she arrived.

"I'm afraid that's yet to be seen," the old teacher replied.

It wasn't the answer she was hoping for, but there wasn't anything she could do about that,

"Tell me about your family, child."

Emma told him all the things she had already told Truss, Piers and Mat about losing her mother and moving all over the place, following her father's work. When she was finally finished, Mister Widget and Missus Styrene looked at each other and sighed.

Mister Widget considered the matter for a few moments, and while he did so, Emma felt the root stew settle in her stomach and her eyelids grow heavy. She hadn't realized how hungry she had been earlier, until now, when she was suddenly so very full. She could hear Mister Widget and Missus Styrene speaking to each other. Words like "Wanderer" and "unfinished" and "not what I expected" floated by as she felt herself drifting off.

The last thing she heard Mister Widget say before she fell asleep was: "Yes, I suppose you're right, my dear Polly. Ceres will know what to do. We will send her to Ceres in the morning."

"But for now, let her sleep, poor dear," said Polly. "She will need all the rest she can get."

Far off in the distance, a dark and persistent rumbling crept into her dreams like the grey blight on the roots that surrounded her, and it turned all her happy memories into sad ones.

Chapter Ten: Under World

The path was narrow and sometimes steep. Emma clung to the wall as best she could, because every time she looked down, or even out in the direction of the edge, her stomach tightened up and rose into her throat, so she had even more trouble breathing. The path was just wide enough for her to stand facing forward, but even so, her outer foot landed just inches from the edge, and she could feel the pebbles shifting and dropping into the abyss just from the weight of her footstep.

Rustle, rustle, plink, plink, plink … plink.

Memory of the brownie burrow and all its strangeness quickly faded too, as she tried desperately to keep moving forward without panicking. She had slept, but for how long she did not know: it could have been hours or days. She was still groggy.

Rustle, rustle.

Far below, the rocks and air meshed into a reddish grey haze. Warm air wafted upwards from deep below, so Emma had to fight off drowsiness on top of dizziness. Worst of all was when the path suddenly twisted hard to the left or right, vanishing from sight until she was standing practically in the middle of the turn. Up to that point, it looked like the path just stopped and dropped off into nothingness, and she couldn't tell if she was walking straight off the cliff.

"Hurry! Hurry! We must leave now if we are to reach Ceres in time!" Piers had told her as he shook her awake at the Academy that morning.

"In time for what?" Emma asked, still rubbing the sleep from her eyes. No one responded. No one heard. They were all too busy making preparations for some other journey. The arrangements had all been made while she slept, though explaining them to Emma did not seem to be on the agenda.

Plink, plink.

Emma clung to the wall and tried to focus on breathing, moving forward one step at a time. She was glad they had rested, even if Missus Styrene's root stew was now doing strange things to her tummy.

They continued to descend, and the landscape gradually changed from dark, rich brown soil and grey, slate–like rock to darker, blacker soil and redder stones. Some time after that, the soil disappeared entirely, leaving only granular sand and gravel. Then the rocks grew jagged and splintered every which way.

"Do be careful, child. Your skin is more tender than our own," Truss cautioned. A split second later, Emma brushed her arm against one of the razor sharp rock slivers. The stone cut into her skin like a vicious paper cut. She cried out, even before she felt the pain shoot through her arm, nearly blinding her.

"Goodness Gravel, you'll be cut to ribbons, girlie," Piers exclaimed as he leaped back on the path to inspect the wound. He quickly pulled off his belt sash and wrapped it around her arm. "There, that should hold until we find a doctor."

"Will the doctor know what to do with monster flesh?" Mat asked.

"Foundation knows," Piers replied. "We'll have to ask the doctor when we find one."

"Perhaps Ceres knows about such matters," Truss suggested.

"We'll see," Piers replied. "Now, let's just try to get this one down to the valley in one piece, shall we?" He reached into his tunic and pulled out a large overcoat. He threw it over Emma's shoulders, saying, "That will keep you safe from the razor rocks, girlie." Piers was definitely in high spirits, especially since he'd been reunited with his steaming hot bowl of gravel and pegs.

Emma still wondered how these brownies managed to tuck so many things inside their very small pockets. It was a great trick, one she'd like to learn, especially since her storybook seemed to be getting heavier by the minute.

"Figures we find a Wanderer, and it turns out to be breakable," muttered Mat, who was now blaming Emma for making them leave the burrow, and more importantly, the Academy. Emma could hardly fault the young brownie, and she was sure she would never want to leave school if they had a Translations Room, too.

They continued their descent, more carefully now they were all aware of Emma's relative fragility. Emma moved forward awkwardly, trying to avoid the rocks, but the oversized longcoat was stiff and inflexible. She clutched the book in front of her for protection.

"Do you suppose she'll be able to help us?" Piers' wavering voice floated up the path.

"What? The monster?" Mat replied.

"No, silly. Well, yes, er … I mean, I was thinking of Ceres, but you pose a valid question …"

"What question? Did I ask a question?"

"Well, er, you mentioned the monster, didn't you?"

"I am *not* a monster," Emma put in, crossly. The vibration from her voice dislodged a small cluster of pebbles, which slid off the edges of the cliff side in an insistent rush.

Rustle, rustle, rustle.

"Shhhhhhhh. We'll all be killed!" Master Tect scolded.

"I *told* you she was trying to kill us," Mat hissed.

"Who, Ceres?" Piers asked. "Why would Ceres want to kill us?"

"No, the monster."

"Oh, the monster," Piers nodded sagely. "But why would Ceres want to hurt the monster?"

Plink, plink, plink …

Another rush of pebbles and small stones slid off the cliff into the unknowable bottom below. Silence fell over the travellers.

They crept along the cliffs for what seemed like forever, eventually coming to a long shelf that widened enough for them all to walk forward comfortably. Soon, they could walk two by two and then, after a time, the razor rocks vanished altogether. The air grew hotter and gradually began to swim with steam and moisture, while the light became more intense, darker and redder, flickering off the brownies red faces like Christmas tree lights.

"I'm hungry," Piers whined softly.

"Again? You just had breakfast," Truss replied.

"Can't help it. When's lunch?"

Emma could hear a twinge of nervousness creep back into Piers' voice.

No matter how far down they went, the abyss continued to drop into nothingness beyond the edge of the path. Now that the shelf had widened a little, Emma found herself able to look out from time to time without feeling sick to her stomach. Her knees still wobbled, but only a little. The rock gradually became softer and rounder, until it began to resemble a smooth, continuous wall. It was, in fact, a delicate brickwork of enormous, flat stones seamlessly crushed and blended together. And yet, even this far below, tiny vines grew out between the cracks and crept up the side like ivy trying to take hold.

"What is that?" Emma asked Truss, who was walking close behind her.

"Those are house roots, child," the brownie replied.

"So far down?"

"The strongest magic runs deep and touches every part of the earth. Our burrow is the last, but it is also the most powerful. It has taken many years for the witch's poison to infect its roots, and still it continues to fight back."

Emma looked at the roots. The delicate green tendrils pushed their way between the cracks in the rock, seeking heat from the cavern core. They seemed so tender and fragile. Emma wondered how they could possibly withstand any attack at all.

They continued to hike even further downward as the air grew hotter and hotter. Emma was practically melting in the heat, and the heavy coat was making her steam.

The rock began to lose its smooth, polished softness again. It started to droop, then drip, oozing a dark, viscous fluid that looked like lava, but was cool and slimy to the touch. And wherever the rock dripped, long, bulbous rock icicles formed, sometimes splintering into many prongs like upside down candelabra. Wherever there was a level surface underneath the drip, the fluid would collect, pool, and eventually build up into a point, like a funhouse image of the downward spiral above it.

"Mmmmmm," lowed Piers. "Looks like rock candy."

"Piers, are you ever *not* hungry?" Mat grumbled irritably.

"No, no, of course not. I mean, yes," Piers scratched his head, trying to understand what Mat was asking. "I mean … I wasn't hungry right after I finished off that bowl of polished pebbles this morning. Does that answer your question?" He looked up hopefully.

"And how long did that last?"

"At least until we left the burrow," Piers asserted.

"Piers, that was five minutes after you stopped eating," Truss said with a frown.

"Well there, you see? I wasn't hungry for five whole minutes!" Piers seemed to be quite proud of this achievement. Mat sighed heavily and decided to just stop talking.

The path became increasingly treacherous and slippery. They had to step around the wet, dripping pillars while trying to avoid the larger puddles, which still threatened to send them sliding right off the ledge. It was possible there would be something to land on, now that ledges and outcroppings had reappeared in the cliff–side, resembling mushrooms on a prehistoric tree, but it was equally possible they might slide right off into the abyss. Or worse, get impaled on one of the spiral points.

Emma began to fret.

"Is something the matter, child?" Truss asked.

"My book … it's getting wet."

"Well, girlie, why don't you just put it in your pocket?" said Piers with a shrug. "The coat will keep it dry, sure enough."

"The book is too big," Emma said, growing frustrated. "It won't fit in there."

"Of course it will. Just think about the book being in the pocket, and it will fit. Try it."

Emma looked dubiously at the pocket and then at the large picture book she still held cradled in her arms. She shrugged, then stuck the corner of the book into the pocket.

"See," she said, looking back at Piers. "I told you it wouldn't fit."

"But it already has, girlie. Just look."

Emma looked down, and to her surprise the entire book was somehow inside the coat, except for the corner she still held with her hand. She let go, and the rest of the book vanished from sight.

I must learn how that works, she thought to herself.

They slid past the enormous pillars silently, concentrating on their footing and sometimes clinging to each other for balance. Emma was very glad now to have the outer protection of the long coat, which seemed to be made of some strange fabric that never once tore or caught on the rocks around them. She was also glad to have the use of both her hands for balance.

"Is it much further?" Emma whispered to Truss as she gripped the solid brownie's sleeve.

"Nearly there, child," Truss whispered back in the hot, damp air as she reached across to pat Emma's clutched fist reassuringly.

They continued to walk.

The dangling spires and soaring towers grew larger, longer and more convoluted. They also grew closer together, and it became difficult to find sure footing. The heat was unbearable, and the thick, hot air made Emma feel faint. The heavy overcoat started to feel more like a liability as it weighted down her shoulders and trapped the heat inside. She considered taking it off and passing it back to Piers, but its outer shell was coated now in the same hot, dark slime that dripped from the walls of the cave, so she left it on.

Good choice, she thought, as she slipped sideways between two enormous pillars that had grown so large they nearly blended into one double-wide partition, leaving just a small opening between them. *Slipping through,* she thought. *I'm just slipping through the cracks.* She would have laughed, except the space was so small, she could barely breathe. Her arm was still aching badly from the cut she had received higher up on the cliff side.

Oddly, neither Truss nor the very round Master seemed to have any trouble with the narrow width, and Emma wondered once again how they could seemingly change shape to fit whatever sized passage presented itself.

She was still edging through the narrow crevice when the ground started to shake. The two pillars on either side of her began to shift. The stones began to squeeze together. Terrified, she tried to call for help, but she couldn't breathe. She could feel the weight crushing her chest flat.

The brownies sprang into action. Master Tect grabbed her arm, and Piers grabbed a leg. They both yanked hard, trying to pull her out. This time, Emma got the scream out, and they both flew backward in surprise.

"Hey! I'm attached to those!" Emma gasped at them. She wanted to get out, and fast, but she preferred to be removed all in one piece. The entire cavern started to shake again. Dark grey patches began to appear all over one of the pillars. Truss looked at it in horror as it began to crumble.

"The roots! They're sick to the core! The witch … she's found us!"

Truss cried out, nearly in tears.

"Please! Help me!" Emma gasped.

"I've got you, girlie!" Piers called bravely, as he leaped across the path toward Emma. Rocks and pillars began to crumble everywhere. He slid his arms into the crevice and wrapped them around her as best he could. Several large stones fell from the ceiling and narrowly missed his head. Mat, Truss and Master Tect ducked and dodged more falling debris, as they lined up behind Piers and all grabbed onto each other.

"Ready, girlie?" Piers said.

"For what?" Emma gasped. She could barely breathe under the crushing pressure.

"OK. On the count of three, think, 'I'm through.' Got it?" Piers said earnestly. She nodded, weakly. Piers began to count down, "One … two … THREE!"

All four brownies pulled very hard, and Emma shut her eyes. *I'm through*, she thought. *I'm through*. And suddenly she was.

The brownies all fell to the ground like bowling pins.

Another horrible screech filled the air.

"Run!" Master Tect cried out and began lumbering down the path, slipping and sliding in all directions. Grey patches began to appear on the pillars all around them, and soon after, the roots and walls began to crumble. Within moments, they were running for their lives as an avalanche of stones fell all around them.

"Look! There!" Piers called out, pointing a gangly hand to one side. A portion of the wall had collapsed, leaving a pile of rocks and a space the size of a keyhole. Beyond the space, something cast a rectangular shaft of light across the pathway. The brownies scrambled toward the light and one by one disappeared through the crevice.

It was a tiny space. Emma looked at it fearfully, wondering what to do. The walls were collapsing all around her. She had to go. *Now*.

Emma closed her eyes and dove toward the light. She passed

through easily, and suddenly, she was clear.

To her relief, the geography changed dramatically on the other side of the crevice. But it also took her a moment to realize that although she had escaped the slimy spindles, the path had completely vanished.

She was standing on a tiny ledge just large enough to hold the five of them. At the same time, a blinding light caused her to recoil against the cliff side. It was part of the reason she hadn't noticed her surroundings, and luckily, also the reason she hadn't fallen off. It took her another moment to realize they were no longer in the bottomless cavern, but had crossed over to someplace else.

A deep red ball of flame hovered on the far side of an enormous cavern that was so large and vast, the flame appeared to be a setting sun on the far horizon. Below, a wide river glinted darkly as if refusing to allow light to penetrate its murky surface. The farthest side of the river disappeared into a grey fog, from which rose an enormous, ornate stone gate. Something equally large paced in front of it, dark as night. A cold chill ran down her back.

Emma squinted in the light and shadowed her eyes. There appeared to be a steady stream of creatures moving toward a pier on the side of the river closest to her. The light caught the top of a billowing wave on the water, where she detected a large boat.

"Oh. Hell." Emma didn't exactly speak the word. It was more a gasp or a whisper. It was a statement, not a curse.

"Not Hell, child. Hades. A land of the dead, to be sure, but Hell is a different place altogether." Truss explained.

"Different part of Under, too," added Mat. "We do try to keep our afterlives separate. Helps keep the place neat and tidy, if you know what I mean. It just wouldn't do to have the dead all running around, mucking things up for the living. Not that we have anything against them, mind. It's just that they get to be a bit of a nuisance with all that free time on their hands. Anyway, we're looking for Ceres, not Hades, so we're not crossing the gates."

Emma paused for a moment, searching her brain, which was already befuddled from the interminable walk and was now trying to grasp the idea that the Greek myths she'd read might be true, too. But since another portion of her brain was also still trying to process the existence of brownies, and since her stomach was still churning from root stew, her brain just ceased to function at all.

"Well, ok, then," she replied dumbly. "So, how do we get down?"

"We catch a lift," said Mat, as blasé as someone declaring they were waiting for a bus.

Before Emma could ask what sort of ride they could possible expect all the way up there, an earth–shattering caw shattered the air. She threw her hands to her ears and cowered, though none of the brownies flinched. Another shriek followed, and with it a blast of warm wind battered the travellers. Emma staggered backward, glad that the weight of the longcoat helped keep her from blowing over altogether. None of this seemed to faze the brownies, though their hair and loose bits of clothing all blew backward horizontally. Master Tect's cheeks, which were more pudgy than solid, rippled in giant waves from the violence of the blast. Then, without warning, it all stopped.

"What was...?"

Emma never finished the sentence, for in response, an gigantic, dark form rose up from beneath the ledge.

It was a bird, or at least, it was bird–like: part eagle, part prehistoric pterodactyl. It rose vertically, as if hoisted on an invisible wire that lifted it into the sky. Its wings beat a slow, rhythmical beat and made a sucking noise as they lifted and pulled air into the pockets underneath. It was so large it could have lifted an elephant easily in a single talon, had there had been any elephants around to be lifted.

Time stood still as the wings crested the top of each beat and hovered silently for a moment before thundering down again, forcing cascades of hot air against the cliffs.

The Master inched forward and hollered something to the creature.

Emma couldn't hear a thing except the wind battering her ears.

The bird rose even further into the air, bent its back and neck forward, and cawed with another ear–splitting shriek. When Emma recovered, she saw the brownies in front of her, hopping up and down, waving at her frantically. She had to read their lips in order to understand what they were saying.

"Come on! Come on!"

Come on where? she wondered.

Instead of explaining, Piers wrapped his long fingers around her arm, and Truss took her other hand and led her forward to the very edge of the cliff. Emma had to lean heavily into the blasts of wind coming from the bird's wings, just to keep her balance.

Piers pointed to something directly ahead of them, and Emma struggled to see where he was pointing. Then she saw it. A rope ladder dangled above the ledge in front of the bird's wing, reaching up the beast's back. Emma stared at it for a moment before realizing that Piers wanted her to climb.

She reached out a shaking hand and somehow managed to wrap her fingers around a rung. Truss released her other hand and guided Emma to the next one.

This is crazy, Emma thought to herself. *I'm in the middle of the earth with a bunch of basement brownies, trying to climb a prehistoric bird.*

Luckily, the wind was blowing so strongly in her ears that she couldn't hear her own thoughts.

She took a deep breath and lifted her foot onto the bottom rung. She looked up. Mat and the Master looked down at her from something that seemed to be a large basket on the bird's back. They waved her up, shouting loud words of encouragement, though not loud enough to be heard over the roar of the wind and the wings and the cawing.

Slowly, as steadily as she could, she climbed the ladder, shaking the whole time, until the Master was able to reach her hand from above and pull her inside. Emma sunk to the bottom of the basket and cowered in a corner until the other two had clambered up.

"All aboard?" Mat cried out gaily. "Then off we go!"

The bird bobbed its head several times then lurched upwards into the air. Emma clung to the edges of the basket for dear life.

The bird pivoted without warning, and Emma felt herself lifting right off the ground, or more accurately, off the bottom of the basket, which was already far above the ground, and they all suspended in mid–air for a moment.

Her knuckles turned white as she clung even tighter to the edge of the basket, not daring to look out even after her feet touched down again, half expecting they would plunge straight down again any second. She waited and held her breath. She waited still longer. Finally, she dared to look and discovered they were coasting safely in large, slow, lazy circles.

"Come, child, have a look–see," Truss called out to her genially, stretching a hand out to help. Emma took the brownies' solid hand and slowly stood up. She gasped.

They were still cruising far above the large red ball that filled the valley with light on the distant horizon. From her perch Emma felt like she could almost reach out and pluck the ball from the air and roll it in her hand. Behind them, the red light bounced off the cliffs with a brilliant metallic glow that in turn reflected into the eastern part of the valley and kept it filled with a soft light. Emma looked back and watched as the tiny ledge they came from disappeared from sight.

They coasted and banked above the long, winding river that split the valley in two. Below them, the solitary boat came into full view on the river. It was an oddly shaped Viking longboat with a beautifully ornate figurehead carved in the bow. Emma could see hundreds of people filling the deck, but no one seemed to be at the helm. The ship sailed in a perfectly straight line. The sails were full, but there was no wind in the air, other than the airflow from the bird's single set of beating wings. In fact, except for the rhythmic *whoosh thump* from their ride, the valley was eerily silent, especially considering the number of beings gathered by the shore.

"They're so quiet and still," Emma shouted at Truss as the bird's wings suctioned air up and then pounded it back down.

"Yes, child. They are waiting their turn to cross."

"Cross where?"

"To Hades, the ancient Greek version of the afterworld."

"There used to be many more of them," Mat added professorially, "back in the days when Greece was the center of the known Universe. These are the last of the Greco–Roman souls. It's rare that a new one arrives here now."

"Where did they all go?"

"To other religions and other gods, child," said Truss, "It's gotten quite crowded down here, what with all the different ideas of the afterlife. There are new ones cropping up all the time."

"Yes, quite annoying sometimes, too," Mat added. "Do you remember the Everlasting Resting Place of Jebediah Funkleblister?" The other brownies nodded and shuddered. "They had to move his entire utopia to the lower limits because the parties were keeping all the other Underlings awake."

Emma looked back out at the valley. The enormous beast she'd seen pacing in front of the large gate stirred as they passed overhead, and one of its three enormous dog heads perked up and snapped at them as they passed a good distance overhead. Beyond the gate, the land was an amorphous detail–less grey, as though someone had started a painting and forgotten to fill in a part of it.

"That's Hades, child," Truss said, noticing her questioning look. "You can't see anything because you have not yet passed through the gates. The land is only visible to those who know its secrets."

"Not that you'd want to," Mat interjected. "Not so easy getting back out again, if you know what I mean. The exit clause always comes with a tricky catch."

The bird cawed loudly, as if in agreement. Then it banked heavily again and turned gracefully in the air, heading back toward the cliff.

"There it is!" Piers shouted, pointing to a large, dark spot at the base of the cliffs. Emma guessed it was a cave of some sort.

"Prepare for landing!" Mat called out.

"This could be a bit bumpy!" added Truss.

Oh, dear, Emma thought to herself.

Her fingers tightened around the basket edge, and her toes curled in her shoes, as though she were trying to grab onto the bottom through the soles. Piers draped a long arm over her shoulder and held onto the basket on either side of her. Somehow, this made her feel safer and more secure.

The bird cawed once again and dipped its head. The rest of the bird followed suit, and soon they were in a nosedive, hurtling toward the ground. In spite of herself, Emma felt a wave of euphoria sweep through her as they plummeted down, and instead of feeling afraid, as any sensible girl would, she found herself laughing and screaming as if she were at the amusement park.

They hurtled toward the earth with increasing speed, and just as it seemed as if they were too close to pull up in time, the bird's great wings lifted and arched simultaneously. The creature raised its head and dropped its tail. The switch from near free fall to the sudden pull up was like suddenly stepping off the moon onto earth, where gravity is six times stronger.

Just as the pressure got to be so strong she was sure she would burst, they leveled off and the weight eased up. The enormous bird cruised forward, barely skimming the ground as they approached the cave entrance.

"Hold on!" Piers cried out as the bird arched its wings again, this time to brake, and stretched out its taloned claws to brace against impact.

"Landing isn't exactly his strong suit!" Master Tect confided, leaning toward the girl and shouting at the top of his lungs.

They touched the ground, and the back of the bird's claws gouged the earth. They jolted and slowed a bit, then bounced back up again. On the second touchdown, the bird dug in deeper and curved its back against the impact. Emma and the brownies all managed to hang on through the second bump, too. The third bump, however, sent them all flying every which way.

Emma felt herself hurtling through the air like a gymnast and wished she'd paid more attention to dismount techniques in gymnastics class. She braced herself for impact as the ground closed in on her. Luckily, though, she landed in a big patch of soft, cushiony moss.

She sat up and waited for the world to stop spinning. She finally regained her bearings enough to catch her breath and picked herself up to survey the damage. The bird had regained its composure already and was busy preening its feathers and setting itself right. Truss had fallen into a large pile of brambles, which appeared to have broken her fall without breaking her.

Mat was clinging to the Master's leg, which was stuck up in the air over his head. They had flown out of the basket as one and then rolled down a sharp incline, heads over heels, until coming to rest in a crumpled heap by a large boulder. Piers had crested the one bit of vegetation resembling a tree and had landed on the far side of it. He dangled upside down from one foot caught in a small fork in some branches.

It took several minutes for each of the brownies to right themselves and regroup in the center of the small clearing. Once they were all assembled, Master Tect looked at the cave, then turned his gaze back to the wobbly crew. He tugged on his tunic to straighten it out and adjusted his medallion, which had gone all crooked in the fall. Then he waved his arm, gesturing toward the dark entrance.

"Shall we?" he said, in his most officious tone.

And they did, hobbling toward the cave with as much dignity as they could muster.

Chapter Eleven: A Strange Ceres of Events

The five of them half–strode, half–hobbled into the cave, while the enormous bird found a nice, soft indentation in the brush and nestled down to preen itself.

"See you in a bit, George!" Master Tect shouted toward the creature, waving a friendly goodbye. The bird partly lifted its head, squinted, then squawked in acknowledgement and went back to preening. Emma glanced over her shoulder just in time to see it re–bury its head under its wing. It seemed to be either cleaning itself or preparing to sleep. Either way, Emma thought to herself, George was an awfully plain name for such a strange creature.

A few steps further and they plunged into shadow.

At this point, Emma was pretty much prepared for anything and would not have been surprised to discover that the cave was yet another portal to another plane of existence, or if it was oddly larger inside than seemed plausible, or even if the whole arrangement could be folded up and placed in her dress pocket. It was, however, simply a cave, with all the cave–like features one might expect.

The walls were rocky and a bit damp in places. Some of the deeper crevices contained small amounts of moss and smelled vaguely of mold, especially where it was wettest and farthest from the light. The cave was shaped like a cave, smelled like a cave, and for all intents and purposes, was a cave. Emma couldn't help but feel a little disappointed. Frankly, after all she'd been through, a plain old cave was a bit of a letdown.

Truss hustled her along toward the back, which was cloaked in murky darkness. Once again, Emma braced herself for something strange, but it turned out to be nothing more than a plain, ordinary tunnel. They continued to make their way forward cautiously, into what should have been total darkness. It took Emma a few moments to realize the walls were lit, in fact, with a soft green glow. She looked at the walls questioningly.

"Glow worms," Mat said, matter–of–factly.

They continued to walk until they rounded a sharp corner, where their path ended abruptly at a solid wall of rock. They came upon it so suddenly that Emma barely had time to gasp and exclaim, "Oh, dear!" before she ran her nose right into it.

"Nothing to worry about, child. It's just the first gate," said Truss.

The Master stepped forward and presented himself to the wall, as if addressing himself to a foreign dignitary. He lifted his right arm, made a fist and then cleared his throat loudly before bringing it down to knock soundly on a particularly round rock. Emma rubbed her own knuckles instinctively, but the Master gave no indication that knocking on the stone was anything but normal. The sound was thick and heavy, like bashing two boulders together.

Master Tect paused for a moment and tilted his head, listening for some sort of response. None came. He rapped again on the rock, a little harder this time. Emma winced. Still nothing.

Just as he was raising his hand to knock a third time, Mat leaned forward, tugged on the Master's coat sleeve and whispered urgently. Master Tect listened intently, frowned, then looked at Mat, who in turn nodded frantically at him and pointed energetically at the wall. The senior brownie blushed and half–turned toward Emma.

"Er, so sorry. Wrong rocker, it would seem."

He stepped back and scrutinized the wall. He pointed to a stone. Mat scowled. He pointed to another stone. Mat frowned and turned an odd shade of purple. Finally, he pointed to another large stone and looked at Mat quizzically. Mat nodded emphatically, followed by a great deal of eye rolling as soon as the Master turned away.

Master Tect knocked again. This time, the knocking produced a deep, hollow echo that rang through the cave.

Nothing happened.

The echo faded into the distance, and a faint, muffled sound replied.

The sound grew louder; it was very rapid footsteps, something like a pitter–patter, but with an odd, offbeat shuffling sound which Emma could not identify.

Clackity–clackity–swoosh–thump–clackity–clackity–swoosh–thump.

The footsteps grew louder, then stopped suddenly on the opposite side of the wall. A low rumbling sound filled the cave, followed by the hiss of displaced sand. The same boulder the Master had knocked on rolled backward, like a bowling ball down a gutter, until it vanished from sight and was replaced by a roundish head of approximately the same size. The head was round and pudgy, a mirror image of the Master's in some ways, but although it was similar in shape and consistency, it was decidedly green. Its chin and nose both managed to be flat and squishy, yet the nose ended in a sudden point and the chin pointed upward to meet it. The head was wearing bright pink lipstick and brilliant metallic eye shadow.

It had pointy ears like the brownies, and they popped out from the hole, effectively locking the strange little head in place, as though it might somehow roll away by itself.

The face squinted and scrunched as it scrutinized the visitors. It turned its gaze toward the Master, who struck a pose normally reserved for Renaissance era courtiers and diplomats. The yellow eyes narrowed further, and the mouth turned down in a surly frown.

"Yes? What do you want?" it demanded.

"We seek audience with her Magnificence, the Earth Mother and Goddess of All Things Green and Growing," Master Tect declared grandly. He jiggled about in a ridiculous manner. Emma gathered this was meant to be a flourishing bow. It looked more like the hokey pokey.

"What's that? What? Who, by Olympus, do you think YOU are? The Goddess is entirely consumed with grief at the moment and expects to be so until spring." The head tried to beat a hasty retreat into the tunnel, but its ears got caught and stopped it in its tracks. Furious, it invoked a torrent of words, none of which Emma understood.

She looked questioningly at Mat, who happened to be standing beside her, and who she figured was enough of a smarty pants to know what was going on. Mat just shrugged and whispered, "It's all Greek to me."

Master Tect took advantage of the green head's ear predicament to renew his suit. "If we could please beseech your eminent … er … *greenness* to inquire within. I do believe Her Leafiness is expecting us."

"Expecting? Expecting?" the green head echoed shrilly. "Who is expecting? Her?" She pointed her long nose at Emma. "That's ludicrous! She's far too young."

"No, well, I mean, that is … no, that's not what I meant at all," the Master said, clearly unnerved. "We humbly beg that you tell Her Regal Rootificence that the envoy from the Grand Poobah has arrived."

"Ooooh, the envoy from the Poobah, is it? What does he want? Another favor? Tell him she still hasn't forgiven him for requesting she sprout that pomegranate bush in the middle of the Poobah Palace courtyard. Now go away!" The head pulled back again, struggling to free its ears enough to retract. The Master stammered on.

"We're on urgent business here, please! We bring the Wanderer by express order of the Premonitionary Review Council!"

The green face stopped wriggling around. "The Wanderer, you say? Well, well, well, well, well, why didn't you say so immediately? Come in! Come in!"

The head pulled back into the tunnel with a loud suction–y *POP* as its ears finally gave way. A low rumbling sound filled the hall, and the original bowling ball–shaped rock rolled back into place, quickly replacing the head. There was a moment of silence after the ball clicked into place, then a deeper rumble, longer and louder than the previous one.

"Best you stand back, child," whispered Truss. Emma did so without bothering to ask why.

A hairline crack shivered down the center of the wall. The stone wall split in half and began to slide open, like a stage curtain. The ground shook so hard the travellers all bounced up and down like Mexican jumping beans. Emma thought her teeth might shatter from all the clacking.

The stone wall opened to reveal another tunnel, almost exactly like the one they were already in.

No, not almost, Emma noted to herself. *Exactly.*

The green head turned out to be attached to a potato–shaped creature, vaguely resembling a troll, or what Emma imagined a troll would look like. Emma had already seen its pointy nose and pointy ears when they were poking out of the hole in the wall. By contrast, the creature's body was very round and decidedly fat, unlike Master Tect's, which was almost identical in shape but mostly solid. It was like looking at two sacks filled to the bursting point, but one with gelatin and the other with wet cement.

The creature was dressed, surprisingly, in a rainbow colored gossamer gown, which seemed – and Emma tried to think of a way to describe it without sounding too cruel – ill–fitting. The dress was clearly made for a much smaller, daintier creature. In this case, the fabric bulged and stretched awkwardly, as if a sumo wrestler was stuffed into a prom dress. And to make matters even more bizarre, the creature had chicken legs. Green ones.

Emma found herself staring.

"Old–school nymph. Used to be a siren. The whole lot of them were sisters. Stunners, the lot of them, really gorgeous creatures, until Ulysses passed by and ignored them. Kind of gave up caring and went to pot after that. A few hundred years of depression after that, and now, well, let's just say she's a few noodles short of a tuna casserole, if you know what I mean. Still fancies herself to be irresistible to men," Piers whispered as he leaned toward Emma. "No one ever has the heart to tell her otherwise."

The green creature noticed Emma staring and seemed affronted.

"Our deepest apologies, oh caretaker of She–Who–Nourishes–The–Earth!" the Master flourished. He hemmed and hawed rather loudly, gesticulated wildly and bowed repeatedly. "No offense was meant. It seems the Wanderer's education is incomplete. She is unfamiliar with our ways and appearances."

The once beautiful but now decidedly lumpy nymph squinted at the Master while she considered his statement. Then she swivelled her head heavily toward Emma and stared at her for a long time. Emma squirmed.

"Doesn't look much like I'd expected," the nymph finally grumbled. "Awfully pale, isn't it?"

"That's *exactly* what I've been saying," Mat chirped.

Unfortunately for Mat, the nymph's attitude flipped like a switch, and she turned suddenly bright and cheerful. She waved them all to follow her down the duplicate cavern until they reached yet another solid wall. The nymph stepped forward and rapped on a particular roundish stone, which immediately rolled back and was replaced by another green head almost identical to the first.

The first nymph stepped forward and whispered something very quickly and furtively in the second nymph's ear. Every few moments, she would stop, look meaningfully at Emma and then continue. The second nymph responded by inspecting Emma as though she were some sort of livestock. Emma squirmed again. Finally, the two nymphs paused, looked at Emma together, looked at each other, then burst into hysterical giggles. Emma blushed so hard, she turned as red as the brownies' normal skin tone, though she wasn't really sure why she was blushing in the first place.

The second head disappeared abruptly into the hole with a *POP*, and the rock wall opened just as the first one had. Yet another identical cavern appeared beyond the gate. They passed through the barrier and met the second trollish nymph, who was just as oddly dressed as the first, but instead of a gossamer gown, she wore a checked gingham dress with a flouncy skirt and a white apron. She carried a small instrument that looked like a miniature harp. They walked on.

Let me guess, Emma thought to herself as they rounded a familiar looking corner. Sure enough, this cavern also ended abruptly at yet another rock wall.

This time, the second nymph knocked on the round rock and whispered to a third green nymph head that appeared in its place. The second and third nymphs took turns looking at the first, who nodded affirmatively, then looked at Emma, who continued to turn crimson under all the scrutiny. The nymphs all burst into spontaneous giggles. It sounded like three goats bleating, a trio of wild hogs and a pack of whinnying horses, all at the same time. Emma grimaced. Even the brownies looked uncomfortable.

The stone wall finally ground and scraped open, revealing the third nymph, who was dressed in a long white nightgown. Her enormous green, talon–shaped feet stuck out under the delicate lace hem. She carried a wooden flute. Behind her was yet another identical cave. The Master sagged and sighed. Piers groaned audibly and bent down to rub his foot. Even Mat whined a bit. Only Truss seemed cheerily unaffected.

"Come along, everyone! One brick at a time builds the wall!"

And so they proceeded onward, now with the trio of green trollish nymphs leading the way. Eventually, to no one's surprise, they came to another wall, but this time, instead of knocking, the three nymphs gathered in a circle and began to dance, kicking up their heels and tossing their heads back. The effect might have been delicate and charming if they had been petite, or even athletic, but their feet struck the ground heavily, causing it to shake. The three nymphs seemed oblivious to the rock falling all around them, and they leaped about merrily with their bellies jiggling in a direction that did not quite follow their choreography.

A rumbling sound started from somewhere deep within and

gradually grew louder. Emma and the brownies all clung together in fear, with memories of the recent avalanche still fresh in their minds. Emma cowered in her heavy overcoat, hoping nothing would fall from the ceiling and knock her on the head. Piers shook like a jumping bean, partly from the quake and partly due to fear, so that his gangly knees knocked together, doing a crazy percussion solo. Master Tect collapsed on the floor with a thud and curled up as tightly as his rotund body would allow. Emma thought she could hear him whimpering.

There was a sudden shift in the wall, and a waterfall of sand began to pour through the cracks between the most prominent stones. As the sand fell, it also began to spread apart like a curtain, until the opening was wide enough for them to pass through. The first nymph broke from the dance just long enough to gesture to the travellers, waving at them to enter. Truss took Emma by the hand and led her rapidly through the sand. The others followed close behind.

As soon as they cleared the passage, the singing stopped abruptly, and the wall sprang closed behind them like a soldier snapping to attention.

The travellers found themselves in yet another large cave, this one not at all like the others. Where the first three caves were bare and glowing green, this one was filled with jungle vines and exotic flowers. A small waterfall along the back wall connected to a small pond that later unraveled into a small bubbling brook and filled the air with a soothing, trickling sound.

The light here was also green, but different from the tunnels. This turned out to be caused by millions of fist–sized emeralds embedded in the walls, which magnified and splintered the glowworm light into a brilliant green kaleidoscope of colour.

A small rustling sound to their right startled the travellers. They looked over and to see a curtain of vines parting and the three nymphs prancing toward them. Two thoughts crossed Emma's mind simultaneously: first, why on earth did they have to go though that whole dancing and showering rock spectacle if they all could have just used the side door; and second, that while the other two nymphs clomped and stomped about, the third nymph was surprisingly graceful.

The nymphs danced over to the five dumbfounded travellers, singing "tra la la la la" over and over again. The second nymph seemed to be sweating profusely and wheezing a bit, but forged on nonetheless. She began to play her harp, and the third nymph chimed in with her flute.

They traipsed over to Truss, hand over hand, as best they could, while they played their instruments, in a bizarre dancing daisy chain. The first nymph in line grabbed Truss' hand and half pulled, half pushed her along until Truss was leading the chain herself and dancing along with the nymphs in a wide circle around the others.

After a few rounds, the first and second nymphs swooped in and picked up Piers and Master Tect, and, once they got their footing, the lean and lumbering brownies bounced and pranced as best they could to keep up. Piers' long legs bent and knocked every which way, while the Master gave the nymphs a run for their money as far as thumping and plonking were concerned. The three brownies and three nymphs pranced around Emma and Mat, spinning faster and faster, making Emma dizzy as they flashed by in a blur.

Without warning, a green arm reached in and snatched Mat's hand, and the little brownie was swept into the swirling dance. They spun around and around. Emma could barely see beyond the blur of bodies, and just as she thought she was going to fall over from dizziness, she felt herself being swept up, too. Two different hands clasped each of her own, one large and sweaty, the other small and pointy. They were all spinning so fast, it seemed as if the brownies and nymphs and Emma were all dancing in one place, while the earth spun around them.

Finally, the first nymph let go of Truss' hand, and the heavy set brownie whipped away, dragging the others along with her into a long line, the ones on the end weaving back and forth like a thrashing tail.

"Tra la la la la," the nymphs sang out as they danced down the path, into the exotic jungle, across a bridge that spanned the bubbling brook, and into a wide clearing filled with flowers of every kind imaginable.

At the far side of the clearing lay an enormous bed, decked out with fine silks and a canopy made of wild orchids. Gallons of brightly colored flower petals were strewn in front, creating an organic oriental carpet. The bed was flanked by two giant peacocks. A giant, multi–colored lizard slept on the wide platform step in front of it. Small puffs of steam rose from its nostrils when it exhaled, and this turned out to be the source of the mysterious looking mist that surrounded the base of the bed.

Truss leaned over to Emma and whispered, "Whatever you do, DON'T mention her daughter!"

Before Emma could reply "Who …?" or "What …?" the three nymphs struck a grotesque pose that vaguely resembled a picture on a Grecian urn. The second and third nymphs began playing their instruments, and the cave filled with a precious, tinkly sort of music, that evoked angelic harp music, but slightly off key and off tempo.

Suddenly, the bed moved. Or rather, something very large and bulbous on the bed moved. It had been so still and so large and, well, so lumpy, Emma had thought that it was part of the arrangement.

The mountain sighed heavily. Then it moaned. Then it sighed again.

The nymphs dropped their instruments with a *thunk* and a *plink,* and all three ran to the base of the dais and arranged themselves in a line. Then each of them struck a unique pose that was meant to be dainty, but which was, in fact, rather grotesque.

The first nymph raised her arms in a ballerina pose, but the effect was somewhat ruined by the fact that her arms splashed up against her face, even with her elbows angled out sharply. Then she pointed her right foot forward and leaned backwards, in what was meant to be a graceful back bend. Unfortunately, this effect was ruined as she grunted and snorted and tried to hold the pose without falling over. Sadly, her chicken legs did not seem to be built for the task, so the effect was decidedly off the mark.

The second nymph was in a similar mess, but with her arms spread over her head in a V–shape, one in front of the other with her left leg kicking back into the air behind her. She made heavy wheezing sounds as she tried not to lose her balance.

The third nymph bent forward in a tenuous lunge. Aside from a little problem with her balance, she looked quite lovely.

The mountain on the bed sighed a third time and stirred. Then it spoke.

"Ah, my dainty darlings! Come to me! Come, love me tendrilly!" The voice was moist and warm. Emma felt the hair on the back of her neck and arms tingling, almost as though there were some sort of vegetable spores taking root under her skin. It was a very odd feeling.

The three oddly shaped nymphs dropped their poses and scurried up a pair of side ramps, nearly knocked over the peacocks, and began fussing at a spot that looked roughly head–shaped. A great, contented sigh emanated from the lump. Two enormous, doughy eyes opened and gazed around the room, finally lighting on Emma and her companions. The eyes were an uncommonly brilliant emerald green.

"What's this? Leucosia, you did not inform me we had guests," the big blob hummed. "My apologies, gentle visitors, I've been caught totally unawares. I'm afraid you've found me in my dormant state. How terribly rude."

The nymph who greeted them at the first gate dropped the heavy fold of cloth she was rearranging and scurried forward, wringing her hands and bowing so deeply, she nearly hit her head on the floor. She threw herself in front of the shapeless form, which Emma had now rightly guessed was the goddess Ceres. Emma found herself wondering why they kept calling the goddess by her Roman name, when they were in Hades, which was Greek. The nymph curtsied deeply, which had the unfortunate effect of hoisting her oversized, feathery bottom in the air, causing all of the visitors to gasp and step back involuntarily.

"Eternal apologies, O, Earthy One!" the nymph exclaimed from deep within her bow. Emma couldn't help but think that the goddess wasn't the only earthy thing around here; but fortunately, the nymph stood back up, and a bit of decorum was restored.

"Behold! The Wanderer From Over sent hither to rescue the denizens of Under, in accordance with the prophecy that was foretold by, um … the foretellers … in the, um …" The nymph bit her lip, stared at the ceiling and dug a toe into the ground while she tried to remember the next part. Finally, she gave up and simply added, weakly, "… the, um … foretelling thingamabobby?"

The second nymph stepped forward to assist.

"Lo, but she comes in the company of the … um … little folk, as foretold by the … um …" She tapped her foot rapidly for a moment. "The … um …"

The third nymph stepped forward triumphantly and cried out, "The foretelling thingers!"

The other two nymphs bobbed their heads up and down in enthusiastic agreement.

Apparently this made some sort of sense to the goddess. The emerald green eyes in the big blob shifted back to Emma, where they rested for a moment. Her gaze made Emma feel strangely grounded in an unsettling kind of way.

The goddess began to unravel, or so it seemed. Her head and limbs sprouted from the indiscriminate blob and organized themselves into a humanoid form. She didn't stretch so much as grow. Her arms and legs crawled out from her body like vines and took shape as they extended. Her head swelled up like a pumpkin, the dark emerald eyes rising along with it, though they became less prominent as the goddess' features became more defined.

The goddess was uncommonly beautiful. Middle aged, perhaps, or a bit older. She had kind eyes and a Roman nose and long, flowing hair with a greenish brown tinge that rippled like a tree branch in a summer's breeze, and you could barely see the dark streaks of grey in it. Beautiful though she was, there was a deep, familiar sadness in her eyes.

"So," the goddess said, once she had taken form. "The prophecy is upon us. Tell me, child, what do you make of this hurly–burly? I expect you are not a little confused."

"No, ma'am, not a little. A LOT!" Emma exclaimed. She hurriedly curtsied in response to Truss' urgent pantomiming.

The goddess' laughter shook the cave. A thousand blossoms bloomed in a great explosion of color, and Emma thought she detected some of the goddess' crows feet quietly vanish. Ceres flicked her head, and her hair grew darker and more lustrous. Emma felt the tingling sensation in her skin again, as though she were being tickled by thousands of tiny vines.

The goddess leaned backward and raised her arms, and suddenly the bed sprouted into a great throne. Ceres sat back comfortably and casually in her seat.

"Let me look at you, child," the goddess said, beckoning with one long, oddly gnarled finger. Her skin glinted faintly green.

Emma stepped forward, helped along by a gentle nudge by Truss and a rather more aggressive shove by Mat. She stood at the base of the dais, feeling somehow both settled and relaxed, but also oddly nervous, as if something undetectable was in constant flux under the surface of her skin. The cut on her arm tingled strangely. It didn't help that up close, she could now tell that the big lizard sleeping at the goddess' feet was actually a small dragon.

The goddess studied Emma for a moment.

"So small and unfinished, aren't you, seedling," Ceres smiled as she spoke. Then a look of astonishment crossed her face. "But you are not the one we were expecting. Not the Wanderer of the prophecy. No, but yet so full of power you do not yet realize." She leaned in conspiratorially. Emma stepped forward to hear what she had to say.

"You feel it, don't you," Ceres whispered.

"I feel … something … ma'am," Emma replied tentatively, as the uneasy feeling in her stomach grew stronger. The goddess stared into her eyes for several minutes longer than Emma thought she could bear. Then Ceres smiled broadly, and as she did so, several more wrinkles vanished and a tiger stripe of grey hair turned to lustrous brown–green with a flick of her head.

"The Wanderer is lost," the goddess said to the brownies, without taking her eyes off Emma. "This child also searches, but does not know what it seeks. Do you know what it is you feel, child?"

Emma did not.

"That, my child, is change. Few have the power to sense it, and even fewer have the power to control it. When you are ready, you will be able to stop a rosebud in mid–bloom, bid vines to do your bidding, cause a heartbeat to slow until its rhythm is nearly imperceptible. You will have great power, child. But not yet. Not now."

"But why?" Emma finally stammered. "Why me?"

"You are not yet the Wanderer, child, but you have the power, nonetheless. For you, few things are immutable. There is no permanence with you. Change is in your nature. But there is something within you that does not change, and once you discover it, you will gain your power to affect nature. You will be able to change change, as it were. And with this power, you will release Under from danger, you will free the enslaved prince so that he may be restored to reunite Under against the witch that has ensnared us all.

"But always remember, child, that the power to command nature comes with the power to destroy it. If you use this power before you have discovered that which does not change within you, terrible things will happen. Nature itself will wither and die. Sadness will overtake the world, and darkness will fill the hearts of all living creatures."

As she spoke, the goddess began to shrivel and age. Her hair turned grey, then snow white. Her emerald eyes grew dark and dull.

"Oh, my child," the goddess moaned. Emma was not fully aware that the goddess was talking about a different child.

"Oh, my child, taken from me. My Persephone! My Proserpine!" The vines and flowers surrounding the dais began to shrivel and fade. The glow worms took flight into the crevices of the cave, and the walls grew dark.

It began to snow.

"Come, child," said a voice, and it took Emma a moment to realize it was Truss. "It's time to go."

"I didn't say anything about her daughter. She just …," Emma whispered in alarm.

"It's alright, child. We know," Truss replied in a soothing voice, while she steered the girl back toward the entrance.

"Where are we going?" said Emma, suddenly empty, cold and confused.

"To find that which does not change," said the Master.

"Come now," Piers said.

"Come now," the other brownies echoed.

Emma felt a deep, painful ache in her heart as the cave grew darker and the flowers around them continued to wither and die. She did not know what else to do, so she turned and allowed the brownies to take her hands and lead her back out of the cave.

Chapter Twelve: A Stone's Throw

They carried the goddess' depression with them like a dark cloud and barely noticed when they emerged from the dark cave into the brilliant red glow of the valley. It could have been dawn or dusk, but whichever it was, it was unchanged. The red ball of flame had not budged, and the shadows lay on the ground exactly where they were when the travellers had entered.

All except George's shadow, that is, for the giant, scaly bird had since rolled over onto his back and was now sleeping in a most undignified and unbird–like fashion. One wing drooped over his belly, and the other splayed out to the side. His taloned legs stuck straight upwards, and Emma was sure she could hear him snore.

In fact, that's exactly what he was doing.

Snoooooooooort

[*pause*]

Wheeze

[*whistle*]

Blub blub blub BLUB blub.

Over and over again. It was a most peculiar series of sounds in the first place, but quite unexpected coming from a bird.

"George! George! Wake up, good fellow!" Master Tect stomped on the ground near the bird's head, trying to wake him up. The bird did not budge, though the Master's thumping shook the ground so hard that the one scraggly tree lost half its remaining leaves. The Master stamped harder, but with similar results. He tried again, which was unfortunate for the tree, and this time flapped his arms a bit, his fingers nearly grazing the top of George's beak.

"Yoooohoooo!" the Master called out in a loud, piercing, tenor voice. Nothing. He tried again.

"Yoooooooohoooooo!"

This time he blew the "oooo"s directly into George's gaping beak, where the sounds bounced around like a demented ghost in an empty oil can. George snorted loudly, rolled over and continued to snore.

The brownies gathered around George's head to consider their options. They were so deep in discussion that only Emma noticed Leucosia, the first nymph, or siren as Piers called her, waddling out of the cave, waving her arms and hollering for them to wait. For a Greek deity formerly known for having the most alluring voice in creation, Leucosia had a heck of a set of lungs on her.

"Yoooohoooo!" Leucosia hollered toward the group. Master Tect frowned, then stuck his head into George's open beak, trying to figure out how *his* yoohoos were suddenly echoing back to him from *outside* George's head. He stood back up and scratched his head.

"Yoooohoooo!"

Emma thought perhaps it was not a coincidence that the nymph should also be known as a siren. She shook her head to stop it from ringing.

"Yoooohoooo!"

The brownies stopped consulting each other and turned to see where the hullabaloo was coming from. Leucosia ran toward them as quickly as her heavy bird legs would allow. A large figure dressed in a brown hooded cloak followed behind her.

"You hoo–hoo–HOOOOO!" Leucosia scuttled into range, breathing heavily. She stopped for a moment to catch her breath, and she scratched the earth with her talons. She looked an awful lot like a dumpy green chicken.

Leucosia bent over with her hands on her feathery thighs as she gasped for breath.

"Yooooo … yuuuuuu …" she wheezed.

Just then, George let out a particularly loud snort and wheeze, too.

The siren inhaled sharply.

"You must forgive me. Just a tad out of shape. Haven't been to the gymnasium in several millennia, you know. Got myself a membership and simply stopped going, just like that. Always meant to, but things get in the way. You know how it is. Always one thing or another. But there's a discus class on Tuesdays I keep meaning to join. Hear it's full of good–looking Greek athletes, too. There must be a new session starting soon, I imagine. I'll have to look into that."

George snorted in his sleep again. The exhalation blew the siren's pointy ears forward, and they flapped rapidly against her cheeks like laundry in a gale force wind. She responded by turning to the bird and bellowing so loudly the bird's eyelids rippled in the sound waves. The giant bird twitched, then snorted, cracked an eye open just a smidge, then settled back down with a comfortable "Mmmmmmmmmm" and made a loud smacking noise with his beak.

His tiny bird brain took its time processing the image of the green faced siren, with her stubby, hooked nose, pantaloon–shaped bird legs and misshapen gossamer gown. His eyes flew open with a start, and he rose onto his haunches with a great fluttering of wings, as though awaking from a very bad dream. Luckily for Emma, she was standing next to a small bush at the time, so she was able to grab hold and hung on. Mat was less fortunate and went flying through the air like a tumbleweed.

"Well met, cousin," Leucosia said. George snorted several times, then peered at the siren intently. "It's me, Leucy, you big galoot. How's your mom doing? The rest of the family?"

George replied with an ear–splitting squawk that closely resembled Leucosia's holler.

"No kidding? With an ostrich? Well, I'll be. Well, she never was the roundest egg in the aerie, was she. An ostrich, you say? Tsk, tsk. Your father must be devastated."

George lowered his head mournfully and whined. A few enormous tears welled up in his eyes, filling the lower lids like a pair of bathtubs with the taps left running.

Leucosia stroked George's beak reassuringly. She turned to face the others, who were all standing around, feeling a bit left out.

"Her Fertileness sends her regards and offers assistance in your quest," she said, resuming her 'official' tone of voice. She gestured to the cloaked figure that had followed her out of the cave. They had all been so distracted by Leucosia, no one had paid any notice to the figure with her. It had taken a position near the outside of their circle and remained immobile and silent since they approached.

"What is it?" Emma asked, only half aware that calling it an *it* might be considered rude.

"She is a stone goblin, sent for your protection. Her goblin name is unpronounceable, so we just call her Amulet. She will travel with you until you find what you seek, and she will help protect and guide you on your way."

Emma looked at the cloaked figure. The creature was tall, broad shouldered, didn't move unless necessary and never spoke. The hood kept the goblin's face in shadows, so Emma couldn't see any details beyond a narrow strip of bluish tint where the light glinted off the bridge of the goblin's nose.

"Well, all right then," Mat interrupted impatiently. "Can we get on with it?"

"Yes, by Foundation, let's go!" the other brownies chimed in.

The brownies all leapt into action. Piers prepared George for flight, the Master began a series of complicated and flourishing bows and pronouncements pointed in the general direction of the cave, and Truss hustled them all into the basket on George's back.

"I say, are you coming too?" Piers exclaimed.

Leucosia had hustled herself into the basket along with the rest of them. She squawked, apologized, squawked once more and then picked her way to the ladder, past the Master, who was now on board but still genuflecting and flourishing with arm–dislocating energy. Leucosia wobbled back down the rope ladder to the ground.

"Then we're off!" shouted Master Tect, over the growing rush of wind George was generating as he plumped his wings in preparation for take off.

"Great! Let's go!" shouted Mat, holding on to the edge of the basket.

"Onward, HO!" yelled Truss, looking for all the world like a general urging her troops to battle.

"Fare well! Be safe!" Leucosia hollered above the din. Emma could hear her with perfect clarity. The green–faced siren jumped up and down, waving goodbye with nearly as much vigor as the Master, who was conducting his final ceremonial flourishes.

George reared onto his legs, his wings arching like billowing sails over their heads. An enormous squawk tore from his throat. Emma leaned over to the Master, who was standing beside her, still flourishing.

"Um, excuse me, but … where are we going, exactly?"

Master Tect froze and looked at her, as did the other brownies. George paused mid–squawk and hovered half–raised on his talons. Down below, Leucosia's big, beaming smile froze and subtly turned to surprise and then to embarrassment, and then back to surprise.

George plunked back down with a bone–jarring *thud*, and Truss hustled them all back down the ladder to the ground. They reassembled around a medium sized rock. The brownies all looked at each other, then at Leucosia, who shrugged, then at George who lowered his enormous beak and blinked back as if to say, "You're asking me?"

"She said I need to find that which does not change," Emma piped in, trying to be helpful.

"Right! So let's go fetch it now, and then we can go home," Piers exclaimed, making a move back toward the ladder on George's back.

"Fetch what, exactly?" Emma asked.

"Fetch. It means to go get something and bring it back," Mat instructed her.

"Yes, I know that," Emma said, flustered. "I mean, what exactly are we supposed to fetch?"

"Well, that thing that does not change, of course," Piers replied. "So, why don't you just tell us what it is, and we'll shake a tail feather. One of George's, I expect," he added. By now he was rubbing his belly and licking his lips in anticipation of the pot of gravel his mother was certainly cooking up at home. Emma was starting to feel a bit hungry, herself.

"But I don't know what it is," said Emma.

The brownies looked at her with astonishment, as if they fully expected her to know all about such matters. Some heavy sighing and eye rolling came from the direction of the smallest brownie.

"Fire and brickstone! What do we have to do to get us a real, useful Wanderer? Huh? Huh?" Mat danced around the others, stamping and flailing. Emma didn't know why, but she was reminded of Rumplestiltskin, and this made her giggle.

A concerned expression crossed Truss' face as she leaned toward Emma and put her hand on the girl's shoulder.

"Think, child. What do you suppose it might be?"

Emma thought as hard as she could, but nothing came to mind.

"Maybe it's something you keep on your person or in your house," suggested Piers.

"Maybe," said Emma and tried to think of what it might be.

"A piece of clothing, perhaps?"

"No," Leucosia interrupted. "Clothing fades and tears and wears out. And fashion changes all the time, too." She looked forlornly at her dress, which had last been fashionable in 342 BC.

"A piece of jewelry, then? Or a trinket of some sort?"

"Trinkets can be lost," said Master Tect. "And jewelry, too. And of course they can be broken or tarnished."

"A person? A parent?"

"People grow old, and sometimes sick," said Piers.

"And people die," Emma added very quietly. The brownies hushed for a moment, and a pall cast over the group.

"Maybe that's it. Maybe it's death," suggested Mat. The other brownies frowned and nudged the tiny brownie as if to suggest the subject was not appropriate.

"No, really. Everyone dies. Death is constant," the little brownie insisted. "No one said it had to be a happy thing."

"Ceres doesn't die. She's a goddess," said Leucosia. "Come to think of it, neither do I. Though I must admit I am looking a bit worse for wear lately."

"A book?" Piers piped in, trying to change the subject.

"Books wear out and fade," said Truss with a frown.

"What about the ideas in the book?" Piers persisted.

"Ideas change all the time," Truss replied.

"I say, what about Universal Truth?" the Master chipped in.

"Can you find two people in this universe who agree that that is?" said Mat grumpily.

"Wait, that's an idea," said Emma.

"Universal Truth?" Truss asked.

"No, the book. The big book that Mat carries. What does it say? Maybe it will tell us where we should go."

"The book only tells what has already happened and what we know to be true," said the Master.

"What if one of us knows the answer but doesn't know it's the truth? Won't the book know that too?"

"I dare say it's worth a try!" Piers said. Mat was already reaching into a tiny vest pocket to pull out the enormous tome. The book expanded and unfolded until it fell to the earth with a heavy thud and kicked up a massive dust cloud that sent them all coughing and sneezing.

Truss and Piers each grabbed hold of the corner and lifted it with a great deal of huffing and puffing. George lent a helping beak as soon as it was high enough for him to wedge his beak underneath. He gave the cover a gentle prod, just strong enough to allow it to stand straight up and fall back down heavily on the other side.

Mat heaved page corner after page corner up and over, looking for the right page, and Master Tect plunged his head into the space beneath them and crawled inside to help flip the pages over. This was much more difficult than flipping the cover because the pages insisted on bending and wobbling in every possible direction. Finally, after a great deal of fuss, the brownies managed to open the book to the correct page.

"Let's see," said Mat, speed reading the text. The tiny brownie had to lean across the book on tiptoe in order to see the top part of the page.

"'*Mumble mumble mumble* … **Wanderer,**' yes. Check, got that. 'Then *mumble mumble mumble mumble* **witch**,' check. '*Mumble mumble mumble* walk walk walk *George*' – oh, that's you," Mat muttered, half nodding to the giant bird.

George bobbed his head appreciatively.

Mat resumed, "'So then … *mumble mumble mumble* **goddess** cavern **Amulet** …'"

Emma smiled at the hooded figure but there was no response.

"'In the basket … *wherearewegoing* …'" Here, Mat shot a frown toward Emma. Emma frowned back. It wasn't her fault if she asked sensible questions.

"'Out of the basket … opened the book … and the basement brownie known as Mat' … Hey, that's me! … 'began to read the history of the travellers to date, but in a very mumbly voice and skipping over all the details.'" Mat finished reading the passage, then realized the last part was not very flattering turned a much darker shade of red.

"What does it say next?" asked Emma. She leaned in, trying to see the text.

"'And then the child Wanderer–That–Wasn't leaned forward and inquired what came next in the recounting, and the brownie known as Mat grimaced impolitely and said, 'Nothing. That's as far as we've gone.'"

Mat looked up from the book with a frown and said to Emma, "Nothing. That's as far as we've gone."

Emma looked at the spot in the book where the little brownie was pointing. Text and ornate decorations filled the pages up to that point. Beyond it, the page was blank, much like the landscape of the valley beyond the gates to Hades.

"You see, child? The book only says what has happened, and only what we already know," said Truss gently. As she spoke, text began to appear on the page. It reminded Emma of a time when she and her mother had made invisible ink out of lemon juice. The lemon juice disappeared when it dried, but warming the page over a candle made it turn brown, and the text reappeared on the page as if by magic. The text in the book read:

Then the portly brownie by the name of Truss consoled the Wanderer child and explained the workings of the book. And the child was amazed and astonished by the strange magic she saw unfolding before her.

"Well, I don't know about amazed and astonished," Emma said with a frown. "But certainly very curious." At this, the last sentence dissolved, and it reappeared like this:

And the child looked at the text with curiosity and wondered how it came to be.

"That's better," said Emma.

Thank you.

The text appeared on the page and vanished again so quickly, Emma wasn't sure if she had read it correctly. The letters continued to fill in:

And so the mighty adventurers considered their options.

Just then, Piers said, "So, I guess we need to consider our options."

"Yes, indeed," agreed Master Tect. "It would certainly help to know where we are going."

The text narrated:

Sadly, none of them had the faintest foggiest idea where they were going.

"Maybe we're looking at this all wrong," suggested Leucosia. "Perhaps, instead of trying to guess what doesn't change, we should find someone else who actually knows."

"A wise woman!" said Truss, excitedly.

"Or a wise man!" said Piers, crossly. "Why does it always have to be wise women, anyway?"

"A wise thingermawhatsis, then," said Leucosia. Piers seemed satisfied and nodded happily.

"Yes, someone unbelievably clever, at least," added Mat.

"But who?" asked the Master.

The brownies all fell into silence. Emma watched their conversation appear in slightly altered form and in a heightened epic language that made it all seem much more important than it was. Then the text wrote:

Sadly, the travellers could not know that the answer was contained among them, for the impassive stone goblin Amulet held the answer in a locket she bore on behalf of the earth goddess, but they could not know this, for the stone goblin did not speak.

Emma looked at Amulet, who hadn't budged since they'd arrived, except to climb into the basket and climb back out again.

"Amulet has the answer," Emma said quietly. "Don't you."

The stone goblin remained still. The brownies, Leucosia and even George looked at Emma in astonishment.

"It says so here. The answer is in the locket Ceres gave her."

"Could it be?" said Master Tect.

"Well, it's written, so it must be true," said Mat.

"As far we know," the Master corrected.

"Have you got a locket?" Truss asked. The goblin did not respond.

"Perhaps she doesn't speak," Emma suggested.

"There's a bright observation," Mat snipped.

"But she got into the basket when Truss told her to. Maybe she only responds to commands." Emma turned to the cloaked figure. "Amulet, give me the locket."

The goblin reached into her cloak and pulled out a beautiful locket on a gold chain. The locket was made of white and yellow gold and had a multicolored stone in the center. The goblin held it toward Emma in her enormous, blue–tinged club of a hand. Emma extended her own tiny palm, and the goblin dropped the locket into it.

"Thank you," said Emma.

The cloaked goblin stepped back into silence.

Emma looked at the locket.

"Open it," Mat urged. Emma couldn't find the release.

"I don't know how," she said. As she said this, her thumb brushed over the multicolored stone. A rapid clicking noise came from inside the locket, and the stone turned blood red, then emerald green, then pure white, like a translucent pearl. Then the locket opened with a hiss.

A small roll of paper fell into Emma's hand.

"What is it?" said Mat, on tiptoe, straining to see.

"Looks like a scroll," said Piers. "What does it say?"

"Give the girl a chance to open it," Truss fussed.

"I can't see," Master Tect whined.

"Squawk," George croaked.

"I dare say you're right," Leucosia agreed, nodding to the bird.

"[…]," said Amulet.

Emma inspected the piece of paper. It was indeed a tiny scroll, a piece of parchment rolled around a tiny rod with jewel tipped ends. It looked like a miniature version of the scrolls she had seen at Mister Widget's Academy. Carefully, she unravelled it and read the inscription aloud.

> *"Daughters of the great white whale,*
> *Dark witches of the Night;*
> *One eye, one tooth betwixt them all,*
> *They're blessed with extra sight.*
> *Though they're known for old grey eye,*
> *They see not black nor white.*
> *They know your path, but don't forget*
> *They know not wrong from right."*

As she read, an image of a large black stone appeared above the scroll. In the center of the stone, a large flame burned brightly.

"What does it mean?" said Piers, rubbing his forehead with the back of his hand, trying to massage his confuddled brain.

"Wait!" Leucosia jumped in excitedly. "It's a riddle. What's that part about them having grey eyes?"

"'Though they're known for old grey eye'" Emma re–read the phrase.

"It's a trick!" said Leucosia. "Not known *for* grey eye, but *AS* grey eye. The Graeae, of course!" She looked around excitedly, as though expecting everyone else to be just as excited as she was.

"The Grey–who?" asked Master Tect timidly, after a pause.

"The Graeae. Three old women. Prophets. Anyone? What do they teach you in brownie school anyway?"

The brownies darkened and dropped their heads in shame. Then Emma remembered the Graeae were part of the Perseus story in her book. She couldn't help herself. She giggled.

"HEY!" Mat cried out suddenly. "Something just fell on my head!"

Something hit Emma on her arm. "OUCH!" she cried.

"It's hailing!" shouted Truss. "It's hailing … pebbles!" The ground beneath their feet began to rumble.

"Oh, no! Another quake!" shouted the Master.

"It's an avalanche!" Leucosia cried out. The ground continued to rumble. Pebbles and small stones began hitting the earth. The rumbling grew stronger.

"What's going on?" Emma shouted, trying pull the long coat over her head to protect herself from the shower.

A hideous shriek cut through the valley like a giant fault line ripping it apart.

"It's HER!" the brownies screamed in unison. George responded by rearing up on his haunches and screeching back across the valley.

"Come on! Everyone!" Truss bustled around them, quickly hustling them all back into the basket on George's back as soon as the prehistoric bird lowered his body back to earth. They scrambled up the ladder. The falling pebbles and small stones gave way to larger stones and then to even larger ones. The entire cliff was starting to crumble. Piles of stones collected on the ground where they fell. Leucosia fluttered in alarm as rocks and boulders began to pile up in front of the mouth of Ceres' cave.

"Quickly! Go!" she shouted, pushing the Master so hard up the ladder, he nearly fell off and ended up dangling from the top rung by one arm. The others reached down to help him and pulled him in, amid much grunting and groaning. The cliffs continued to collapse around them.

"What about you?" Emma called out to Leucosia.

"I'll get back to Ceres and help protect the grotto," Leucosia hollered back.

"Go! GO!" Then she turned and waddled back toward the cave as fast as her claw–footed legs could take her.

Another shriek shattered the air. George lifted his neck and raised his wings. Emma and the brownies clung to the basket rim. Amulet simply stood in the center of the basket, without moving or losing her balance once.

Emma looked down at Leucosia, who stopped and turned to watch them fearfully as they took off. The ground shook again, hard enough to knock the siren off her chicken feet and send the brownies lurching in the basket.

George cried out. His wings thundered as he drove them toward the earth, and they took off hard and at a horrible angle. Down below, Leucosia staggered to her feet and began picking her way across the rubble near the entrance of the cave, which was quickly disappearing behind the falling rock.

George lifted his wings again, and the downbeat sent a great blast of wind across the basket. It blew Amulet's hood right off her head.

Another screech rocked the valley as Emma looked at the blue–faced stone goblin in surprise.

Half stuttering, half shouting over the wind, Emma called out, "Madame LaRoche?"

Chapter Thirteen: A Bit of Bad Luck

The flurry of George's wings continued to generate a high force wind. It battered Emma's face and ears, deafening her. It wouldn't have made much difference anyway because Amulet, or Madame LaRoche, or who– or whatever she was, did not respond to Emma's surprised cry.

Not that there was time to respond. Emma and the brownies all clung to the basket rim for dear life as George lifted off the rumbling earth. The hailstorm of stones was starting to knock larger rocks off the cliff, and now whole boulders and rocks fell all around them.

Another screech filled the air, but this one did not come from George. This one ripped through the valley from somewhere deep within the cliffs. Emma caught her breath as George lurched upward, then she promptly lost it again as he veered sharply to avoid a large rock. They zigzagged upwards at great speed. Meanwhile, Emma's brain was working overtime, trying to figure things out.

What was Madame LaRoche doing here, she wondered. How could Madame LaRoche be a stone goblin? No, wait, that point actually made a bit of sense. She had thought the woman was a bit … boulder–ish, right from the start. She didn't speak much back home, either, and she was so formidable at school. But here to protect her? Come to think of it, it was curious that she always seemed to appear just when things were particularly difficult.

But how could she be here? Why didn't she say anything now? Maybe it wasn't her after all. Maybe Amulet was a stone goblin who just looked a lot like her school principal. Maybe Emma was just going crazy. Maybe she was getting too light headed from the altitude and from getting the air knocked out of her over and over again. Maybe she … was … blacking … out …

When Emma came to, she was flat out on her back on the floor of the basket. Truss and Piers both hovered over her with worried expressions. If they were still moving, Emma couldn't tell. She couldn't see anything overhead except an unbroken slate grey, and she was too low down to see over the edge of the basket. She tried to sit up, got dizzy, and felt a moan escape her lips.

"Shush, child. Stay down and rest," said Truss.

"Where are we?"

"Out of danger," said Piers soothingly.

"The witch … the earthquakes …?" Emma looked at Piers weakly.

"Far away. For all her power, no one can keep up with ol' George here," Piers smiled and nodded toward the bird's head.

George raised his head and squawked appreciatively. As he did so, he lurched slightly, just enough that Emma could tell they were still airborne. She turned her head slightly. Master Tect was slumped in a corner, snoring lightly, while Mat was perched gaily on the corner of the basket, both feet swinging merrily below the rim. Amulet, or Madame LaRoche, was still standing impassively in a corner.

"Madame LaRoche?" Emma stammered. It was only half a question.

"Amulet is her Under counterpart," explained Truss. "Many of the beings that exist in Over have parallel form in Under."

"Helps keep the balance, you see," Piers added. Emma didn't.

"Then I have a counterpart here, too?"

"No, child. You are a Wanderer. You travel through both Over and Under. You are unique," Truss replied.

"And the witch?"

"She is a rogue, like you, but dark and unpredictable. She is destruction and carries chaos with her wherever she goes," Piers said. His voice warbled with fear.

"But if I am a Wanderer, aren't I unpredictable, too?"

"Unpredictable, yes, but not destructive, unless you choose to be. Change is sometimes good, sometimes bad. The wisdom to know the difference is a formidable power indeed," said Truss. Piers nodded gravely in agreement.

"Then Madame LaRoche isn't a stone goblin?" Emma was still trying to catch up.

"Not as such. But she embodies the same principles," Truss continued.

"The principal's principles," giggled Mat from the corner perch.

"She exists on earth to protect you, just as Amulet exists to protect you here," said Truss.

"Balance of nature and all that," Piers repeated.

Emma sat up slowly. She was still a bit dizzy, but that might have been altitude as much as anything else, and her arm still throbbed a bit where she had cut it on the rock. She checked the bandage. There was no blood, so she figured it was best to leave it alone.

Mat had dropped back into the basket and stood lookout, scanning the sky, looking for something.

"Where are we?" Emma asked, groggily.

"Far above Hades. We had to cross over it to evade the witch. It's also the fastest way to the Graeae," Truss said.

Emma rolled onto her knees and managed to climb onto her feet. Truss and Piers held her elbows for support. She reached out for the basket rim and used that to help steady herself. Finally, she looked out.

They were suspended in grey for as far as she could see. They were flying high and since they were also technically underground, there was no sky, though the endless grey slate cavern roof almost passed for one. Below was simply grey. When she had seen Hades from the valley, all she had been able to see was a foggy haze as if someone had simply erased the landscape and left nothing behind. Now they were flying over that same void, and it seemed to stretch forever in all directions, until it blended into the grey slate cavern ceiling, seamlessly, somewhere in the distance.

There was no color to be seen anywhere past the tips of George's wings, except for the glowing red ball of flame that still hung on the distant horizon straight ahead.

Truss saw Emma staring intently at the light.

"That's the center of the earth, child," the brownie said. "Some say the Graeae live at the end of the earth, but here in Under, we can find them at the center, at the place where you are no longer going in and suddenly find yourself going out. Here in Under, that place is the end, but it is also the beginning."

Emma looked out into the field of grey. The red ball gave off a pulsating heat wave that was a bit hypnotic. She blinked hard and looked away.

Staring out into the greyness that surrounded them, Emma felt odd. She wasn't used to having nothing to look at, and she found that all the sounds became amplified instead. She could hear the sound of the air passing through each of George's feathers. She could hear herself breathe, and her heartbeat began to sound off in her ears.

Ba bum, ba bum.

Without even trying, her breath began to synchronize with the air beneath George's wings.

Ba bum, ba bum, whoosh. Ba bum, ba bum, whoosh.

All around, the sky above and earth below surrounded them in a blanket of grey.

No, not a blanket, she thought, *but like … nothing.*

She began to think about people she knew, friends she'd had at other schools, relatives she rarely saw. With a bit of effort, she discovered she could make them appear like ghosts out of the nothingness. There was Amy, her only friend when they lived far out in the country, looking just as she did that day when they'd run barefoot into the river. They'd felt the fish nibbling at their toes and went running back into the fields, laughing hysterically. She could see Amy looking at her now, still laughing. Then there was Uncle Louis, sitting down to the table after a long day at the office, his tie off and the top button of his starched white business shirt undone. When he leaned over the table to help himself to more potato, his enormous belly would always get in the way. He would crack the dumbest jokes, and they would all laugh as though they were the funniest things in the world. Then she saw her father, sitting at the same table, but it was somewhere else. He was in their new apartment. He was sitting alone and sad, just as he had been in her dream.

Papa! she cried out.

She felt a warm hand on her shoulder and cool breath on the back of her head, and a voice whispered, "Shush, child, it's all right. Everything is going to be all right."

Emma looked up. A swirl of faint color and form hovered above her.

Momma? Emma spoke questioningly.

The form sharpened, and her mother's face smiled down at her. Emma felt something stroking her hair the way her mother used to do. Then the form swirled and fluttered off, back out into the grey. Emma cried out and chased after it.

"Whoa there, girly!" Piers called out. His long arm snagged the back of her collar, and he dragged her back into the basket just before she plunged over the side.

Emma fell back onto the basket floor with an *oof* that made her stomach ache. The thud helped shake her out of her dream–like state. A terrible sense of loss and disconnection overtook her.

"Land ho!" Mat cried out excitedly. "Land ho!"

The brownies all ran to the front of the basket to see, and even Master Tect stirred and staggered to his feet, rubbing his eyes. Emma sat for a moment, not sure what she wanted to do, but curiosity finally won out, and she climbed back onto her feet and looked out over George's back toward the fiery red ball which now filled nearly half the forward sky.

"Land? Where?" she asked. She couldn't see anything besides the pulsating red glow. It was so intense that when she looked away, all she could see was a big dark green circle of the same size, like a photo negative imprinted on her brain.

"There!" the Master pointed into the flame. Emma tried to shade her eyes with her hand, but she still saw nothing but red light. George banked suddenly, then started to descend. The air was unbearably hot. They leveled off, and soon George was gliding just above the surface of the red–hot ball, which spread like an infinite field of hot, bubbling lava, gurgling and steaming beneath them.

"Where are we?" Emma asked.

"The center of the earth!" Piers announced cheerfully. He sounded like a train conductor announcing stations. They were close enough to the surface now that Emma could see the red molten surface rising and falling like an ocean. Great waves curled and crashed back down with a firework display of flame and sparks.

"Land Ho!" Mat called out again. This time, their destination stood out clearly. A floating mound of dense, dark, volcanic rock floated in the lava like a surfboard in a hurricane. The island tipped and careened violently whenever a molten wave struck against it.

George squawked loudly over the hissing steam and thundering waves. Emma and the brownies prepared themselves for landing, each remembering the prior landing's acrobatics and none of them feeling too keen on taking a chance at tumbling over the edge into the fiery ocean. George seemed to compensate better this time, too, perhaps also aware that a misstep would be costly to them all. Still, it was a pretty bumpy landing.

"*OOF!*" said Master Tect, as they touched down, his heavy body once again acting as ballast and helping him to a heavy, but mostly stable landing. Truss echoed him with an *OOF* of her own.

"*Urkle,*" said Piers, whose landing sent an impressive shock wave through his long, lean body. Mat did a good impression of a paddle-ball being knocked around, but somehow managed to keep a firm grip on the rail. Even Amulet grunted a little.

The island rocked and shifted in the hot lava waves, and it took Emma a moment to get used to the rocking motion before she was able to climb down to the surface, where the others waited. She felt a bit seasick. Apparently, Amulet did too, for her normally blue skin turned a noticeable shade of blue–green.

Truss reached out to Emma as she stepped off the rope ladder, and Emma was very happy to have something solid to hold onto.

"What is this place?" Emma asked.

"The end and the beginning. Home of the Graeae," said Mat.

"The grey eyed what?" asked Emma, feeling nauseous.

"Graeae, dear. Wise women and prophets. Able to see the future as well as the past. Sometimes both at the same time," Truss reminded her.

"Oh, yes, I knew that," Emma gasped in the heat.

"And they're dangerous, too, so watch your step, child," the Master added.

"Come on," Mat said impatiently, waving them up a small path that led up the hill–shaped mound at the center of the island.

They picked their way up the treacherous path and had to weave and bob their way around harsh outcroppings and pools of steaming lava. Every few minutes, a large wave bashed the island, the ground shifted and rocked, sometimes subtly and sometimes violently, and great clouds of steam and sparks erupted into the air. Luckily, as the path rose higher, it also cut into the stone and formed a regular footpath, though it was long ago abandoned and forgotten. Soon the travellers were flanked on both sides by walls of rock, and Emma could reach out and use them for balance. The rock was dark and burnt, and the black rubbed off on her hands and coat. Once again, she was very glad to have the heavy overcoat to protect her.

Amulet followed silently behind, forming another wall to break her fall, in case Emma should slip backward. Luckily, she did not.

The top of the hill hadn't seemed far from the landing where George remained waiting for them, but Emma was soon exhausted, both from the climb and trying to keep her balance at the same time. Soon her legs wobbled beneath her, even when the island wasn't shifting and jolting. She was very glad when the path finally opened up onto the flat, open hilltop.

She looked around. The view was quite spectacular with the dark black rock rising above the dark red and orange ocean, but she still couldn't understand why they were there.

Then she saw them.

The Graeae were three in number and crouched under old, ratty blankets on the far side of the highest outcropping. They were so shrivelled and still, Emma had mistaken them for part of the rock formation. Despite her exhaustion and the suffocating swelter inside the heavy long coat, Emma shivered and felt her blood run cold.

They were women, though they were so old and shriveled it was hard to tell, one way or another. They might have been triplets, or they might have aged so much that their features all blended together into a strange, pruney sameness. Each of them had a heavy, furrowed brow that shadowed their deeply set eye sockets, long hooked noses with more bumps and wrinkles than a winter squash, and wide, thin lipped mouths that smacked loudly when they spoke, as though their jaws were loosely hinged and controlled by some invisible puppet master.

There was something else, though, something odd that Emma couldn't quite put her finger on, something not quite right. As if on cue, a large lava wave crashed against the cliff below them and sent a spray of sparks across the level plain, lighting up the area with perfect clarity.

Emma took a step back in horror and lost her balance as the island shook from the powerful wave's shocking crash. Emma fell to the ground, but could not take her eyes off the old women.

They had no eyes or teeth.

The first old woman reached out a long, gnarled finger and pointed directly at Emma. The girl's heart stopped, and she scurried backward, looking for shelter. Amulet was directly behind her, so she crawled behind the goblin's leg and hung on.

The old woman clawed again at the air, until Emma realized the woman wasn't pointing, but feeling for something. The gesture seemed feeble and weak, and Emma suddenly felt less afraid.

"Sisters, do you smell what I smell?" the old crone croaked. The other two tilted their heads back and began sniffing the air like dogs. Then the second clutched the first woman's arm and tugged on her sleeve. The first woman reached into her mouth and plucked out her single tooth. She passed it to her sister, who took it and put it in her mouth.

"Smells like food," hissed the second crone, once the tooth was in place. Then the third sister pawed at her, moaning, until finally the tooth was passed down the line.

"How long has it been since last we ate, sisters?" the third woman said.

"I want to see food. Sweet, tender, tasty food," the second growled, having regained the tooth. "Give me the eye! Who has the eye?" She passed the tooth to the first sister.

"No!" said the first. "I sensed food before sisters. I want to see food before sisters!" They continued to pass the tooth between them.

Emma was horrified.

"So long since we last ate ... " said the third.

"I'll say," said Piers, rubbing his belly. Truss nudged him in the ribs and motioned for him to be quiet.

The three old women cackled and screeched as they fumbled on the ground, looking for their eye, which seemed to be missing. Meanwhile, something was bothering Emma, something other than the fact that she was standing on top of a mountain made of lava rock, in the middle of a lava ocean in the middle of the earth, accompanied by four basement brownies, a stone goblin that looked just like her school principal, and an enormous, leathery bird, while a trio of old women sat around planning to eat them.

The answer flashed in Emma's mind like the sparks off the cliffside.

"The eye!" Emma whispered urgently. "We must get the eye before they do!"

She knew the story of Perseus well. They had to get the eye before the old women found it. Only then would the old women tell them what they needed to know.

Emma saw a flash as something glinted in the corner of the level area where the three Graeae crouched. The third crone felt along the ground with her gnarled fingers. Her long and yellowed nails scraped and clacked on the stone. Her pointer finger grazed the eyeball, and she screeched in glee as she pounced on it, but as she was lunged forward, a wave rocked the island, and the eye spun and rolled across the dais.

One of the Graeae screamed, and the other two sisters wailed as she dove blindly toward the rolling eye, sweeping the ground with one hand and baring the other like a claw, swiping at whomever might try to come between her and the precious object.

Emma saw her chance and took it. She dove into the middle of the slashing fingernails, toward the small, round sphere. It looked and felt like a large, wet marble as her fingers closed around it.

Almost at once, the three old women recoiled backward, knowing they were compromised.

"The Eye! The Eye! Give us the Eye!" moaned the second old woman, who currently had possession of the tooth.

"No!" Emma shouted. "If I give you the eye, you'll eat us!"

"Never! Never, my precious, tender morsel. We have no designs on your sweet, soft flesh." The other two women licked their lips with narrow, lizard tongues.

Emma did not believe her.

"Tell us what we want to know, and I will give you the eye," Emma said, trying to remember the storyline to avoid making a mistake. Inside, she felt nauseous and seasick. A river of sweat ran down her back.

The three women shrieked and hissed. Mat cowered behind the Master and even Amulet took a defensive step backward. Emma did not.

"Tell us!" she called out. Then she had an idea. She walked over to the edge of the cliff and held the eyeball out with one hand. "Tell us, or I'll drop it into the sea."

The witches shrieked and wailed. Emma looked down. It was a very, very long way to the bottom of the cliff, and there was nothing but rock and molten lava below if she fell. A wave hit the side, and the island rocked. The eyeball nearly flew out of her hand. She struggled to keep her balance, but the rock surface was too slick and uneven.

She lost her footing.

She felt herself starting to tumble off the cliff, but as she did, Amulet stepped forward, grabbed the overcoat by the belt, pulled her back toward the center and yanked Emma back onto her feet.

Emma felt the eyeball roll out of her fingers, almost in slow motion. It hung, suspended in the air for a second, then began to drop. Her heart stopped.

"Got it!" cried Piers, as he plucked the orb out of the air. He passed it back to Emma then rubbed his belly from the exertion and mumbled, "Is it time for supper yet?"

"We're going to *be* supper soon, if we're not careful," said Truss. Piers gave the eye back to Emma. She took a deep breath and advanced toward the old women, who were now cowering in a whimpering heap.

"Tell me!" Emma was starting to lose patience.

"The thing you seek is not far!" the first crone stammered. She passed the tooth to her sister.

"It travels with you, wherever you are!" said the second.

"Look to your heart, child. Your heart is what you seek!"

"More riddles?" Mat cried out in frustration. "I'm so tired of these blasted riddles!"

As if in response, the air filled with a crashing sound, like thunder directly overhead. The sea turned dark and extinguished the light with it. Emma and the brownies found themselves surrounded by darkness.

"The Eye! Give us the promised Eye!"

The island began to rock and spin. Waves crashed wildly against the cliffs, sending sparks like rocket flares into the black sky.

"The Eye! Sister is coming! Give us the Eye!"

Emma fell to the ground, still clutching the eye in her hand. The brownies fell around her like bowling pins, grabbing hold of each other like a daisy chain and latching onto the rocks where they could.

The island continued to spin, caught in a sudden vortex in the sea. The Graeae continued to scream.

"The Eye! Give us the promised Eye!"

Both sky and sea turned completely black. Emma could barely breathe. The air had filled with thick, black smoke, making each breath harder than the last. She felt herself sliding along the ground every time the island shifted. One leg slipped over the edge, then the other. She gasped for air, struggling to hold on. The cliffs were high and the lava below was hot, whether she could see it or not.

"She's coming!" the Graeae chanted in the dark.

"Sister's coming. She's coming for you!"

Chapter Fourteen: Between a Rock & a Hard Place

The sky thundered, and something that felt like small stones or hail pelted the travellers. Emma dug her fingers into the ground, trying to stop herself from slipping or sliding completely off the edge of the cliff. She had no idea where the bottom was. It was so dark that when the sparks and flares shot off the surface of the sea, they blinded her rather than helped her to see.

The island began to spin in full circles, faster than before, and Emma felt her fingers losing their grip. She reached out wildly, trying to find something to hold onto, anything at all, but it was too dark, and the only reward she got was more cuts on her hand. The older cut on her arm ached inside her sleeve.

Another lurch, and she slid again. Her legs hung helplessly above the raging sea. She swung her lower body side to side and almost managed to get one leg up, but then the island heaved, and her leg slipped off again. Her stomach hurt where it pressed against the edge of the cliff. She scrambled even harder, still trying to find something to hold onto, but her fingers slipped on the hard, flat surface of the lava rock and chalky black soot. Finally, her fingers brushed against a small, hook–shaped rock sticking out of the ground. She grabbed it and held on tight.

A particularly large wave struck the cliff below her and lit up the sky. Emma looked up to see a large, dark figure descending onto the rocky ledge where the Graeae crouched.

Everything else seemed to slow down as the figure lowered to the ground. The island spun slower, the waves crashed less often, and the sparks shot into the sky in slow motion. In the extended light, Emma could see the brownies still holding onto each other for dear life, flailing in slow motion. Emma tried to catch a glimpse of the dark figure, but all she could see was a silhouette. Whatever it was, it seemed to be cloaked in darkness.

Behind the dark creature, four other creatures hovered like armed guards. They were smaller, but no less frightening, for while Emma could not see any detail on the leader's face, she could see the four others perfectly.

It was the Gorgeous Gang.

No, she corrected herself, *these are definitely worse.*

They had the same beautiful, perfect faces as the school bullies, but behind the perfect grins and smooth skin was something Emma couldn't name, other than to call it pure evil. And while these creatures looked perfect at first glance, their mouths were too wide, and their eyebrows arched just a little too much, while their nostrils flared like wild, angry horses. Their hair twisted and turned in the air, like a bed of snakes.

Emma looked back at the ledge to see about pulling herself up to safety. She was still holding onto the little jagged piece of rock, unusually small and curved, which closed around her fingers. It was the only thing preventing her from falling off the cliff.

Then the sky lit up, and Emma noted that the rock was shaped just like a hand. A hand–shaped stone. The sky lit up again. It wasn't a hand–shaped stone at all, it was a hand turned to stone, and it was attached to Piers. Emma let go so suddenly, she almost fell off the cliff again. The lanky brownie lay on the ground, his arm stretched out toward Emma to help stop her from falling, but his face turned toward the dais behind her. His face was frozen in a contorted look of surprise. She had a split second to either fall or grab the stone again.

Gorgons, Emma thought. *The Gorgeous Gang are all gorgons.*

Her brain began to spin a mile a minute. The girls, with their perfect blond ringlets, had the ability to stop a student dead in their tracks with a single look or off–the–cuff remark. Of course. They had reminded her of gorgons right from the start. She'd had the Perseus story stuck in her head that day at school. Perseus killed Medusa, a beautiful but evil woman with a hissing bed of serpents on her head instead of hair. She was a gorgon, and gorgons could turn a person to stone just by looking at them in the face. The three old women were the Graeae, the dangerous seers who told Perseus how to find her.

She grabbed Piers' stone hand and held on for dear life.

Emma wracked her brain, trying to remember the rest of the story. Things were starting to fall into place. Perseus had avoided Medusa's deadly gaze by only looking at her reflection. Piers must have looked up and seen them just as he was reaching out to help Emma, and now he'd turned to stone.

Emma squinted and looked around the landing as best she could. All of the other brownies were frozen like stone statues, too. She quickly wiggled her toes and rubbed her fingers together and was thankful when all the parts moved. But how? How could she be alright when the brownies were not?

Then she understood.

The brownies were all facing the opposite way. The hail had covered the rock surfaces with sheets of solid ice, and the heat from the ocean was making it melt. The result was a shiny, reflective, mirror–like surface. Emma had been facing the other way with a sheer rock side in front of her. She was seeing everything in reverse. She was safe. So far.

The gorgons screeched. The leader resembled the golden haired Thena so much it was uncanny, except instead of curls, the her head hissed with hundreds of live snakes. She shrieked and led a furious charge toward Emma's back, trying to run her off the cliff altogether and into the hot, boiling sea below.

Emma saw their reflection growing larger in the rock in front of her. Half cringing and desperate, she grabbed a tighter hold on Piers' stony hand and screwed her eyes shut, just as afraid of being turned to stone was she was afraid of losing her grip and dropping off the cliff. But she couldn't stand not knowing. She cracked open her eyes and discovered she was hanging straight down the cliffside. A wave of vertigo overtook her. She clamped her eyes shut again, but not before looking up, just in time to see the shadows of the four gorgons descending on her.

She cringed breathlessly, waiting for the attack. But nothing happened. Instead, she heard a great THWACK, followed immediately by the sound of the gorgons crying out again. But it wasn't the sound of triumph. It was pain.

Fearfully, Emma opened her eyes again and saw all four of the creatures somersaulting head over heels into the reverse distance. A dark shadow fell across her face. She looked up without thinking, then realized what she'd done. Her heart stopped.

It was Amulet. The goblin reached down and hooked one large hand under Emma's armpit and lifted her to her feet.

"But how?" Emma stammered unevenly.

"Already stone," Amulet croaked in a voice unaccustomed to speaking. It had the deep, grumbling sound of rolling gravel or castanets. "Kan't turn stone to stone."

The Gorgon Gang regrouped behind the witch, while the Graeae cowered in a corner, taunting Emma.

"Sister has come! She has come for you!"

"The Eye! The promised Eye!"

"Sister will restore us the Eye!"

"Evil, nasty creature. Took our Eye!"

"The all–seeing Eye!"

"Sister will restore it!"

"Sister will destroy nasty creature!"

"Dainty, tasty morsel. Tricky little creature food."

"Took our eye! Give it us, dainty creature!"

They scuttled along the stone ledge, waving their arms in front of their faces like antennae, hoping to catch Emma. Luckily, she was well out of reach. Emma found a nook between two protruding rocks and crawled inside, barely daring to breathe.

A flash of flame sparked up from the waves below. She was face to face with something grotesque. It was a frozen face, mid–scream, frozen as the tiny creature peered through the rock toward the gorgons behind her. Mat. One hand was clutching the rock, while the other was raised, trying to shield the brownie's face. Then the sky filled with light again, and Emma saw the foot of another brownie sticking out behind the rock. It was large, so probably belonged to Truss or Master Tect. A thunderclap filled the air, followed by the witch's wicked cackle.

"Come out, child," the witch's voice was no longer a feeble croak. It had grown powerful, as if she were drawing energy from the primordial oceans that surrounded them. Every time a wave crashed against the island, she grew stronger as though the sparks were charging her, until she had absorbed so much power that she began to glow. The entire island began to fill with light.

But the light wasn't pure, and Emma didn't want to see. It was better staying in the dark, rather than chance casting her eyes on the witch or the Gorgon Gang and ending up just like the brownies.

"Come out, child!" the witch repeated. Her voice grew stronger and more commandeering by the minute.

"Come out! Come out! Wherever you are!" chanted the gorgons behind her.

"Give us the promised Eye! Our Eye!" the Graeae followed like a distorted echo. Emma tucked the eye deep inside one of the coat's many pockets and buttoned it down, to keep it safe.

"I will have you, child. One way or another. Come out and surrender to me."

"No pain! No pain! We promise no pain," the Graeae growled.

"We can wait!" the gorgons whispered. "We can wait! Wait for the horrid creature to fall asleep, and then she's ours!"

"Ours to eat! But first, our Eye!" the Graeae responded.

"Leave her there to starve, sleepless, and then she's ours!" the gorgons hissed hysterically.

"*Before* she starves!" the Graeae insisted. "Get her while she's still sweet and succulent and easy to eat!"

There was a pause as the tooth passed from one sister to the next.

"Yes! Sweet and succulent and easy to eat!"

Emma huddled between the rocks, feeling blindly in front of her with her hands, hoping to find a smooth surface so she could see what was happening behind her. She needed to know, but at the same time, she was terrified to find out. She tried to keep her head turned away from the voices while she felt blindly along the rock. She fumbled and crawled, trying to stay close to the mound of rocks that was sheltering her.

She was trapped.

The sky lit up, and there in front of her, clear as day, the witch's face filled the air: gigantic, clear and perfect in every detail. The bed of gorgons re–grouped behind her, the snakes on their heads writhed and radiated in all four directions. Emma recoiled instinctively, then realized she'd found her mirror – a tall, wide patch of flat lava rock that looked like it had once been a gigantic boulder with a large piece splintered off. The entire wall was perfectly flat and covered in quickly melting hail. A wave hit the cliffs and lit the sky with lava sparks. The reflection was perfect. Emma slipped behind a heap of large rocks, her heart pounding louder than the waves crashing below.

"Feed us, sister!" the Graeae moaned. Their voice mingled with the howling wind.

"In good time, sisters!" replied the witch. "The creature must be destroyed."

"But why?" Emma whispered. "Why me?"

"The prophecy!" the gorgons chimed in unison. The end of the word 'prophecy' was long and drawn out, like a serpent's hiss.

"The prophe–seeeeee!" echoed the Graeae.

"Silence!" the witch commanded. The sky lit up in a fiery display of lightning sparks and thunder.

Emma didn't know what to do. She couldn't look around to find something to help her. She was too afraid she'd accidentally come face to face with a gorgon, and then it would all be over. Amulet must be nearby somewhere, she thought, but she couldn't see where. And she wasn't about to look behind the rocks to find out.

The air continued to crackle. The gorgons cackled. The Graeae moaned with the wind. Emma wondered what had happened to the witch. She closed her eyes and tried to listen. The noises combined like a strange symphony of sorts: the viscous, molten lava rising and falling and slapping against the rocks, the strange wind that didn't seem to come from anywhere in particular, just displaced air forced to move as the hot ocean surged and flowed. A hymn of lightning crackled and hissed, with a call–and–response led by the firework sparks lifting off the lower cliffs. Individually, the sounds were frightening and terrible, but together, Emma could hear a perfectly structured orchestration, with a clear and logical message.

She had an idea. Emma reached into the pocket of her overcoat and drew out her storybook. She'd completely forgotten about it. Each time the sky lit up, she flipped the pages as quickly as she could, trying to find the section on Medusa and the gorgons. The book would tell her how to get out of this. It was a brilliant idea.

She finally found the passage just as the third flash of light was starting to fade. She sat in the darkness, waiting for the next one. It felt like forever. The sounds thundered around her. She had to move quickly. She had no idea where the gorgons or the witch were. Then she heard a loud thud and a gorgon's wrenching cry.

Well, she thought, *at least I know where Amulet is.*

Quietly, she thanked the stone goblin for protecting her. The sky soon lit up again. She read quickly.

Perseus, the story said, was half god and half man, born to Danae, the daughter of a powerful king. When he grew older, Perseus bragged he could find and kill the gorgon Medusa, and he was sent off to prove himself. With the help of the goddess Athena, Perseus found the Graeae, who have the gift of sight, though ironically they only have one eye and one tooth between them.

Yeah, yeah, thought Emma. *I know this part.* She skipped past Perseus stealing the eye to trick them into telling the truth, because, after all, she'd already been there and done that herself.

Once he had tricked the Graeae, Perseus went off to find the gorgons, using his shield as a mirror to avoid being turned to stone.

Nice trick, Emma thought. *Too bad I didn't think to pack a shield. Plus,* she thought, *the gorgons were sleeping when Perseus showed up, and it is far too late for that now.*

Then Perseus cut off Medusa's head with his sword and carried it away with him in a bag.

Ewwww. I am so not cutting off anyone's head, thought Emma. *Anyway, it's not like I happen to have a sword handy. Or a bag to put the head in afterwards.*

She slammed the book shut in frustration and shoved it back into the pocket of the greatcoat, where it vanished instantly. The witch didn't really look much like Medusa, anyway. She wasn't at all beautiful, and she didn't have snakes for hair, like the Gorgon Gang did. Then again, maybe the myth was wrong. Maybe only the Gorgeous Gang were gorgons, which would make the witch safe to look at. Except all of the brownies had already been turned to stone, so if she was wrong, she wasn't sure if she could be turned back, or if Amulet would be able to help her. And again, if the witch was a – what was it they had called her? – a rogue, and if she had no power over Emma in Over, then maybe, just maybe, she didn't have any power over her in Under, either. But, the risk was too great and the stakes too large, and Emma never was much of a gambler.

The light failed and darkness overtook the island just as another gorgon rushed toward Emma's shelter. Emma cringed as it approached, then jumped nervously at the sound of another large THWACK, followed by a different sort of screech getting smaller and smaller. *I guess that explains Madame LaRoche's obsession with softball,* Emma mused. For some reason she couldn't explain, Emma found this very funny.

She waited for the next flash of light, but none came. She tried to listen for sounds that might tell her what was going on, but there was no sound. This was even more disturbing than having no light. She could feel her heart beating hard in her chest like a jackhammer, but she couldn't hear it. Not even that *thump, thump* sound in her ears. She could feel them though, both her heart's *thump* and an immediate, smaller version in her ear drums, but it was all pressure, no sound. No waves crashing, no gorgons screeching, no Graeae moaning, and no bone crunching thud of Amulet's club–like arm making contact with the gorgons' chests. No wind in her ears, even though the air continued to swirl hotly around her, making it hard to breathe. She was sweating horribly in the heavy overcoat. She could feel chaos all around her, but there was no sound and no light. For a moment, Emma thought that maybe this is what it felt like to be dead.

"Come out, child. You can't hide forever," the witch whispered across the silence. "You have no place to go. No way to escape. Your companions cannot help you."

The sky suddenly lit up, and Emma could see a perfect reflection of the tableau behind her. The witch stood on the dais, her robes lifting in a serpentine dance above the rising heat waves. Below, against the rock, was Amulet, all four of her limbs pinned to the rock in a giant X, with one hissing gorgon on each limb. The Graeae crouched on the rock above them, clawing the stone and sniffing the air with their heads tilted upward like pig–faced dogs.

"Child, my patience wears thin. Surrender yourself."

Emma sank further into the rocky crevice, knowing all the while it was a futile move. She was quite sure the witch could come and pluck her out anytime she wanted.

And yet, she hadn't.

Why not? Emma wondered. Then she did something unexpected, most of all to herself.

"Come and get me, then!" Emma cried out defiantly. Amulet struggled to break free from the gorgons, but neither they nor the witch budged.

It's me, Emma thought. *There's something about me they're afraid of. But what? Ceres said something about power. I must have something they're afraid of. That thing … something that does not change. It must be HERE. It must be here somewhere!*

She began to search her pockets, but all she found was the storybook, a few strange coins, a button, some lint and the Graeae's eyeball. She tried again from the top, systematically, then again more frantically. Perhaps there was something she'd missed. But there was nothing. She tried yet again, this time desperately and randomly, the way people look for things they know they've lost, but aren't yet ready to admit are gone.

The witch began to chuckle.

"What's the matter, child?" the witch rasped. She inhaled sharply. Then she began to laugh even harder. "Don't know the source of your own power?"

Her laughter was horrific. The gorgons joined in.

"Doesn't know? The creature doesn't know its own power!" they hissed.

"Stupid creature! Can we eat it now?" the Graeae chimed in.

"My sisters will all eat and eat well," said the witch. "I promise my sisters, none will go hungry tonight."

The Graeae laughed again. "We told the creature the answer, you know. Too stupid to listen. Maybe too stupid to hear," said the first old crone.

"We have but one eye and one tooth between us. Perhaps the creature has only one ear!" the second Graeae laughed.

"Certainly it has no brain," the gorgons joined in. "Will you still eat it, sisters, if it has no brain?"

"It took our Eye, the nasty creature. Took our Eye and did not give it back. Get our Eye for us, sister, so we can see our delicious food!" said the third Graeae.

"Told it everything, though we wanted not to," added the first.

Emma began to shiver in spite of the intense heat. She looked up, just in time to see the witch strike the crones with a violent wave of her hand. They wailed and scrambled into the farthest corner of the stone platform, where they cowered in fear.

"Silence, idiots!" the witch screeched at the Graeae. "If the stupid child doesn't already know, there's no point in helping her, now is there?" The Graeae moaned and cringed further against the small embankment. The witch turned to face Emma, and suddenly her voice softened and mellowed until she sounded like someone close and familiar.

She sounded just like Emma's mother.

"Come, child. Let's put an end to this nonsense, shall we?"

"I don't know what you want from me," Emma replied. She tried to sound firm and strong, but instead it came out sounding weak and frail. The gorgons cackled.

"She's afraid! She's afraid! Are you going to cry, Princess?" they chanted. "Princess is going to cry! Cry! Cry!"

Emma thought maybe she might do just that.

They continued to taunt her. Amulet took the opportunity to try to escape. There was a brief and violent struggle, but the stone goblin was no match for four angry gorgons. At least the gorgons stopped chanting.

Instead, the witch continued to call to Emma. Her voice was cloying and sweet. It was amplified and strong, and it tugged at Emma in a way that confused her. It drew her in, hypnotically. The voice wrapped around her like a soft blanket at first, but then it tightened, making it hard for her to breathe. Every time she opened her mouth to reply, it filled her lungs, suffocating her.

"What are you going to do, child? Escape? There is nowhere for you to go."

Emma knew this was true, and she felt her resolve starting to weaken. The voice was too seductive, too insistent. And there was something Emma couldn't pinpoint, but it was drawing her in. It was true, though. There was no place to go. She didn't know how to fight magic or witches or even school bullies. Most of the time she'd slipped by unnoticed. She stayed out of trouble by sidestepping it. Now she was stuck in an actual crevice at the end of the world, and there was no place for her to go.

"That's right, child. Come to me. You know you must." The voice caressed her and pulled her in. It sounded just like her mother, and Emma was terribly confused. It beckoned to her, but it was also wrong somehow. Ceres had said there was something about her that did not change, and now, for the first time, Emma wondered if maybe it was the horrible sense of sadness that she felt. Her heart ached with it. The Graeae had said it was something in her heart.

"That's it, child. You are so small and weak. Come to me now, child."

Emma looked up and saw her reflection in the rock. She was tiny and frail and lost, hiding between the rocks in a ridiculously oversized coat. She didn't look so different from the Graeae, she thought, as she looked up at them, cringing in the shadows behind the witch. They crept forward on all fours, heads tilted in anticipation, waiting like wild animals stalking their prey. Emma looked back at her own reflection.

"Yes, child. It is time."

She knew the voice was right.

Emma looked up again and saw the reflection of Amulet, still struggling to free herself from the gorgons. The stone bodies of the brownies stretched and contorted along the hard rock. Emma didn't know if they could still feel or see anything, or even if they were alive.

"I'm so sorry," Emma whispered to her friends.

Amulet stopped struggling and went limp. The witch spread her arms to embrace the girl, and the Graeae laughed triumphantly from the darkness.

"Stupid child doesn't know. She's weak. She's ours."

"Knowledge is power, but only if you know what to do with it."

"Doesn't know. Doesn't know. Look at her."

"She's ours. Doesn't know."

"She's ours!"

Chapter Fifteen: Taking Root

The witch seemed to know the instant Emma had made up her mind to surrender. She threw her arms out. Streaks of lightning filled the air, radiating from her fingertips and surrounding the entire hilltop in a ball of electricity and blue light.

"Come, child. Let's be done with this. Come to me, and I promise to do you no harm."

The Graeae laughed in the same way girls sometimes sniggered behind Emma's back at school.

"Come to me, and your friends will go free." The witch said.

The Graeae laughed again.

Emma shivered, in spite of the heat. The witch's voice was somehow hypnotic and convincing. The timbre that sounded like her mother made it possible for Emma to ignore the part that sounded so wrong. She couldn't fight it anymore. She didn't want to.

"Momma?" she whispered in the dark.

"Yes, child," the witch replied. "Come to me, child." The voice turned soft and crept over Emma's skin and filled her with longing. She knew she had to stand up, but she couldn't bring herself to do it. The witch called to her again, and all Emma wanted was to crawl into her mother's arms and feel safe. Her mother's voice wrapped even more tightly around her. In the reflection, Emma could see a mask of her mother's face projected where the witch's face should be. The witch called again, and her mother's face grew stronger and better defined.

"Come to me!" The words rolled over and over again in Emma's mind. She broke them down and put them back together, over and over again, until they repeated in her mind in a crazy jazz syncopation.

Come. To. Me. Come to me. Cometo. Me.

She started to hum.

"Give us our Eye!" the Graeae called out, impatient, almost breaking the hypnotic spell. Emma felt in her coat pocket and removed the grayish white orb. She held it in the palm of her hand and looked at it. It looked back at her.

Emma could feel something inside her snap. She stood up. There was no way to put it into words, but she was no longer afraid, and the sense of relief was so strong, she couldn't help but giggle. It rose up from her stomach and exploded from her like a hysterical hiccup. Then again. And again. And all the while, the strangely familiar tune ran over and over again in her head. She continued to hum, even with the hiccups.

Come. To. [hic!] *Me. Come to me. Cometo.* [HIC!] *Me.*

In the reflection, the Graeae looked at each other with confused expressions, and the gorgons were distracted just long enough to lessen their grip on Amulet. The stone goblin threw them off with a roar that sounded like a ton of stone being smashed to bits. The gorgons went flying in all directions.

Something strange was happening to Emma. The giggling hiccups faded as her humming grew stronger, and as it did so, her mother's reflection in the rock also grew stronger and stronger, until it was no longer a projection of the witch, but something separate. The witch, feeling the apparition slipping from her grasp, tried to pull it back, drawing heat energy from the lava sea. But it was no use.

Emma didn't really know what she was doing or even what effect it was having on the witch. All she could do was concentrate on her mother in the reflection, singing her into existence.

Come to me. Come. To. Me.

As she sang, the reflection grew stronger and heavier, until finally it stepped right out of the stone and stood in front of her, three dimensional and solid, glowing softly in white light.

"Momma?" Emma whispered.

The witch screamed and brought her hands together. She pulled more energy out of the air and began to collect it between her fingers. Soon she had a bright blue ball of light in her hands. She hurtled it at Emma.

Emma saw it coming and ducked. The ball flew over her head and smashed into the wall in front of her. The force of the blast sent Emma flying backward. As she slammed against the rock face, the chain around her neck broke, and the locket flew off, hit the ground and sprang open. Something small and brown fell out. The ice covering the rock in front of her shattered like a broken mirror, and shards of ice flew in all directions. The reflection vanished. So did Emma's mother.

Without thinking or knowing what she was doing, Emma stood up again. She could barely breathe. She felt something rising inside her. Something that was tired of being bullied at school. Something that was tired of being sad and alone. She missed her mother, but she also missed her father, who was still up there somewhere, missing her, too. She had no idea where he was. He was probably sitting alone at the table, lonely and worried, just as she dreamt. She was tired of not knowing what was going on. Tired of avoiding conflict. Tired of being treated like a child. She was tired of being threatened, and most of all, she was tired of being afraid.

And she wasn't.

She turned just as the witch hurled another ball of electricity toward her head. This time she did not duck, and the ball flew straight toward her head. The Graeae rose on their haunches in anticipation. The gorgons hovered in the corners, waiting to pounce.

Inches away from her face, it stopped.

Emma looked down at the locket, which had fallen to the ground and sprung open, revealing a compartment. The small brown thing turned out to be a seed. It had taken root in the harsh lava stone and was growing rapidly, quickly turning into a sapling. The ball of blue light was trapped in its branches.

The witch recoiled and gasped, "It's not possible!"

And the gorgons, who were creeping forward from the four corners of the hilltop, whimpered and began to creep back into the darkness.

Emma stared at the little tree with its branches filled with blue light, and she reached out to touch it. The light flared, and she pulled her hand away again, quickly. But she was drawn to the tree as it grew in front of her. The trunk twisted and turned as it continued to stretch and grow, strange patterns dancing in the bark. Once more, Emma saw her mother's face, this time embedded deep in the organic design of the tree.

She began to sing again.

Come to me. Cometo. Me.

She threw her arms around the trunk, trying to pull her mother out, but contact with the tree just made it grow faster and taller. The ball of light trapped in its branches turned from blue to yellow to white and then to emerald green. The light radiated in all directions as the tree continued to grow. Vines and green shoots began growing out of the rock, starting close to the base of the tree and moving outwards across the lava rock.

Vines sprouted in the cracks of the rock, all over the top of the island. The witch screamed in fury and frustration, until a fast growing vine wrapped around her ankle. She fell, and the vines quickly enveloped her entire body. She kicked and screamed, while the remaining ice covering the rocks shattered and melted into a gentle mist. Soon, there were so many vines and fresh leaves, the witch disappeared altogether.

Amulet kept the gorgons at bay, battering them with her club–like arms, but they just kept coming, like balls in a batting cage. As soon as the stone goblin saw the witch disappear, she started throwing the gorgons into the thicket, which quickly enveloped them too, one at a time, until they were all gone but one.

The last gorgon was the one who looked like Thena, and she just wasn't going to give up that easily. She hunched over and hissed at Amulet. Then, seeing Emma alone by the tree without cover, she leaped across the thicket and landed right in front of the little girl. Emma was surprised and froze, but she did not turn to stone. Instead, the image of her mother inside the tree trunk reached out an arm; a shaft of light shot out, struck the gorgon in the chest, and sent her flying over the edge of the cliff.

The air filled with an ear–splitting cry. It came from George, who rose from below and caught the gorgon in his massive talons. The gorgon shrieked, but her cry was drowned completely by George's squawk. George banked sharply, headed out over the sea, and dropped the gorgon into the hot lava sea below.

Flowers began to bloom everywhere, filling the island with explosions of color. As the petals brushed against the stone statues of the brownies, they too turned from pale grey to dark brick red, and soon they were shaking off their imprisonment.

Master Tect rolled up to a seated position and rubbed his head, wondering what had happened. Truss and Mat both climbed uneasily to their feet, wondering at the beautiful oasis that now surrounded them. Piers took a deep breath.

"I must say, I'm famished." The lanky brownie rubbed his belly. "Where's supper?" He didn't have to ask again, for soon the entire island was covered in exotic vines, flowers and fruit. The tree spread in a glorious array of green across the rocky peak and offered cool shade to the entire island below. The Graeae, meanwhile, were nowhere to be seen.

Emma blinked, then peered into the tree trunk, looking again for signs of her mother in the bark. A hand rested lightly on her shoulder. Startled, Emma turned. Her mother stood before her, as three dimensional and solid as Emma remembered her. The child's eyes filled with tears as her mother's arms wrapped around her. The white gossamer sleeves of her mother's dress brushed Emma's cheeks, and she was crying so hard, her entire body shook.

"Hush, child. It's all over now."

The sound of her mother's voice – her real voice – made Emma cry even harder. She felt her mother hold her even tighter than before.

"It's ok, darling. She's gone."

Emma looked up at her mother's reassuring face. She had so many questions.

"Is she … dead?"

"No, dear. But it will take her a long while to recharge. It's time to take you home."

"But I …"

"Shhhhhh …"

Emma pressed her head against her mother's shoulder. Her mother laughed, and the air filled with the sound of wind chimes.

"You've grown so tall."

"But how …"

"The Tree of Life, child. Anyone could have brought the seed here, but only you had the power to make it grow."

"The Tree of Life?" Emma looked up at the great expanse of branches and greenery that stretched over their heads like a canopy. She didn't understand how she had made that happen.

"You will understand, soon enough. In the meantime, we've got to get you home. It's way past your bedtime, young lady," her mother said with a smile and another tinkling laugh.

The brownies danced and somersaulted on the green grass, and Piers discovered a particularly rich grouping of exotic fruit, which he was now sampling with great glee. He seemed particularly pleased with the pits.

"But, the brownies? Their homes?" Emma looked up at her mother with concern in her eyes.

"Safe, darling. The Tree of Life is restoring the root structure as we speak. The witch has been banished from her lair in Over, and forces are already on their way to release the Prince."

"Then it's over?"

"For now, child. Let's get you home."

"Aren't you coming too?" Emma almost couldn't bear to ask.

"No, child. I must remain here, to protect the tree. That is my destiny. My time in Over is … well … over. But I will be with you always. I promise you that."

She smiled kindly, before Emma could protest, but with a deep, familiar sadness in her eyes. It was the same sadness Emma often saw in her father's face.

"Take this, Emma."

She held out a beautiful golden apple and pressed it into Emma's hand. "If you need me, call, and I will be there for you."

"Come now, your friends are waiting for you."

The brownies greeted Emma with great excitement and even greater confusion.

"You did it!" Piers called out as he munched happily on a strange looking fruit.

"I say, I say, smashing good job!" Master Tect agreed.

"Emma! Well done!" Truss bustled up. "So glad that's all sorted out, then. And who's this? Oh, my!" She stopped abruptly and gasped. "But YOU're the …"

"Yes, I am," Emma's mother said with a kind smile.

"But if you're the … then … how …?"

"It was too late for me to help you, little one," Emma's mother smiled again, but more sadly this time. "But Emma's power will be greater than mine, some day. It was her turn to bring it forth."

"Wait, so you mean she really wasn't the Wanderer after all?" Mat blurted out, all signs of shyness suddenly gone.

"I was, and she will be," said Emma's mother.

"AHA!" Mat cried out triumphantly and began marching around the island singing, "I knew it! I knew it!"

Astonished, Truss, Piers, Master Tect, George, Emma and her mother all watched the little brownie prancing and singing, until Emma finally started to giggle. Within moments the other brownies and her mother had joined in, and soon Emma was laughing so hard her stomach hurt. She began to hiccup, but that just made the brownies laugh even harder, until they all began to hiccup too.

Then they sat under the tree and listened, rapt with attention, while Emma told them what had happened.

The brownies could not remember a thing, except that one minute they were sliding around on the dark, slippery rock, and the next they were waking up in a beautiful garden on a hilltop, surrounded by orange sea. Then, when Emma's mother explained to them that the roots of the Tree of Life would replenish their homes and restore health and prosperity to all the basement brownie burrows, not just their own, they all got up and danced a special brownie jig, much to Emma's delight.

Soon, Emma felt her eyelids grow heavy and her head fell on her mother's shoulder as she struggled to stay awake.

"It's time to go home, child," her mother said, lightly stroking Emma's hair.

"Can't you come home with me? Please?" Emma begged. "We miss you so much. Papa needs you." A huge well of sorrow opened in her throat. "I need you."

"I'm sorry, child. My time is finished. It's your turn to look after Papa. He will be fine, with you to look after him."

"But why me?"

"Who else, child? Your father needs your love, and that is something you carry with you always." She wrapped her arms even tighter around the little girl. "Don't cry, Emma. I will always be there when you need me, in spirit if not in flesh."

Emma wrapped her fingers around the golden apple, which glinted at her in her lap.

George wiggled and rolled happily in the grass. He executed the closest approximation of a yawn a prehistoric bird is capable of making, and he rolled onto his belly, though perhaps it would be more accurate to say he flopped, like an fish out of water. But George was no small fish, and when he flipped, the entire island rocked like a rowboat about to tip over. The basket on his back had been pressed flat like a pancake and took several minutes to get its shape back. A few more moments of wing flapping and random preening passed before George presented himself to the others with a satisfied squawk.

Emma looked at her mother with mournful eyes.

"I'll come with you to the farthest gate," her mother said, and she reached down to brush a lock of hair off Emma's face. Emma nodded and sniffled. When they stood, she threw her arms around her mother and would not let go, not even as they climbed the rope ladder into the riding basket on George's back.

Take off was easy. George simply lumbered forward a few steps and sauntered right off the edge of the cliff with his wings outspread. Their free fall was gentle because the heat from the boiling ocean provided additional lift, and they coasted right off the cliff and drifted for a while before George slowly began to ascend.

Before long, they were crossing through the grey void, and Emma began to see faces from her past forming once again out of nothingness. This time, they seemed to recognize her, and they smiled and waved as the giant bird and his passengers coasted past. Once, her father's face appeared, still sad and withdrawn, just as he had been in her dream. But slowly, he lifted his face until his eyes rested on Emma. The corner of his mouth turned upward, and his eyes sparkled like a fireworks display. His gaze shifted to her mother, his wife, and the same eyes filled with sadness and longing and happiness all at once. He reached a hand out, as if trying to touch them both. Emma's mother reached back and brushed the back of his hand with the tips of her fingers.

"You can see him?"

"Of course, child. He is a memory we both share."

"Can he really see us, too?"

"Not as such, child. This is the sea of memory, which surrounds the valley of death. This is where the memories of the dead are kept and protected forever. The memory of the living is a trickier thing."

"Why?"

"Flesh does strange things to memory. Pain and joy both alter it. When you are happy, you remember things one way. When you are sad, you remember them another. And sometimes the flesh does not admit that memory is real at all or plucks false memories out of thin air."

"Then he can't see us?"

"I think perhaps he can. When a human catches a true glimpse of the sea of memory, sometimes the feelings can be so strong the dead are stirred to respond. Humans usually see these things as ghosts, hallucinations, or most often, dreams."

Too soon, the pale, dry valley came back into view, and the red ball of flame receded so far away that it now hung once more on the distant horizon like a setting sun.

George coasted to a comparatively gentle landing in a level area beside the river. It was bumpy enough, but at least no one fell out when they touched down.

Up close, the river was dark and moved swiftly, the red light barely glinting off the surface and showing no hint of what lay beneath. They were all clambering down the ladder, when a high pitched voice shattered the air.

"You're back! Well, praise Ceres! We were all so worried, of course, well, you know, who wouldn't be. We waited, naturally, but then for the longest time nothing happened and nothing happened, and we thought for sure the witch had got you, and that it was all over for all of us, and that meant no more gossamer gowns for the likes of me, you know, since gossamer doesn't grow in dark times, and anyway, we all watched and watched and waited and waited for something to happen, and then the roots started to change, all of a sudden like. Well, not completely, or radically, of course, but unexpectedly, and well, they stopped dying and then one of them even sprouted a new little root, and it was so cute and curly like a pig's tail, but green, naturally, so we knew the witch was down, but we still didn't know if you had all survived, but now here you are, so you must have!"

The green faced siren paused for a moment, but it was only to inhale. "Anyway, we're all just so relieved that it all worked out, and that you're alright. And, oh … hello … who are you?"

"Leucosia, this is my mother," said Emma. Leucosia leaned forward to examine the newcomer.

"Not from here, are you? Not Over, not Under." She sucked on her teeth while she continued to pace around Emma's mother, inquisitively. The siren sniffed and touched the soft, flowing sleeves of her dress, then stepped back to admire the style with the studied air of a true fashionista. Then she gasped and recoiled a bit.

"But YOU're the …"

"Yes, I am," Emma's mother said with a kind smile.

"But if you're the … then … how …?"

Emma's mother tipped her head toward her child, who was still holding her hand, afraid to let go.

Leucosia thought about this for a moment, scratched her head, adjusted her dress and snorted twice, most unbecomingly. Then she made a strange noise at the back of her throat. It sounded a bit like cooing.

"Well, then welcome to the club, sister! Glad to have you on board. You need anything, just sing! Call me Leucy. Everyone else does."

Emma's mother thanked her, then turned to Amulet and nodded her head. The stone goblin walked to the river's edge and picked up a large horn which hung from the branch of a scraggly bush. She lifted it high into the air and blew into the mouthpiece. A pure, clear note filled the air, then floated down–current like driftwood. The valley became quiet as though everything in it had suddenly died, including the air. The sensation lasted longer than Emma felt was comfortable.

Just as Emma thought she really would die if she couldn't take a breath, a boat came into view. A strange wind blew across Emma's face, and the travellers slowly began to breathe again. As the boat approached, she saw that it was the same longboat she had seen earlier on the river, the one that carried the dead to the opposite shore. It pulled alongside the shore, and a long plank extended outward, guided by unseen hands. Amulet stepped to the side of the plank to help Emma and her mother onto the boat, then followed them both on board.

"Wait!" Emma cried out. She ran back down the plank to say goodbye to her friends.

"How will you get home?" she asked tearfully, as they gathered round to hug her and say farewell.

"George will take us up. There are other entrances to the brownie burrow, and new ones may have opened up after the avalanche," said Master Tect, trying to sound authoritative instead of sentimental. It worked for a few seconds, but as soon as he shook her hand, he started blubbering like a baby. He quickly retreated to the back of the pack, dabbing his eyes with a fresh handkerchief.

Piers stepped forward. "N ... n ... no, you keep that," he stuttered as Emma moved to return his overcoat to him. "You never know when it might rain." Then he belched so loudly, the sails on the longboat rippled. Quickly blushing, the tall brownie rubbed his belly and mumbled something about tomorrow's breakfast, then belched again. The brownies all collapsed into laughter.

Once she had regained her breath, Truss stepped forward. "You be careful, child. The witch is down, but she's not out. Always keep your eye turned outward."

Emma nodded. There was no time to ask questions.

Mat and Leucosia both stepped forward together. Leucosia hugged the girl so tightly Emma thought her back would break. Mat stood on the side, digging a hole in the ground with one toe. Then George cawed mournfully, and Emma patted his beak and scratched him just above his right brow.

"Emma, it's time to go."

Emma turned back toward her mother and Amulet, who both stood patiently waiting for her at the top of the plank. Her eyes were so full of tears, she had trouble walking straight. Once, her foot slipped right off the plank, but Amulet caught her arm and guided her the rest of the way. They were just about to cast off when Mat ran up the plank and hugged Emma as if there was no tomorrow, much to everyone's surprise. The little brownie would not let go until the very last moment and had to jump back across the widening gap to shore. Emma leaned over the railing, her tears disappearing into the river below, and waved until her friends vanished from sight.

The boat rocked gently as it passed up current toward the opposite shore, propelled by some unseen force. A heavy, warm mist rose from the river and enveloped the boat. Emma wasn't sure if it was protecting them, or simply hiding them from view. It was a familiar mist, though, one that made Emma feel like she was floating in a bath of warm air. Her mother's face faded in and out of view, but this time Emma knew it wasn't a shadow or a dream and that her mother was here and was real, at least in this place.

The boat ground to an unexpected stop, and the mist quickly parted to reveal the opposite bank close at hand. The plank extended once more to guide the passengers to shore, and Emma and her mother joined Amulet, who stood by the gangway the entire time, silently remaining on sentry duty.

Emma's mother stopped and turned to the captain of the vessel.

"Many thanks, kind Charon," she said. Then she pressed something into the palm of his hand. Emma couldn't see what it was, but it glinted brightly in the valley's odd light. The ferryman nodded gravely, then turned to look at Emma for the first time. Emma gasped. His face was exactly like the grocer's, the one near her school. The old man's face crinkled into a smile, and his eyes glinted more brightly than the golden apple he held in his hand.

Emma and her mother crossed down the plank to the shore, followed by Amulet, who quickly circled around them and struck a defensive pose.

"What's wrong?" Emma asked, wondering what else could possibly happen to them.

"You are going to cross through the gate, child. The way is dangerous. Amulet will protect you."

"Protect me from what?"

As if in response, the valley filled with the terrible howl of a pack of wolves gone mad.

"Wait, is that what I think it is?" Emma gasped.

"It's the most direct way, child. You must go now. Your father is calling to you."

As if in a dream, Emma heard her father's voice, clear as a bell, calling to her. He sounded sad, frightened and alone. Fathers were not supposed to sound that way. A shiver ran through her bones.

Another howl filled the air, and everything turned dark. Amulet looked up, and Emma followed her gaze. There appeared to be some sort of enormous black wall stretching into the air, and she figured it must be the dividing line between the valley and the land of Hades. The wall was wide and loomed overhead at a crazy angle. She looked further up, higher and higher, then stopped when she realized the wall was looking back at her.

Two enormous yellow eyes on top of a snarling, drooling snout blinked twice. Then another set of eyes. Then a third.

"It's time to go, Emma. Now. Stay with Amulet. She will take you through the gate."

"But where will you be?"

"I must return to the island. The tree needs to be protected, and that task now falls to me. Here, take this," she said, producing an oddly shaped piece of wood. "It's a root from the Tree of Life. It will protect you from the hound. Carry it in front of you, and stay close to Amulet. You will arrive at the gate safely."

Emma wanted to ask what would happen next, but her mother leaned down and kissed her on her forehead.

Then she was gone.

The three–headed dog howled, and Amulet took Emma by the shoulder and guided her past the beast. At first, it snarled and growled, but Emma held the branch in front of her. The beast whined and backed off. They crossed the dusty plain to the enormous gates that stood on the opposite side of the monstrous animal. Amulet extended her hand.

"Eye. Tree."

Emma was momentarily confused. Eye? What eye? Then she realized she still had the eye of the Graeae. She dug into her coat pockets and pulled it out. In daylight, it looked even more like a marble, except it still blinked at her. She placed the orb and the tree root in Amulet's hand. The stone goblin wrapped the root around the eye and tied a complex knot, then placed the bundle into Emma's hand. She wrapped her arms around Emma. Then she clapped her hands together, with Emma's hands clasped between them.

There was a monstrous flash of light.

Everything went black.

Chapter Sixteen: Moving House

Emma opened her eyes but found she still could not see. She was surrounded by darkness. She tried to move, but couldn't. She tried to remember where she was, but she was confused, as if she'd been bumped on the head.

Bits of memory came back. She had crossed the gate into Hades with Amulet. Was she dead? She struggled to move again, but she was totally pinned. She tried to speak, but her voice was muffled. She had trouble breathing. Something was pressing against her face. She thought that maybe she was buried in the avalanche in the valley. She started to panic.

She opened her mouth again, but no sounds came out. A crushing feeling constricted her chest. Then, a deep moan filled her ears, and this confused her more, since she wasn't exhaling at the time. She tried to repeat the sound, but nothing came out. Then she heard the moan again, and this time it sounded more like a groan. The groan came again, accompanied by a scraping noise, like heavy furniture dragging on wood floors.

All at once, the pressure on Emma's chest released, and a shaft of light cut across her face.

"Emma?"

"Daddy?" Emma thought she was shouting, but the voice in her head sounded small and weak. The light blinded her. A series of shouts and groans followed as the rescue team moved some more debris off the tipped over piano and cleared a small space. She tried to crawl through the narrow opening, but for some reason she couldn't move her arms or legs very well. Her father shouted at her to hold on and said he would be there soon. In less than a minute, he was able to reach in and pull her out through a narrow crevice in the debris.

"Daddy?" Emma said. She collapsed into his arms, confused and feeling a bit lost and found all at the same time. "What happened?"

"The roof collapsed, princess. I was at work. The whole neighbourhood came to help. We've been trying to dig you out for two days." He reached down and carefully removed her storybook, which she was still clutching to her chest.

"You're a lucky little girl," said a man dressed in overalls and work boots. He wore a yellow hard hat on his head. "It was like the building didn't want to let us get to you. Strangest thing I ever saw. We were about to give up, but your dad here wouldn't stop, no matter what."

"Yep, yer dad kept saying he knew you were alive. That he could see you or some such. We all thought he'd lost his mind," said another.

"If that piano hadn't tipped over and sheltered you like that," the first man paused ominously.

"And that there book looks like it kept your chest from being crushed," said a second.

"Never been so glad to be wrong, though. That's for certain," the second man added. "Say, that's a nasty scratch you've got there," he added, pointing to her arm.

Emma felt weak and tired and dizzy, and her arm was throbbing.

"The boy ... there was a boy in the apartment down the hall."

"We got him, Princess. He's safe."

"Old lady wasn't so lucky, though," said one of the other rescue workers as he cracked open a bottle and took a deep swig. "Can't say I mind. She always kinda gave me the heebie jeebies."

"Jack ...," Emma's father said with a frown.

"What? OK, so maybe she wasn't home. But if she got away, you'd think she'd have come back for the boy. Anyone takes off and leaves a kid like that, they're going to wish they was dead if'n I get my hands on them."

"She's dead?" Emma asked.

"We haven't found her yet, princess. We just don't know. There's a lot of rubble to sift through. Say, what's this?" She fumbled with one hand and weakly tipped her head up to see what he was pointing to.

She was wearing a strange necklace. It had an exotic blue stone shaped like an eye, wrapped in a complex knot of metal twisted into the shape of a vine, or maybe part of a tree. It hung on a piece of coarse string, tied around her neck.

"Momma gave it to me," she replied, still weak and exhausted. "Yesterday." Her father looked at her with a peculiar expression.

"It's beautiful. I don't remember seeing it before." He looked confused for a moment, then his eyes filled with tears. He hugged her again. "I'm just so glad to have you back, Princess." An uncomfortable cough came from one of the workmen, who were still standing nearby.

"Ben, the child is shivering," another man cut in. "Here, take this," he added. He passed them a large overcoat, which her father wrapped around her shoulders.

"She misses you, too, pappa," Emma said, suddenly feeling very tired and very weak. Her father rubbed the back of his hand as if touching a distant memory, then another look of confusion flashed across his brow. But before he could ask what she meant, Emma blacked out.

One week later, she awoke in her own bed, or rather, in her new one. They had moved what was left of their possessions into another apartment on the opposite side of the same building, on the same floor. The earthquake had caved in the roof of their old apartment, the old woman's place, and all the apartments in between, but for reasons no one could explain, no other damage had been done to the property.

Sheer bad luck, some folks on the block said whenever Emma and her father walked by. *Imagine moving fresh into a new apartment and having the roof cave in just like that.* Then they would shake their heads and go about their business.

Others would whistle softly and exclaim how lucky the two of them were to have survived, and how it must have been a miracle that stopped the rest of the building from collapsing and killing them all.

Yes, yes, definitely a miracle, they said.

Good foundation, said a select few, with a nod of their heads and a sly wink.

It was a magic time. Emma soon discovered that her father hadn't been home during the collapse because he'd gone to an audition up the street. At the very moment the roof caved in, he was being offered a permanent job playing in a hotel lounge close to home. It was more security than they'd had since her mother got sick. The job paid well, it was nearby, he could be home when Emma came home from school each day, and best of all, he could play jazz every night. And then, out of the blue, a long faced man with a serious expression came from a movie studio and offered to buy one of her father's compositions for a film he was making.

The small windfall was enough to get them properly settled for once, in their new place.

The superintendent, afraid of a lawsuit after the *"incident,"* as he called it, gave them all the help he could muster, and he immediately offered them the end suite on the opposite side of the building. It was much the same layout as their previous apartment, but newer and nicer and filled with sunshine. By sheer luck (or so the superintendent thought), the roof damage turned out to be easily containable, and the destroyed section could be easily cordoned off without causing any problems to the existing piping and electrical system, or even access to the staircase. The rest of the tenants on that floor could stay put. As for the elevator, the superintendent got right to work on fixing that, too.

All that week, neighbours dropped in and helped bring the building back to life. It soon sprang back into better shape than it had seen in decades. The enormous windows that flanked the main staircase were cleaned, and the walls painted in all sorts of bright and beautiful colors.

So, just over two weeks after her rescue, Emma woke up in her own bed, or rather, her own *new* bed. The early morning sun streamed into the room through the cracks in the blind. She nestled under the blankets and felt the cool autumn morning nip at her toes where they'd escaped out from under the covers during the night. The room was a lot like her room in the other apartment, but where the old place had peeling walls and strange, overused furniture, this one shone brightly with a fresh coat of paint, and the furniture, while not new, was old in a quaint and comfortable way. The neighbours had been very kind and generous.

Her eyes drifted to the wall, and she looked up at the air vent, identical to the one in her other room. She looked carefully, but there was no sign of brownies or any other creatures inside. She wondered how the brownies would find her again, and she wondered if they would know to look for her here, instead of the other room, now demolished, or if the house would show them the way.

It was her first day back at school since the cave in, and she was looking forward to it with a combination of dread and curiosity. She stayed in bed as long as she dared, enjoying the warm comfort and basking in the early morning rays of sun on her feet.

Eventually, she knew she couldn't put it off any longer. She threw off the covers and swung her feet off the bed and onto the floor. The wood was cold, so she quickly pulled them back up and tucked them back under the blanket, which was now wadded down by the foot-board. But it was no use trying to avoid it. She'd been out of school for more than a week, and no amount of hiding or procrastinating was going to change the fact that she had to go back. She took a deep breath and hauled herself out of bed.

By now she was running late, so she washed and dressed quickly, then tiptoed down the hall to her father's room. She cracked the door open just enough to see him sleeping in the bed and stayed just long enough to confirm that the odd combination of snores and snorts were actually his. Then she tiptoed down the hall and slipped out the front door.

The street felt entirely different. The last time she'd walked to school, the houses seemed strange and mysterious. Now the odd details and overhanging gargoyles greeted her in a carnival explosion of colors and textures. The homes were filled with dozens of people who had helped out after the quake, so now there were friendly smiles instead of shadowy stares, and women leaned out the windows to ask about her health and to inquire about her father's music. Even the old ladies who disapproved of Emma being raised "like a vagabond" by "that itinerant noisemaker" made a point of checking in to see that nothing was amiss. The only thing that seemed to be missing was the three old women on the stoop, halfway down the block. They had vanished, and Emma didn't miss them one bit.

Emma felt so happy, looking up at the sky and inhaling the fresh air, she barely noticed the cracks in the sidewalk that had once seemed like a dangerous network of traps trying to ensnare her. Instead, when she did look down and take note of them, she saw only a complex, but beautiful pattern in the ground, a series of cracks and crevices linking this world to another, in a special language that only she understood.

Emma turned the corner and hurried down the busy block, then the next, until the grocery store appeared up ahead. The grocer was out front, as usual, hosing down the sidewalk. But he didn't look up as she passed, and this morning the steam didn't rise from the sidewalk. The air was clear, and the wet sidewalk glistened like black ice. For the first time in a week, Emma began to wonder if it had all been real or just a dream. She passed by, but the grocer kept busy, his shriveled face shrouded in a large hooded sweatshirt. She smiled. He didn't seem to notice, so she shrugged and passed by, just as he put out a big sign announcing a sale on apples. Golden delicious apples.

She reached the corner and turned up the dead end road that led to the school's entrance. In a single instant, all her old fears came back in a massive tidal wave of anxiety, pouring down the cul–de–sac. The building still loomed like an evil monster waiting to devour her and the many other children, who were streaming, clueless, through its gates.

She gulped hard. Her throat rubbed against the necklace she wore tight around her neck like a choker. She touched it and felt the smooth marble stone between her fingers. It was cold between her fingers. The metalwork wrapped around it felt warm and soothing, like somehow it was holding everything together.

She gulped again, then took a deep breath and stepped forward. Then another step. Then another, until finally she passed through the gates. She stopped and looked back down the road to the main thoroughfare, where cars whooshed by: an endless school of fish swimming downstream across the surface of a river whose depths could not be seen.

The grocery store sat like a place out of time beyond the rushing waves of traffic. The old grocer stopped unpacking fruit for a moment and turned to stretch. Then he tipped his head to the side, smiled in a way that made his entire face crinkle up prunishly, and then he winked. Emma could see it all the way up the street.

She turned to enter the school.

"Well, look what we have here, girls," a nasty voice hissed in her ear.

It was Thena, standing right in front of her, with a look of absolute derision and loathing on her face. Her arms were crossed and her hip thrown out in a way that was supposed to look adult, and she tapped her fingers against the arm that was crossed beneath them. Behind her, the three others huddled together, whispering, but ready to pounce on command.

"Hey, here's a riddle," Thena said with a sneer. "What do you call a princess without a roof over her head?" She stared at Emma menacingly, but she was clearly talking to the girls behind her.

"I don't know," replied the one with the extra set of dimples on her chin. "What DO you call a princess without a roof over her head?"

"Why, a princess with a roof ON her head, of course!" Thena sneered, and the others laughed as if this was the funniest thing they'd ever heard.

Emma was not impressed. She decided to shrug it off and walk away, but just as she moved to walk around them, Thena shook her yellow curls and cried out, "Hey! What's that?"

She was pointing to Emma's necklace.

Emma was suddenly gripped in a sort of paralysis. She didn't want a fight, but she certainly didn't want them getting their hands on her necklace, either. The other three girls circled around behind her while Thena made a grab for the necklace. A crowd was starting to form. The Gorgeous Gang edged in closer. She was surrounded.

They began to taunt her, knowing they could have the necklace, or anything else she carried, whenever they wanted. No one would help her. No one dared.

"*Princess.*"

"Princess has a necklace!"

"Give us the necklace, Princess!"

"It's OUR necklace now, Princess."

"Give us OUR necklace!"

"You don't deserve it."

"Too nice for you!"

They continued to close in, poking her and pulling her hair. Emma began to shrink away, one arm tightly wound around her books, which she pressed against her chest, and her other hand on the necklace, trying to protect it. She hunched over as they slowly forced her into a crouch.

"Some princess," Thena scoffed. "More like a peasant!"

"Not even a peasant!" growled the one with the large beauty mark on her cheek. "She's not good enough to be a peasant."

"How about dirt!" said the one with the pug nose. "Princess of Dirt!" They broke into peals of laughter.

They continued to poke and punch her for what seemed like forever. Emma wondered why no one would help her, but the crowd seemed to be more interested in the fight as a form of entertainment. She could hear voices shouting out, "Yeah! Get her!" and "Fight! Fight!" Her heart pounded. She wondered where Madame LaRoche was.

Pug Nose shoved her hard, on one shoulder. Emma staggered and nearly fell over, much to the amusement of the crowd.

"Hey!" said Dimples, angrily. "I don't want your dirt. Take it back!" She pushed Emma back toward the other side.

"No one wants her," said Thena. "But this is mine!" She reached out and hooked her fingers under the string and pulled. The cord broke, and Emma felt it leave her neck as if someone had just cut off a part of her own body.

Thena turned to face Emma, as if daring her to even think about trying to take the necklace back. The bully's breath on Emma's face made her wince, and the hair on her skin quivered uneasily.

Emma was rooted to the spot.

Gorgons, she thought. *They are gorgons. They survived the island somehow and have come for me.* Suddenly, she remembered the witch and the island, and the horrible, withered Graeae reaching toward her with their gnarled, filthy fingers. The feeling of desperation and loneliness that came over her in that dark and frightening place. She looked around at the crowd of students gathered around, staring at her. She could almost feel the skin on her legs starting to turn to granite. *I am turning to stone. I didn't finish it. They're back. I've lost.*

Thena pushed her again. "Well," the cruel girl growled. "What are you going to do? Is princess going to cry?"

"Cry! Cry! Cry!" the others chanted.

Emma looked again at the angry looking faces and clenched fists. She felt a deep swelling of sadness in her chest. She really was going to cry. The tears were trapped inside her, and there was nothing she could do to keep them down. She gave in.

But she did not cry. Something else came rising through her throat and found its way into the world. It was a laugh. A confusing, surprising giggle.

A flood of memories filled her head.

She had travelled to the center of the earth and fought an evil witch. She had survived avalanches and earthquakes and eaten some pretty odd–tasting root soup. The gorgons were gone. Swallowed up by the island where her mother now stood guard. And the gorgon who looked like Thena was dead, thrown into the lava sea by George, the enormous, reptilian bird who snored in his sleep. These girls were nothing by comparison. These girls had no power over her. Not anymore. Thena was nothing. And she had Emma's necklace. Emma laughed even harder.

She was no longer afraid.

Emma stood up and felt herself grounded with both feet firmly planted on the ground. "Give it back!" she demanded. "That's MINE!"

Thena was clearly startled. No one had ever fought back before. No one had even dared to try. She didn't quite know what to do. For a single instant, she hesitated. It was only an instant, but it was long enough. Emma saw it, and suddenly all of the nasty girl's weaknesses were as clear as the cracks in the sidewalk. Even worse for the Gorgeous Gang, the crowd saw it too.

Chaos erupted. Kids in the crowd started throwing balled up paper and spit balls. They banged on locker doors. In that instant, Emma was no longer alone. The Gorgeous Gang was outnumbered, and for once, the other students knew it.

The class bell rang, and the confusion increased as everyone started to head off to various classrooms. In the middle of the chaotic swirl, Emma stood, still staring at Thena. Finally, she broke her eyes away to look down as she reached over and plucked the necklace out of Thena's hand. Thena just stood there, looking small, inconsequential, and confused.

"Fine. It was cheap trash, anyway." Thena turned with a huff and started to swagger down the hall, painfully aware that no one was watching, and that no one seemed to care. Halfway down the hall, she stopped and turned, threw out her hip and folded her arms.

"Um … excuuuuuuse me." She bobbed her head around as she said it, mimicking some popular actress she had seen. She looked pretty silly doing it. The three others were still standing behind Emma, looking foolish and dumbfounded. They quickly snapped to attention and scurried up the hall to follow Thena to class, trying not to look deeply embarrassed.

The hall emptied rapidly, and Emma was soon standing alone in front of her locker. The necklace was still in her hand. She suddenly realized she had the hiccups.

"Aren't you supposed to be somewhere, young lady?"

Startled, Emma looked up and hiccuped loudly. She still couldn't figure out how anyone as big as Madame LaRoche could creep up on people so effectively.

"Um, yes, ma'am. I'm … I mean," she muttered. Her heart was still beating a mile a minute.

"Goodness, child. You'll never get anywhere in this world if you don't learn to speak properly. Accident or no, you are supposed to be in class. Now move it."

"Yes, ma'am," Emma stammered. To her chagrin, Madame LaRoche followed her all the way to her homeroom class door and wouldn't stop yammering about the softball team. Emma reached for the doorknob, but the head mistress stopped her.

"I'm sorely disappointed you show so little interest in sports, Miss Sheridan. Nevertheless, one extracurricular activity is mandatory. May I suggest music appreciation classes? Tuesdays after school. Perhaps that's more your element, no?"

Emma nodded, not knowing what to say.

"And put your necklace back on. Always keep your eye turned outward."

The enormous woman threw open the door to the class.

"I've picked up a straggler, Ms. Pheegee."

"Ah, Emma, gu-gu-good to have you bu-bu-back. I'm afraid we have a new student, and he's taken your regu-gu-gular seat. Come here. There's an empty bu-bu-beside him."

Emma walked into the classroom, aware that all eyes were watching. But instead of hunching over and slinking in, she stood up tall and walked proudly to her seat. She could hear whispers. She had faced down the Gorgeous Gang and won. They would be talking about this for some time. Best of all, she'd be around to hear it.

One of her books slipped off the top of the stack as she slid into her seat. It hit the floor with a thud. She bent over to pick it up, but another hand got there first. It was thin and very pale, fragile at first glance, but strong underneath the nearly translucent skin. She looked up and came face to face with the new boy. He had pale skin and hair so blond it was nearly white. She recognized him immediately.

He held the book out to her, and she reached out shyly to take it.

"Thank you," she mouthed, trying not to disturb the class, which was back in full swing.

"No," he mouthed back. "Thank YOU."

His eyes burned with a light that made the whole room feel brighter. Emma smiled as she settled back into her seat.

She was home.

Coming Soon:

Emma and the Elementals: Volume Two

Water Works

Keep in touch

...with Emma and the basement brownies,
and be the first to know when Book Two is released!

Visit the Emma Series Blog:

http://emmaseries.blogspot.com

Or follow us on Facebook:

http://www.facebook.com/emmaseries

CPSIA information can be obtained at www.ICGtesting.com
Printed in the USA
LVOW072001181012

303460LV00012B/25/P